ALLWEAREIS
BOOKS

Cover Art by Chelsey Pettyjohn
www.hideousthings.com

Copyright © 2015 by Roof Alexander
First edition

Allweareis Books
Brooklyn, NY
www.roofalexander.com

ISBN-13: 978-0692504000
ISBN-10: 0692504001

ECCLESIASTES

BOOK

ONE

THE

PRESENT

IMMORTALITY

ROOF ALEXANDER

"All we do our whole lives is go from one little piece of

Holy Ground to the next."

J.D. Salinger

1

THE END OF THE WORLD

A Loose Possibility

The day we were packing our truck with the last of our possessions was the day my grandmother was being buried 3500 miles away on the other side of the country. We would be there at some point, but not that day. I sat on our back patio for the last time, thinking about her, her life, her sacrifice to everyone except herself, and just hoping that she received some sort of validation before dying. Otherwise, what was it all for?

"Come on Ecc, I'm starving." Moll was either always starving or always sick to her stomach or always happy or always sleeping. Balancing her feelings and cravings wasn't exactly her expertise. Twice a year she would get manically depressed for several days at a time, questioning her purpose, but coming up short and eventually forgetting about it. But that day she was just starving, and we were about to go on a long search for some sort of validation.

"Give me a minute, would ya?"

She looked out the back door and could tell that I had finally started mourning, had started to realize that my grandmother was gone forever. "You really should have gone to the funeral. We could have-"

"It doesn't matter if I'm there Moll." I fumbled for a cigarette. "Her spirit is everywhere."

"I meant to share the experience with the others that loved her."

"What the hell do they need me there for? Verification that I can actually care?"

"No jerk-ass, to remember her through the people she loved."

"Did you read that in a magazine?" We had been packing and cleaning since sun-up and the frustration was starting to show. Plus she did sometimes quote from magazines.

"No, it just happens to be true."

"Truth? What do you know about death anyway?"

"It's always the same with you. You use all the great deaths in your life to feel superior."

"Yes, I've been quite lucky to land in such an honorable position."

"Seriously! You use your parents' death to claim expertise on abandonment. You use your childhood best-friend's death to deny spirituality. What am I supposed to do, just because I've never had anyone close to me die? Why don't I just put a bullet in my head? It can be your next lesson in life. Your self-righteousness is just too much sometimes."

"God, Moll. You're so dramatic. Just say you don't know anything about death, and we'll move on. We'll know that I'm right and you're wrong." I smiled.

"The line has been drawn Buster. Get your shit together." The fact that she called me *Buster* meant that we were all right. There would be plenty of fights to come, but we both knew that starting the journey with a fight would be even more destructive than our usual preference.

"Yeah, come on. Let's get the fuck out of here."

I closed the apartment door behind us and shoved the last of the small items in the back of the Bronco. A Polaroid photograph showed its hidden corner from underneath the sleeping bags. It was an image of Moll and me in a mirror. The picture looked as if we were ghosts, our bodies slightly transparent, our expressions uncertain, and the atmosphere solid and unmoved. I didn't remember when or where we took this piece of time. It frightened me to keep it for some reason, probably because of the truth it held in our real lives, so I hid it away underneath Moll's tote bag. As I moved the bag, a small notebook fell out. It was the type I usually wrote in, so I opened it up, seeing right away that it wasn't mine.

It was almost completely empty except the front page that read:

JUNE 1, 1999

HE COULDN'T HAVE BEEN MORE THAN TEN FEET AWAY FROM ME. HE WAS REACHING OUT, AS IF I WASN'T ABLE TO GRASP HIS FINGERS THE WORLD WOULD HAVE JUST CRUMBLED RIGHT THEN AND THERE.

I quickly put it back in the bag.

~

He couldn't have been more than ten feet away from me. He was reaching out, as if I wasn't able to grasp his fingers the world would have just crumbled right then and there.

I went into his arms and knew that this move was going to be the right *move*.

Ecc was mostly impossible, a steel wall with eyes peering out just enough to judge everyone and everything around him. All of his real thoughts were locked inside the pages of his notebooks. He could be one of the most considerate people I had ever met until it came to his secrets, until it came to the possibility of knowing him too much.

"What was that?" I saw him tuck something away in the backseat as if he was trying to hide it from me. He didn't know that I knew that he was constantly hiding things from me, from everyone. But me! I was the closest person to him, yet I barely knew him. I'd never seen him cry. I'd never seen him blow his nose or take a piss. Intimacy starts with being a part of another's body excretions. Ecc liked to believe he loved me, but I don't know if he was capable of loving anything except his ink-filled dreams.

"What was what?"

"You put something in the back, but you did it in your sneaky way."

"My sneaky way?" He laughed, he always laughed when a crack formed in his wall. "It was just an old photo."

He was lying, and I let him.

~

I don't know why I lied to Moll. It would have been easy to explain that I thought the notebook was mine. She's complicated. We're complicated. This was complicated.

We were leaving San Francisco forever. Everything on this journey was going to be forever. Forever seemed so easy, solid, permanent, but it also was complicated. There are those last moments when one is moving far away, that a decision has to be made whether to keep a possession or lose it forever. Sometimes we have to throw one thing away to give another a destination. And then there are some moments in which one cannot make the choice. The universe makes it for us. We're secretly deceived for a higher purpose. I loved when life did this, little slips of moments in time, drops of rain that fall before our eyes, dirt flowing through our fingers, the wind howling by our ears, life, fucking life taunting us, dancing and laughing in our face, and then running away, screaming, catch me if you can!

As we were driving down Fulton Street toward downtown, toward out of town, the Bay's breeze jacked through my tangled hair, the radio appropriately played *Road to Nowhere*, and my heart thumped like I just got away with murder. Hundreds of people flopped through the city, faces sad and shiny, so many lost souls that would never know which way to go. Moll and I stared over the skyline, only thinking about the possibility of the road, the possibility of the people, the possibility of anything and everything, but mostly the possibility of those singular life-changing moments that stay with you forever in the familiarity of a song or a scent or in the sense of pure freedom. Our possession was freedom, and it was ours to defy or embrace. We were smiling in our toes, cruising along in no hurry. I missed my turn on Gough Street and ended up going back in the opposite direction. Moll didn't question me as we passed right by our former neighborhood again, and then back down Fulton Street. Even though the exhilaration of being reborn was still there, it wasn't the same. Those streets had already died for us. We just had to keep on moving.

A Futuristic Disease

We shot through the photographs of Berkeley on 580, and watched the highways change as fast as the towns. It was an overwhelming start, jumping from 205 into Dublin, then 120 into Manteca, and stretching the tightrope through a hundred different one-dimensional farming towns. I inhaled the smell of the California soil, mixed with manure, mixed with the air trapped in between the ocean and the mountains.

I pulled my fingers from Moll's sleepy grip. Her head was cocked to the side, eyes closed, and mouth comically wide open. Moll never had trouble sleeping anywhere. She's a dreamer, just like me, except she remembers her other world. I tend to lose track of reality within memories.

~

I faded in and out while Ecc drove. He was a pretty good driver, but he scared me sometimes like he wasn't the one driving. This one time when we both had cars, I crashed into the back of him while following him home. I totaled my car, and ever since he has been the driver. Just like a man. One mistake while I was drunk and it's never forgotten.

"Let me know when you want me to drive." I told him, but we both knew the game.

"Okay, when we get out of this goddamn state you can take over." Which wouldn't be that day, because we decided earlier to try to make Yosemite Park. It was the only destination that we had decided on so far.

Ever since we decided to leave California our moods all of sudden became much lighter, we became more complementary with each other as if we were a team playing against the whole city of San Francisco, as if we blamed every problem we had on a location. I suppose that's what humans do on all sorts of levels, team up and silently fight against whoever isn't on their team.

I rolled down the window that my head was resting on. The midday sun was beating down on both of us, the team, all for one and one for all.

~

We were just reaching the Sierra Mountains. My hands were a sweaty mess against the rubber steering wheel. Sometimes I have tension attacks when I'm driving close to a ledge, or a bridge, or anything like that. My truck, a rusted-out baby blue Bronco hugged the curves of the blacktop. I'm always in control of which way the tires are pointed, but unfortunately I don't have very much control of the mind that is telling my hands and feet which direction to go. You see, the problem lies within the question, the question being, "What is the right thing to do?" If one has a disease, and it tells this person that he should drive the car toward the ledge instead of the road, well, it becomes difficult. So, what is the right thing to do? My instinct told me to drive us all to our death, but my reasoning side eventually won the battle. My instinct thinks about the jagged rocks below, about the Bronco exploding into flames, about Moll forever dreaming. But fortunately, I've learned to ignore my instinct for the most part.

I exhaled heavily and took the control back. The disease is kind of like vertigo, except it's exclusive to being in an automobile. If there's a ledge, my head gets dizzy, my eyes focus on the open air, and it's all I can do to not drive right off into nothingness. They call this disease Autigo. Of course that's a made up name, but I have several brain diseases, and they all get made up names.

We got back on solid flat ground and I reached out to hold Moll's hand again. She napped away while the thumping in my head continued.

Moll woke up. "Where are we?"

I had a complicated answer, but instead I told her the cold truth. "Stockton, California."

She closed her eyes again. "Thanks Buster." She began calling me *Buster* after she heard this old bluegrass song about a man that crashed his pick-up truck into the ocean. That man's name was Buster, and now I'm Buster when convenient.

"Keep on rolling Buster." Moll put a fist into the air, quoting that bluegrass song. So I did. I kept on rolling.

A Reflection Of Wishes

We pulled into the Yosemite Park welcome center area.
Our goals were easy and limitless, drive until we stop, and
then keep going after we stop. Don't look back and don't
look too far forward. Moll taught me how to do this, but
this, this situation was all my fault. I had no sense of
reality, no dignity when it came to the future, no
compromise when it came to living in the moment, and
Moll had become the by-product of my dreams. She made
me anticipate a spirit, a feeling, a breath of air that if
demanded upon them, "Come over here, slit your wrists,
and fuck me till you die," then it would happen. The spirit
wouldn't question, that spirit that used to be her, and that
spirit that is now me. It would just know that everything

would be fine, because of a higher faith that we all carry with us in our pockets, or at the very least, we lose in between the cushions of our couch. I remember as a kid defiantly questioning our preacher's gibberish about how all we needed was faith, but now I know he was right about what he wanted, and that everyone is right as long they fully believed in whatever the hell they believe in.

I took a Polaroid picture of Moll beside of a domesticated chipmunk. They were both on a stone wall in front of the panoramic view of Yosemite Valley. The chipmunk stared at Moll tying her shoe, like it was something bigger, like when the knot was complete, everything would be complete. This picture epitomized Moll. She was the grand view, the trusting little animal, the flash of light, the thin mountain air, the stubborn stone wall, the disintegrating question-mark clouds, and everything else in between. In short, she could really blow your mind if you really knew her. She taught me all this.

~

We didn't know where we were going, that's what we knew. Ecc said it wouldn't work if we knew. It was something I would have never done before I met him four or five years ago. When we first met he thought I was someone else. Maybe I was? At that time, I could have been just about anyone. That must be something that fades with youth, like being able to eat anything you want, or like perky boobs. At the awful age of 25 my boobs for the first time ever were starting to go down. It's funny how scary that is. Things like that make you hold on to the person you love more, like every progressive fault about you will be the reason they leave. One day my boobs will be down close to my belly and if I told that to Ecc he would put it in a mental list of excuses to get out. Anyway, just like my boobs, we didn't know where we were going and we were going there fast.

~

A woman holding on to a toddler that just learned to walk gave Moll and me the old once-over. She smiled as if we fit. There had been more than a handful of times that a stranger has approached us with the notion, not to say the inquisition of our relation. Nine times out of ten they saw brilliantly dull siblings, and then the one out of the ten, well, they saw two people so in love that it had to be incest. Twice before I've had men ask if they could hit on my sister. Both times I told them to go for it. Moll had no patience for getting hit on. She tore their egos out and pranced off in laughter. Only one of those times did I have to step in and defend the predator away.

I stared into that Polaroid picture, seeing a lifetime of this worthwhile frustration sometimes titled *love* amongst other things. On the other side of the picture, that toddler fell to the ground, slipping from his mom's hand. The little boy looked up at me as if he needed verification to start crying or not. I slightly shook my head to tell him no, do not cry. The mother picked him up and he stayed strong. It would come in handy one day, most days.

"I think the chipmunk farted." Moll waved her hand in front of her nose.

"Fucking eh Moll." I shook my head at her, as I had a million times over.

"What?" She showed her teeth more than she wanted to. She really knew how to bring me back to reality, right as I was about to go inside deep thoughts about love and falling toddlers and moments trapped on paper. Most times if it wasn't for her, I'd be aimlessly floating along in this old grandiose dream, aimlessly floating along until she opened her mouth to yawn every few miles of our life.

A Crucial Fate

We were almost at a campground, and the short five-hour drive from San Francisco was getting to me. Car after car passed by, stinking of air-conditioned sweat, staring out their windows, feigning a concern for nature, and all the while thinking how they were going to live forever, taking pictures, forgetting the laughter of the wind. It was all I could do not to cross the Bronco over the yellow lines and surprise them all.

"Are you alright?" Moll stared at me while holding a book in her lap.

It took me a few seconds to turn my demons off. "Yeah." I half-chuckled, "I was just thinking about how all these people think they know where they're going."

She avoided this statement like the plague. "Do you even know where we're going?"

"Yeah, something should be pretty close." I didn't really know, but it didn't matter. We could stop anywhere and set up a tent, we could sleep in the Bronco, or we could have just kept on rolling until that ledge got us.

I calmed down and just focused on the wild patterns of the sun. Rays of light were weaving through the trees and forming flashing geometrical shapes over the thin layer of California dust on the dashboard. The Bronco's old gray interior had seen better days. We're going to go down in flames together one day on this search.

~

We drove over the winding roads and through the forest while listening to the radio. That 4 Non Blondes song, *What's Up?* came on and it reminded me of my time in Amsterdam about a year before I met Ecc. I had just become friends with some girls in my dorm and we went out to a club after getting drunk in our room. That song came on and we all sang it together at the top of our lungs. Later on that night I kissed one of them, my first girl hook-up. After that I was only into girls all the way up until I met Ecc.

31

The song made me emotional. I stuck my head out to the edge of the window so Ecc couldn't see my tears. And the tears weren't for the girl, shit, I don't even remember her name. The tears were for the moment that was forever gone. I suppose I'm afraid that everything fun and free in my life has passed and there wouldn't be any special people left, there wouldn't be moments left in which I could hear a song and cry from remembering such a beautiful time. All the hope I had left for this was about to come up on this road trip and then... then?

~

Moll wore this black cord around her neck that held a glass raindrop piece. She always played with it whenever she had something important on her mind. As I pulled into a camping area she kept her face toward the window, away from me, and held on to that raindrop. She probably already regretted leaving behind walls, a roof, a job, friends, and all the other stuff that makes one forget that they can do anything in the world at anytime. Comfort makes cowards out of the best of us.

As for me, my favorite part was happening. This is the part in which I build a temporary home in the woods. We were setting up camp, the tents, the chairs, the stove, the radio, and the supplies for dinner. It was as if we were building our whole new life right there within the constraints of a trunk and a sunset. I looked around at the other campers and their own little temporary homes. It was so goddamn organized that the dirt seemed confused.

A Poor Witness

After we quietly set up our newest home there wasn't much to do except have a drink. The beauty of not having was all around us, and yet *having* was right at our fingertips, literally on and around our fingertips, mankind's greatest ability since opposable thumbs. I took out the beer and whiskey and took a bit of both. Moll was fidgety, looking for things to do.

"I'm going to go collect some firewood." She told me walking away.

"It's apparently illegal here to take from the ground. We're supposed to buy it."

"Get my bail money ready then."

"That's my gal. You show'em."

She needed something to do to get whatever was bothering her off her mind. I used the booze to do this. It was almost dark, there was a light haze surrounding us, and the temperature was just cool enough to start a fire.

~

I brought back two armloads worth of firewood, which isn't much, meaning my arms aren't that big. I used to build stick forts in my backyard as a kid, so I'm at the very least, efficient with my limitations. Ecc had the bottle of Jack Daniels out already. It was one of a few bottles that were leftover in our apartment. The other bottles, a raspberry vodka and a cheap gin, were practically undrinkable, but we were halfway to being alcoholics, so we couldn't bear to throw out any liquor.

"Here we are." I meant the sticks, but Ecc thought I meant us.

"Yep, here we are. This is what it's about. Here, now, the not knowing what's next, but we know that here we are, in the forest under a billion stars."

"I *meant* here's the wood dip-shit."

He sprayed out the mouthful of whiskey, almost choking on his laughter.

"Ah, you think I'm funny."

~

The story at the campground could have been titled *American on Vacation*. I loved it. It's my people at their best: No business, no war, no video games, no lottery tickets, no politics, no progress, no one whipping, no one being whipped, no fashion, no television...

A woman that seemed to be alone occupied the campsite that was in between the creek and us. Every time she moved around to get something from her car, or adjust the fire logs, or go into her tent we both looked up and stared without talking about it. Maybe because it was so quiet we were afraid she would hear us. I'm not sure what Moll thought, but I had already made up her story in my head. It was tragic of course, abused wife that left her home in the middle of the night, she used to have a kid, but it got sick and died young, and now she was completely on her own, trying to figure life out. I thought about inviting her over to get the real story, which at that point no one would have been able to convince me that my version was anything but the truth. I thought about how we would all get drunk and stoned, and I would convince her that life is nothing but this moment and nothing else in an attempt to make her feel better about all the shitty past. I must have spaced out while thinking all this because when I came out of my thoughts, she was staring at me staring at her. Then she slowly put up her hand and flipped me off.

A Sensible World

We settled in to the late night camp, the coals of the fire burning heavy and bright, beers in hand, and radio playing. The flames flickered in front of Moll's face and I couldn't help but to think of the concept of Hell, of what I was taught as a child in church. Now that I was sort of an adult and sort of knew how an adult could think, it baffled me that adults would teach children that they would go to a place of eternal burning if they didn't abide by a set of absurd rules that were made by an invisible and perfect god. I suppose being invisible is about as close to perfect as one could get.

As I looked over at Moll I got a hollow feeling in my stomach. Our infinity was under the guillotine. One day soon we would both be invisible.

"Hey!" I said in an animated way to convey an uncomfortable lead-in.

"What motherfucker?" She reminded me of one of those precocious five-year old girl's in the movies that use curse words incorrectly.

"You think you know me?" I asked her this because she had still been fondling her raindrop all night and I had to break it up.

She was thrown back, because this is *her* kind of question, and the kind that I would dance around until eventually not answering. "Of course. Why, do you have a secret past?"

"Secrets… we all have secrets, even from ourselves."

"Like what?"

"Like things that we haven't figured out yet. They're already there just waiting to come out. But I'm referring to the things we *don't* know about each other."

"Like what though?"

I thought for a couple of minutes of what I actually meant. We were pounding cans of Natural Light. One great thing about camping is that there isn't a hurry to do anything except the conquering of a 12-pack. "I don't know. Like reincarnation."

"What do you mean?" She yawned and a burp came out violently. As serious as we sometimes got, she always found a way to make it comical.

"Like, what do you think you will come back as, if for some reason we're put into this world again."

"Like an insect or something?"

"Yeah, whatever... everything... an animal, anything in nature, or a possession, or maybe a vice, anything." I had written a story about this before, but threw it away shortly after finishing it. Sometimes you instinctively know to destroy the evidence.

She pondered while I got up to change the compact disc in the boom box. I put on Garcia and Grisham's *The Pizza Tapes* and went back over to the fire.

~

Ecc just asked me a question that made me question his motives for this trip. This was not the kind of question he asks. It wasn't in my nature to be suspicious. I had a bad habit of trusting just about any one, any thing, and especially any question. But this particular question had suspicious undertones.

I always imagined being a willow tree, every time I saw one I thought it would be a good life. In the rare times or possibly only one time that I've seen a willow tree in a thunderstorm I thought that's what happened when god invented perfection.

~

Moll took a while to come up with an answer. She probably wanted this moment to last, since I'm the kind of person who never talked about the future. I liked to think that we had our whole lives to get to know each other, but... that doesn't ring as true as it used to. I started realizing that all we have is this moment, this little page of paper, and then off we float away on our lifeboats. Nothing lasts and it was fine, it would have to be fine. I'd seen this movie once about the future and all the humans could practically live forever because they had cured disease and stopped wars and all that stuff. The main dude hero-type said, 'The point is that it ends, otherwise there's no reason for living.' I took that he meant the word *living* lost all its meaning without the word *dying*. I would have ended the movie with everyone killing themselves, but that didn't happen. It was an obscure low-budget ending, like they ran out of money and just ended it with the hero watching the sun come up.

"I think, or maybe hope that I would come back as a willow tree, or a thunderstorm, or a rabbit." Moll exhaled like she'd been underwater the past two minutes. "That's what I'd come back as."

"Thunderstorm huh? I think you already accomplished that one without dying."

"Funny Buster. What about you?"

"I think, and also hope that I would come back as fog, or wind, you know, something that could go everywhere without anyone really noticing."

"That sounds like you want to sneak into women's bedrooms. You want to come back as a goddamn Peeping Tom!"

"Yeah, I guess I do." I laughed at Moll. Of course she would think of that angle.

"What about an animal?"

"I hope I wouldn't come back as an animal, I would be something that would get eaten, nothing cute like a puppy or anything, I don't deserve that."

"Oh come on, you're not that bad." Moll didn't eat meat, and I tried not to also for her, but wasn't so good at it.

"How about a bird." I put my arms out like wings.

"Why a bird, I mean that would be cool, but why?"

"Observing and judging from above."

She grew a smirk, but had no rebuttal. It was a part of me that she loved and hated.

"Also, I'd get to crap on freshly cleaned cars."

That's where we were, one day in, under the California stars, and already talking about our next lives.

I remembered the first time I saw Moll twirl under the stars in Amsterdam. It had been almost five years, gone by like a match lighting and fizzling away, no distinct way to register what happened except over the pages and inside words like days and years. A patient breeze flowed along the dirt path in front of us. It was watching us, wondering if we we're looking back, wondering when it would be set free from wandering the world. I'd like to come back as a tree, grow up toward the sky for a thousand years, get chopped down, get made into a baseball bat, or even better, catch on fire and float up into the Milky Way. But that's Moll's thing. The fog will do for me.

An Invited Thief

A purple coldness hovered near the damp ground. This morning as the past few weeks before, I had to catch the liquid coming out of my nose as soon as I woke up. This time was different though. When the blood came spurting out, it was full of dirt. I stared at the tissue and sort of liked it.

A Future Roadside Grave

Packing-up was my least favorite part of camping, preparing to leave it all behind for forever. Even if we came back it wouldn't be the same as staying, it wouldn't ever be the same. Most of the time I didn't think about it because I was hung-over, the perks of drinking. People always say how drinking won't make your problems disappear, but those people don't understand time, they don't understand how drinking makes time disappear.

After making it through the tree shadows, making it through a violent hailstorm, over the snake roads, past the brooks, the flowers, the weeds, the life of the forest, we were back in the desert again. We rode along the edges of red dirt castles, underneath cloud shadows, big cloud spaceships, slipping through cactus fields, ignoring the haze of the long road, and just going and going. There was a hollow fear in my heart as the landscape turned from life to death. I didn't want to leave Yosemite. I didn't want to leave San Francisco. I didn't want to leave any of the other places that Moll and I had been over the years. Who just keeps doing things they don't want to do? Junkies? Preachers? People who are scared to death of stopping?

"Where are we going today?" She asked.

"Don't know. Where you wanna go?"

"Don't know?"

"How about that way?" I pointed at the windshield.

"How about that way?" She pointed backwards.

"Can't do that, no looking back, that's the rule, unless a tornado is behind us, that's the other rule."

~

We had made it through a hailstorm earlier. It came down so hard that Ecc had to slow down to almost a stop. I thought the windshield was going to crack. Ecc was scared, but he wouldn't ever admit it. I watched his hands grip the steering wheel as if it were about to come off, the veins bulging from the top of his hands. If he were to admit being afraid, he would probably have some childhood story of his dog being killed in a hailstorm. He's just one of those people that have things die around him all the time.

~

The first of many roadside gravesites appeared and stayed behind us. The sadder ones had left-behind wreaths of flowers where the souls had been set free. I started keeping count of the graves. It made me feel better to have a number, like I wasn't going to be alone. I used to, like most people when they pass these man-made tragedies, clamp my mouth shut, stare at the remnants of death, and pretend that it wasn't there. But... things are different now. Things are very different now. There's a lump that I can feel growing in my head. Just above my right eye at my hairline, a heavy pulse pushes against the interior of my skull about every five seconds. It bothered me at first, but now I just embrace it. Almost simultaneously with this pulsating came frequent nosebleeds, especially in the mornings when I wake. And I don't know what it means. Death? When? I'm not sure myself. The blood from my nose gets thinner every day, the knot in my forehead gets thicker every day, and the pulsating reminder gets more frequent every day. It's the nice kind of pain that kills the illusion of immortality.

A New Century

Moll was concentrating heavily on the dry road. Every few seconds she pushed her sunglasses back up her sweaty nose. I scanned the radio stations, pausing and passing on all the usual pop station, classic rock station, country station, Spanish station, R&B station, Christian station until getting so low there was even a FM classical station. I stopped on a channel with a woman talking lowly. It sounded like a NPR voice, which is distinctly different because it doesn't sound like someone trying to sell life insurance or tires or McDonald's. They sold opinions that weren't overbearing like maybe they didn't believe them either. The hot topic at the time was what was going to happen at the Millennium. The low voice lady said some experts were predicting massive digital breakdowns that would result in possible worldwide financial ruin.

I secretly hoped that everything would go haywire when the New Year hit. It made me feel better about my inevitable demise to have the world's demise along with it. It was some built-in fear mixed with ego that I couldn't get rid of. I could tell myself that I didn't believe it, but it was there, hiding behind all the good in me.

~

Ecc left the radio on the news channel. He liked words while traveling and I liked soft rock, but neither one of us cared so much that we fought about it. Out in these nowhere parts it seemed to be mostly Christian channels. Christian rock songs always fooled me because it sounds like a good pop-rock song, something I would listen to alone in my bedroom, but never play on a jukebox. But then the lyrics give it away, because they always refer to HIM or HE, overemphasizing this man they follow the teachings of. I don't like the way they must think it's uncool to just say Jesus or God or the Exalted One. If you're going to believe in something ridiculous, own up to it.

So instead of a nice Air Supply song or a song about HIM, we listened to several news voices tell us the factors involving the world going to shit in the year 2000. I don't think Ecc was going to make it in this world, in this new technological based world. He perpetually rolled his eyes at everything without actually doing it. I didn't care either way. I liked nature and gadgets all the same. Ecc tried to separate himself from the herd, yet stayed close enough not to miss anything. He was different to a fault. Exhausting. I'm not sure how much longer we had. It reminded me of one of those soft rock songs that said, "Sometimes love just ain't enough." Of course I've always said this.

~

I turned down the radio after getting my fill of the upcoming world disaster. The religious discussion began about the similarities to Armageddon. One man interpreted that the place God sends Satan is called the Millennium, just like the approaching occurrence is called.

"Do you still believe in the higher power thing?" I asked Moll. I remember she wouldn't use any specific words that conveyed a religion, just the term *higher power*.

"Yeah, I don't know... why?"

"With all of this talk of the world ending, it's good to know what team you're on."

"No, really? Why do you ask?"

"Seriously, maybe you've decided to start worshiping the devil or something. These are things we need to know about each other."

"Uh, I don't know, I think there's, like, a higher power in the universe that we aren't ever supposed to find. It's like, if we find it, the concept would be destroyed. So we go on just believing in... titles through religion or like, whatever people like us believe in, something that we don't want to find." Moll would usually bounce around her answers with too many *likes* and *I don't knows*, but she had been different lately and I couldn't figure out what it was. The sun was beating down on the left side of her face. She pushed her sunglasses back up again. She wiped the sweat off her nose. To me it's obvious. I wanted to yell out, that it's right there on your nose.

"Maybe we should form our own religion or title?" I suggested. "So when the world does end we will go to the same place."

"Don't worry Buster, we're going to the same place. It ain't going to be easy, but we'll see each other there."

We bounced over all those unnamed, unknown roads in nowhere America. The wind coming through the topless Bronco kept us comfortable in the hundred-degree weather. Only the sequenced-out highway gravesites could let a man with destination know he was making progress. The second roadside grave marker came and left. The flowers were plastic, and melting. It reminded me of a line from a young and alive writer named Kerouac. *The candle burns, and when that's done the wax lies in cold artistic piles. —s about all I know.*

A Lost Philosopher

We were almost done with Nevada when night fell. There were supposed to be numerous campsites around the town of Ely off of interstate 5. The darkness came so fast and hard that I became disoriented with decision and direction. Not only did we not find any campgrounds, but we also lost the interstate. The speed limit went from 65 to 20 miles per hour, and the atmosphere from nothingness to country suburbs. Rows and rows of little pink houses passed by our searching eyes. They were the kind of houses that would never have a FOR SALE sign in their front yards.

"I think you missed something." Moll told me.

"I think you're right." Yet I didn't stop or turn around, I kept driving along through the neighborhood, as if there were a reason for this opportunity.

~

Ecc took a wrong turn and I knew he wouldn't turn around. I had never met anyone who hated backtracking so much, as if we would lose some outrageous amount of time. We were both equally stubborn. It would usually take us a minimum of a week to talk to each other after a fight. We would sleep in the same bed, eat at the same table, and drive in the same car without saying one word.

This one time when we got into a fight in New Orleans, or maybe it was Venice, it's all a blur now, but either way I left whatever city it was. Of course he eventually came after me, and found me with nothing but the instinct of where I would possibly go. He always found me, and I can't imagine a world in which he couldn't find me. Even in the afterworld, even if he had to backtrack, he would find me.

~

"Are you going to turn around?" Moll asked.

"I don't know. I kind of want to see where this leads."

"Okay." She said kind of annoyed. "Why?"

It's obvious, I thought. "Because no one travels so high, as he who does not know where he is going."

Her eyebrows and lips scrunched in.

"Cromwell." I admitted.

"Cromwell is stupid." Moll laughed with a snort. She could really crack herself up sometimes.

After going through a dozen identical neighborhood blocks, we came to a stop sign. To the right was a sign for Interstate 5, and to the left in the distance was a larger than life neon sign for the Hotel Nevada.

A Hotel Nevada

Down Main Street was a string of one-star motels and out-of-business storefronts. A smell of 20th century coal and clean sewers hung in the air. We had driven through dozens of these towns, and for every one there was another town just down the highway with construction cranes and a strip-mall with a freshly paved parking lot. For every one of these towns there were a hundred American flags flapping from the wind of traffic passing them by. The American dream unabashedly relinquished.

The sign for the Hotel Nevada dominated the small town landscape. It had a marquee that read, ROLL FOR YOUR ROOM. There was an empty parking space right in front of the hotel's doors. It was fate or either a lack of reasoning. Fate sounded more magical.

Before getting out of the truck, Moll climbed over to me and pressed her lips against mine as if it could have been the last time. We walked into the two-story brick building. The lobby was a casino, or something like a casino. A few withered souls sat at slot machines with handfuls of nickels, the sign of a future ghost town. Maybe I'd appear here when I died? Dust in the carpet, a slot machine dream. Transition seemed so much better than vanishing.

We found the front desk on the other side of the vacant quarter slots. A blue-haired lady with a Virginia Slim shoved halfway in her mouth sat behind a cage.

"We'd like to roll for our room." I said in a very serious fashion.

She didn't respond. She came from behind her iron bars and walked out to the casino floor. Moll gave me an uncertain smile and I just shrugged. We both silently agreed that she wanted us to follow her. So we did. I walked behind Moll, staring at the cigarette-burned and gum-spotted carpet. It seemed to once be a red carpet with flowers.

Old Blue Hair was waiting at the craps table for us. "Thirty dollars on the table. If you roll a 7 or 11 you get your money back and a room. If not, you get a room."

"Sounds fair." I replied.

"Damn right it's fair." She said.

I put down the thirty dollars and studied the dice, making sure they had the right numbers on them. I could never tell if they were weighted. Moll blew on them for luck. I tossed the dice down to the end.

5 & 5

Old Blue Hair already had a key ready. "Room number twelve. It's on the second floor."

Before taking the key, I asked, "Double or nothing?"

"Well, this is a first. I'll have to check with the owner." She said and then just stood in the same spot staring off into nowhere. She seemed to be stuck like her wind-up mechanism had run down. "The owner says to be fair, if you want to do double or nothing, it should count towards another room."

We looked around for someone hiding. The lady was obviously comfortably insane, bored to an advantage. But either way I put down the thirty dollars for the double, and said, "Thank the owner for being so fair, the owner very well could be a crooked casino shark."

"Yes, the owner also could be rich, but…" She faded off and then snapped back in her head. "Can I perhaps get you a beverage?"

"Sure, a couple of beers would be great."

"Hold on, let me get the cocktail waitress." She left the table and a few minutes later came back with two beers on a wooden tray. "Two Bud Lights?" She said like she was unsure.

"Um, yes, thank you." Moll held back her grin.

Then she gave me my beer and stood directly in front of me. I took the hint and tipped her a few dollars.

"A man's integrity is measured by his ability to part with his money." Blue Hair said like she was reading it out of a book.

"Thank you... for the beers and the wisdom." I said.

She resumed her position at the head of the table. Moll gave me another funny smile to tell me she was glad that we had stopped here, she was glad we got lost.

I rolled the dice.

6 & 2

Old Blue handed me two room keys.

"Can I keep going?"

"Well, I'll have to check with the front desk to make sure we have the vacancy." She stood in the same spot and counted on her fingers. "Okay, we have eight rooms left, not counting the two you already have, so you can roll until those are taken."

So I doubled up on my two rooms and bet on another. The few people that were in the casino had obviously smelled the money and made their way over to the table. I was a cash-only kind of guy, never liked dealing with ATM's and banks. I asked Moll to go out to the car and get the rest of our stash. She waited to see my next roll.

1 & 3

"God you suck!" Moll told me before leaving.

~

I went out to the Bronco to get the rest of our cash. I'm not sure what Ecc was thinking, but if I had to guess, he was thinking this was going to save us, or at the very least it was going to give us more time. These were the moments that kept us going over the years, the moments that gave us the validity we were always searching for. I suppose I should have been a little more worried about losing all of our money, but there were bigger stakes than money happening at the time.

Outside the casino the streets were so quiet. I would always remember that serenity I felt right before walking back into the lobby, which seemed to be screaming with bells and sirens.

~

I knew before I rolled that it wasn't time. Moll came back with the money and I handed her the four keys. She gave me the oddest look after taking the keys.

"What?"

"Nothing Kenny Rogers." She cackled.

"It took you all this time to think of that joke?"

"What you talking about Kenny Rogers?" She burst out laughing.

"You're ridiculous."

"Good one."

A small crowd had timidly gathered around. They were much more nervous than I was, even though none of us had anything to lose.

3 & 5 - Five rooms

6 & 4 - Six rooms

4 & 4 - Seven rooms

"Only three rooms left, and it's over," Old Blue told me. "Then you'll own the hotel for the night."

The audience talked amongst themselves about what they would do in this situation. Some literally salivated, some joked, and some winced while I counted out the double of the seven rooms plus the thirty for the eighth room. The money was down. I looked at the dice and knew it still wasn't time. Moll had her black cord necklace wrapped around her finger. I could only control the throw. Whatever it landed on was the beauty.

4 & 5

The crowd moaned. Old Blue didn't even blink. She was visibly unconcerned about the whole ordeal. I started to count out more money. Once I saw how much money was there, I finally became nervous, thinking that maybe the dice were fixed and maybe the odds would never even out. A man behind me who reeked of mothballs told me, "Boy, there's only two chances left. Walk away."

"People hate winners. I couldn't disappoint you guys." I learned how to feign cowboy confidence from all those old Clint Eastwood movies. I felt like a rock star in Ely, Nevada. I could be the hero of a tall-tale, or of a myth of Greek proportions.

Before rolling, a tension gathered around me. I felt an odd sensation against my right arm. I thought it was Moll, but it turned out to be the mothball man. I became worried that Moll had lost faith in me. My eyes scanned around the room desperately while everyone else was staring at my hand. Then she appeared directly across the table with her crooked smile. I thought about how little time was left with that smile. I thought how selfish I was and just dropped the dice to the table.

5 & 6

The audience groaned as if they were all of a sudden against me. It was over. They shuffled back to their own dreams, inspired to live a nickel at a time. Moll was staring at me like I was her rock star. I was reminding myself to breathe, because I almost was taken down by Ely Nevada. I took my money back, and dropped the keys on the table. Old Blue handed me the key to room 112.

"Thirty dollars or roll?" She said, I think joking.

"I can't afford not to pay for it." I handed her thirty dollars.

A Circus Virus

The hall was bleak and smelled of mildew. Moll jiggled the key in and out of the lock. One of the residents was screaming, "shut up" over and over. She was either talking to us or to whoever was dancing, singing, and laughing to

Al Green down the way. The lock finally submitted. When we walked in, I saw a ghost. "That fucking TV." I mumbled.

"What?"

"Isn't that our old TV?"

"What are you talking about?"

"Nothing."

She would think I was crazy if I told her. I looked over it, the details, the chip on the corner, the feel of death. There was a chip on the corner, but I couldn't remember if it was the same corner.

"Are you alright?" Moll asked.

"Yeah, just a flashback."

"I'm going to take a shower." She turned on the bathroom sink as soon as she got in, something she always did whether she was pissing or just putting on deodorant.

Whenever I got a hotel room, I always checked the drawers for the complimentary Bible. It was rare for the one-star hotels to not have the word of God at arms reach from the bed. I took it out of the end table, opened it up to Ecclesiastes, and then randomly flipped through the pages until landing on a passage. FOR THE LIVING KNOW THAT THEY WILL DIE, BUT THE DEAD KNOW

NOTHING; THEY HAVE NO FURTHER REWARD, AND EVEN THEIR NAME IS FORGOTTEN. Which isn't true because thousands of years after Ecclesiastes wrote this, we still know his name. I still carry his name.

~

I pushed up the sink handle to full blast. My biggest fear, besides dying, was someone hearing me do things in the bathroom. Sometimes I would go to bathrooms that had those old sinks with low-pressure hot and cold faucets and I would have to wait till later to do my business. Once I got the shower to the right temperature, I could turn off the sink water.

As I let the shower spray down over me I thought about the whole weird scene down in the casino. I imagined losing all our money. We would have had to settle down here in Ely, find jobs, make friends, never leave, die here in fucking Nevada. But Ecc did it. It was one of the reasons I loved him, he always found a way to get over. It sounds awful saying it out loud, but it must be better than the opposite. Thinking about all this got me revved up. I reached down between my legs and it was all I could do to not run out of the bathroom and go fuck his brains out.

~

———

I flopped on the bed and stared at the blank screen. I closed my eyes and tried to communicate with whatever bigger entity that was between this television and me. What do you want from me? I said over in my head. It didn't answer, so I turned it on and flipped through the six channels. An evangelist with mustard colored pants had a line of sick people ready to come up on stage to be healed. He was the kind of person who had never been beaten up, or who had never been poor, or who had never had a woman cheat on him, and this gave him the ego to "heal" his fellow sufferers. Or maybe all those things had happened to him and it made him into a really clever con artist.

A man that was in front of the evangelist had a lump protruding from his temple. The mustard man put the palm of his hand over the lump, and then asked God to free the man's fears, and free the man's pain, and to take away the affliction. The audience moaned and cried and kneeled and prayed and clapped and ran around and screamed "Amen!" and nodded their heads and spoke in tongues and shook their bodies and held their hands up to the sky. They believed in whatever this person was doing. They had to believe in him or believe in suffering. There wasn't any other choice as far as they knew. The healer finished off by popping the sick man's forehead. All of a sudden I woke up to Moll playfully slapping me on the head. In my confusion I slapped away her hand and pushed her back. "Don't fucking do that!"

She recoiled in fear. My head spun. The TV wasn't on. I gingerly rubbed my skull. She couldn't be the one who killed me.

"I'm sorry, just a nightmare." I said, checking to see if that lump was still in my head.

"Okay psycho." She was breathing heavily. She was naked and wanted to play, but I ruined that.

"Let's get out of here."

A Forgotten Colony

There was a bar down on Main Street that had several people gathered outside. The same brick decorated every building in town, underneath the same desert sky, and below the thick layer of American earth that has infused the blood of all these secluded towns in the middle of somewhere. Moll and I headed that way to get a beer. The name of the place was Twisted Pine. It had to be an old hotel lobby with the hotel torn down. The ceiling was at least thirty feet high, the Sistine Chapel given up. It had that old swirling lobby carpet and that disinfectant lobby smell. I imagined that it was once a big deal, only the most refined of 18th century travelers stopped in to sleep over.

When we walked in, the twenty or so people turned their heads and gave us the once-over. I gave a nod with an uncomfortable smile. They all went back to whatever they were doing except for a couple of men that were getting a better mental picture of Moll. I haven't told you this, but Moll is a beautiful gal. People were always asking her if she was part Asian, or part Native American, or part Italian, or part Egyptian. When people do that they are secretly saying that you are attractive and they don't know how to say it any other way. No one ever asks someone unattractive if they are part Brazilian or Russian or anything like that. Anyway, she could be a real troublemaker if she wanted to, but I've been lucky enough to avoid any major conflict so far.

I grabbed us a couple of beers. Moll chirped at the plump bartender over my shoulder. "Can I grab some quarters from you Larry?" Moll liked to call strangers Larry. She had a solid gage of whom and who wouldn't take it the wrong way.

"If you want quarters for the pool table, you don't need'em, it's free." Larry the bartender paused before explaining further as he probably always did. "A friend of mine donated it to the bar."

We carried our beers across the bar, past the wolves, past a dying bachelorette party, and to this wide-open space where the table sat. Moll went to the bathroom while I tried to get comfortable in the foreign land. There was a piggy bank looking thing with a sign that asked for donations of a quarter a game. I dropped a dollar on to a handful of quarters, planning to play at least four games before the night was done.

Behind the pool table, a giant American Indian danced with this skinny little white gal. They looked like animated caricatures of themselves, not supposed to fit together on purpose. I started to rack the balls and he threw the skinny white gal off to the side. "You want to play me in pool?" He stood about six and a half feet and probably weighed close to three hundred pounds. I wasn't going to tell him no.

"No." I told him.

"What?"

"I'm just kidding." I handed him the pool cue.

"That's funny." He said without laughing. "I'm Lauren."

"Hey Lauren, I'm Ecc."

"Ecc?"

"Yeah like neck without the N."

"Ah."

"How about partners? I've got someone else." Possession is a weird thing.

Without responding to me, he yelled across the room, "Sean!" Another American Indian came across the room. Sean was slightly smaller than Lauren. They were the kind of guys who had never seen celery or a treadmill. Moll came back and they seemed to turn into shy little boys. That is until she said, "Goddamn you fuckers are big! You want to arm wrestle?"

They were confused at Moll's abrasiveness, but still politely introduced themselves. Lauren broke the balls up, and what was going to be a competitive game between Moll and I turned into about a dozen casual games with these guys. Sean kept staring at my bottle, and finally said, "Hey Ecc, what is that? Is it beer?"

"Yeah, it's an IPA, an Indian pale ale."

"Indians make it? My people!"

"Not exactly. The British came up with a recipe that had extra hops to keep their beer fresh for shipping to the Brits who lived in India." This was considered useless knowledge up until that moment. "So they called it Indian pale ale after those Indians way over on that side of the world.

He seemed disappointed, and I regretted telling him the truth as I almost always regretted when it came to truth.

"Can I try it?"

"Of course."

He took a big slug off the bottle and spewed it on the floor. "Holy shit! That's worst shit I've ever had in my life!" He wiped his mouth off with his shirt.

Lauren pointed and laughed at him.

"You try it then!"

"Hell no man! I stick to the good stuff."

"Come on, it's just beer you big pussy. Just drink it." Moll looked almost crossed-eyed.

"Yeah you big pussy!" Sean mimicked.

Lauren looked over the label slowly and then took a baby sip. His faced contorted into a painful grimace, but he managed to swallow it. Moll and I were shocked. We felt like we were on another planet. Lauren ran over to his Bud Light and chugged it like it was a chaser for tequila.

"You guys are fucked up." Sean told us like a psychiatrist. "That stuff will kill you."

The night went on. Moll was running the pool table, Lauren was flirting with some of the girls in the revived bachelorette party, and Sean and I talked in between missing our shots. He and his cousin drove seventy-seven miles every weekend to get to Ely. It was the closest bar from their home of Duckwater, Nevada. "You guys have to come up there! It's really peaceful. We just sit on our porch, drinking beer and shooting cats. You have to check it out!"

"That sounds... great?" I didn't know how to respond.

But Moll did, "You shoot cats?"

"Yeah, it's funny as hell." Lauren said as innocently as the context would allow.

"That's fucking cruel! Why would you do that?" Moll was refraining herself.

"Because they're nasty cats, hundreds of them, shitting and fucking everywhere. It's how we control the population." He laughed.

I gave Moll a *calm-down* look. She was about to start an animal right's argument, which I agreed with, but like I said before; we were on another planet. A planet where we drink commercials, where we go to sleep to dream, where we only know hand to mouth, where we survive and suffer, where we use the word hope, where we praise God and blame the Devil, where we pass the time by shooting cats, where we look ahead to the future, to children, to property, to a better life, to a more convincing afterlife.

~

I went to the bathroom in order to hold my tongue. One of the guys we were shooting pool with happily admitted to shooting cats as his daily hobby. He drank beer, watched TV, and shot cats. Ecc gave me a look because he knows I can't hold my tongue. I turned on the water from the sink and talked to myself in the mirror. "Maybe this is the reason, the validation of this trip, maybe I can save hundreds of cats." Then I heard someone cough from the stall. We both got quiet, and then I hurried out after hearing what sounded like a nose snorting something, cocaine, meth, crank, whatever people snort in the desert.

"I'm going to have a smoke outside." I told Ecc then rushed past him outside. The anger about the cats had been replaced by potential embarrassment of talking to myself. I'm sure everyone talks to their mirror image in the bathroom when they think they are alone.

I lit the cigarette and watched the town not move. Everything that was moving was moving inside that bar. It was like two different worlds. I wondered if anyone else noticed it or if they just saw the same thing inside and out. There was a storefront across the street that you could tell used to be a record store. I imagined that at one time people came downtown to get lunch and then shop for records, and crafts, and clothes, and stuff like that. Now they just do without.

I smashed out the cigarette and took the butt in with me. Everyone was smoking inside, but I liked the contrast of breathing clean air and dirty air together, as if it was healthier. I approached the pool table cautiously until verifying that no one was talking about shooting cats. I was no exception for the out of sight, out of mind theory.

Ecc missed an easy shot. He always played badly against strangers he liked, a forgivable defect.

~

I kept missing my shots, but it didn't matter, no one was paying attention. Lauren was grinding on another girl

70

that was a little meatier than the last. There was a floppy fellow by the bar giving us a look like he needed to tell us something. Beside him was this worn-down woman that had the longest mullet I'd ever seen. It was like she was going for a record. Above her were three girls from the bachelorette party dancing on the wooden bar top. They did the fake-lesbian dance where all three spoon each other while bouncing their butts and crotches together. I highly doubt that even lesbians do this dance. It was addictively pathetic, like watching a kid pick his nose. It's the last thing you want to see, but you stare anyway.

"Cousin, I'm starving. When are we going to eat?" Lauren yelled across the room as he came back to us.

"Soon, soon."

"Where do you guys stay?" I asked.

"In Duckwater."

"You drive back eighty miles?"

"Seventy-seven! But, it's not so bad." Lauren hiccupped.

"It's not bad for you bitch! All you do is sleep." Sean said.

"You guys are wasted, I mean, you shouldn't drive that far. Isn't there someone here you could crash with?"

"Nah, it's fine. We go eat a big meal, get some coffee, and lounge until I sober up."

Lauren laughed at his cousin. "Shit, sober up."

Then Sean laughed at that. "It's been rough a few times."

"A few!"

"I've wrecked five times." He admitted.

"Five times!" Moll punched Sean in the arm.

"Have you ever been hurt?" I asked.

"Just some bruises and cuts, nothing major. I usually just fall asleep and wake up on the side of the road. I've gotten a DUI once. That was the worst." He laughed. "The car wouldn't start back up, so we went to sleep and woke up to a cop knocking on my window."

"That's fucking crazy man." I told him.

"It doesn't matter. I won't be alive too much longer anyway." Sean said, and it reminded me of me.

"What do you mean?"

"Well, I have a bad heart and a hole in my liver. I'm not supposed to be drinking, but I drink almost every day. I'm not supposed to do much at all, but fuck it, what am I going to do, just act like I'm not alive. If I did what the doctor says, then I wouldn't leave my house. I'd rather live right now and then die knowing that I did what I wanted."

"Cheers to that." I put my bottle up to his and hoped that that wouldn't be the sip that killed him. It was sad that he had never been out of Nevada, yet he was convinced that he was living to the fullest. I guess sometimes it only takes a bar in Ely, and shooting cats in Duckwater.

"And that's not the worst part of it. The worst part is my family name is going to die with me. I'm the last of the Hollowbreast." He said with a pause. "You didn't laugh?"

"Is it a joke?"

"No."

"Oh, because of the breast part. Well, it's not really funny. What does Hollowbreast mean?"

"It's Cheyenne for warrior. A man with no heart, a hollow breast. But everybody here knows that I've got a big heart, so maybe the name should die off with me anyway." He killed his beer.

"No man, you should try to pass it on." I said for lack of anything else, like I knew what anyone should do with his life.

He pointed around the bar like he was a lighthouse. "That's why I drive seventy-seven miles." He laughed and nudged my arm like we were old buddies. "See that girl over there that keeps staring at us. I slept with her one night, and she hasn't left me alone since then."

"Well, there you go."

"Nah, not for me. She's crazy... But a few more of these and you never know." He nudged my arm again, almost knocking me over. "What about you? Where is your name from? I ain't ever heard of Ecc before?"

"It's from the Bible book, short for Ecclesiastes. It means gatherer and teacher or preacher. I don't like the preacher interpretation, but sometimes names dictate who we end up being." Sean, the last Hollowbreast silently agreed with me.

Moll brought me another beer that I didn't need. "Hey! Hey you!" She started hiccupping also. Everyone was wasted, just another Saturday night in nowhere town America.

"Sean! I'm fucking hungry!" Lauren was now grinding with the maid of honor to a Bon Jovi song.

"After this beer." Sean said and bought another Bud Light. "Hey! You guys should come back to Duckwater with us!"

I didn't know what to say. "I don't know what to say."

"Yeah, come on, we'll drink more Bud Lights and watch some TV, it'll be fun."

He was so excited that it was hard to tell him no. "I'm about to pass out man. I'll be lucky if I make it back to my bed across the street."

Lauren came back over. "Hey man you got another fucking beer! I'm fucking hungry! God, I'm so hungry."

"Alright man, hold on." Sean grabbed a bar napkin and pen. "If you guys come back by this way, you have to stop in Duckwater and stay with us." He wrote down his address and gave it to me.

"I promise, we will."

"Hey, will you send me a postcard?" His enthusiasm toward us was overwhelming.

"Where from?"

"I don't care, anywhere. I've never gotten a postcard before, and when strangers come through Ely, I always ask them to send me postcard, but they never do."

I didn't feel so special anymore. "I swear to you, that I'll send you one."

We hugged on it, and said our final goodbyes. Moll and I needed to get to a bed. As we left the Twisted Pine, we heard, "Sean man, come on! I'm fucking hungry!"

When we got back to the room, the television was on. We were too drunk to remember if we forgot to turn it off or if we ever turned it on. It was showing an infomercial about real estate. The plaster smile man on the screen told us, "Now you can enjoy the freedom of owning your own land." That's all I remembered before fading off into the night and giving in to another day.

A Trail of Blood

When I woke, the TV was off and my upper lip felt wet. As soon as my fingers instinctively touched my face, I knew the texture. I looked at the blood on my fingertips. Behind my hand was an unfocused room. I told my brain to wiggle my fingers and they did. Things were looking up. I quietly snuck out of bed and into the bathroom. My beard was decorated with a fresh coat of blackish-red paint. I cleaned up and forced the rest of the blood from my sinuses. The little maroon drops plopped against the dirty white porcelain sink, and then disintegrated into a pink nothingness. I had recently learned that blood is actually the color blue until it comes in contact with oxygen. Blue would be a much more pleasant color to decorate a sink. I turned the water up high and watched it all disappear. There was something about watching a part of my body go down a drain that made me happy, as if I was being distributed throughout the system. "The system." I said to verify I was awake.

I went back to bed, and just sat there thinking how it was getting worse.

Moll woke. "Did Sean tell you that he might be dying?"

"Yeah." I cleared my throat. "He told me that he would be dying soon."

"He told you that?"

"Not directly, but he said that if he had stopped drinking and smoking about two years ago, then he could have lived a little longer than *soon*."

"That's so sad." She said with her head under the covers.

"I don't know? If I knew I was going to die early in my life, I think I would be the same."

"What do you mean?"

"I mean I'd probably do everything in my power to kill myself through drugs and drinking and whatever else before my due date. I just like to think that *I* did it, as

77

apposed to things beyond my control, and I'm too much of a coward to do it with a gun or a rope or something."

We sat quietly in bed for a few minutes. I stared at the blank TV, and she still had her head under the covers.

~

When me and Ecc moved to San Francisco, I told him I wanted to stop drinking and doing drugs, and I wanted to maybe have a baby, but I needed to get control of shit first. He was awful at being weak, like if he showed a little weakness and admitted that we were out of control then he would just shrivel up and die. We sort of built a relationship out of this lifestyle, so I can't really blame him for not wanting to change. It was a nice thought though, the sort of thought that lives in the happy-ending movies.

I kept my head under the covers. It made sense under there, in the darkness, in the warmth. We were supposed to be camping or crashing with friends the whole trip, only buying our food in big grocery stores, and only drinking booze outside of bars. If we were going make this endless journey last it would have to be on the cheap. I didn't mind camping, but I loved staying in the hotels, the weirdness of a room that thousands of strangers also stayed in.

Ecc was saying something about hitting the road, but I didn't want to go. If I stayed in a hotel room, I stayed until they made me leave.

"I'm going to read for awhile." I said. "Then maybe take a nap and then get up." Ecc had always tried to get me to read all this old white man literature that I couldn't relate to, so I compromised by finding some old white lady literature. Actually I was reading Virginia Woolf at the time, and she killed herself before getting old, so that didn't count.

"Alright, I'm going to go write somewhere, be back in a bit." Ecc rolled out of bed.

"I like the way Virginia Woolf killed herself. She just walked into the River Ouse with rocks in her pockets, covering her body with water and never coming up."

"Sounds organic." Ecc said as a joke because of the current influx of everything being labeled organic. He argued that everything normally made is organic and doesn't need to be titled it, everything else should be titled *synthetic*.

"Ha-ha, funny. Better than drowning in whiskey."

"Maybe…" He grabbed his notebook and pen, and headed out the door, one of his convenient ways of avoidance.

~

I walked through the casino, head down, not wanting to see the dying people playing penny slots. Outside it was that dry heat that everyone always talks about when they talk about the desert. I walked along Main Street until finding the town diner. The booths were mostly full of senior citizens, the kind that knew everything there was to know about the others around them, and the only thing that ever changed was the weather, and that was so subtle that it was like it couldn't be called change. I ordered a black coffee from a nice mom looking waitress.

"Anything else sweetie?" She said like my mom used to say.

"No thank you, not right now."

I took out my notebook and watched the movement of the diner until the coffee and my pen kicked in. I wondered if any of the people in there thought they had the good life, or if any of them knew how bad they had it, or if any of them woke up one day and knew that it all passed by and there was nothing to do except the exact same thing every day for the rest of their lives. I probably wondered about sadness too much, like it made me feel better about my own short life. I didn't know how to say things to

—

anyone including myself, but if I had to say it, I would just say that I wanted to go longer. Maybe that's what all of these old folks said to themselves also? They got the American breakfast with the endless cup of coffee, and then they would pray to go a little longer.

A Terrible Thirst

From the edge of the Pacific Ocean we had been following a never-ending string of power lines, which is something that could easily be missed. I suppose that was one of the concepts, to make them unnoticeable. Moll believed they caused brain cancer, Alzheimer's, birth defects, and I'm sure if she knew about the lump in my head, that would be added to the list also. Up until Utah the poles had been cross shapes, but then as soon as we left Nevada they turned to the shape of football field goals. We followed these goals along beside the still flat red desert. I envisioned a thousand years into the future. There would be long flat red parking lots with pools and skyscrapers decorating the reflection of the sun. There would be neon-lit dispensers giving out raffle tickets to win a trip to Mars.

I couldn't think of where the power lines would be in the future, it's something they've never invented in science fiction movies.

I saw another roadside grave, the fourth one so far. This one was marked by a plethora of stuffed animals, dusty and ragged like they had been there for years, from some poor parents that probably lost their kid in a car accident. I imagined they made an annual trip to the site to clean it off and organize the toys that now represented their child's spirit.

~

I wish we played some kind of road games like Punch-bug or Eye-spy, something that we could do together, something to remind me that we were both kids once, and not budding grown-ups with issues. The only kids with issues are the ones that are diagnosed by adults. Our game was the silent game; the one who doesn't say what is on their mind the longest is the winner.

I turned the radio from a country channel that we both forgot about several songs too late. I didn't like country music, not even the old stuff in which Ecc claims he loves because "they used to tell stories." Then I found a rap station, but I couldn't get into that either, not even the real

MC stuff in which Ecc claims he loves because "they are actually poets that have found a way to reach a mass audience." Both country and rap have exceptions, but they both have such esoteric motives that how can anyone that doesn't love guns and trucks or guns and ho's be a part of it. That's our game I guess, the one where we have an opinion and the other challenges them to they become irritated.

Then I found a station playing a Blondie song, and in true form, we both silently agreed that this was a win-win game.

~

We were almost done with Utah, hurrying past Fruita, roaring across I-70 in a love-hate relationship with the dead land. It was pretty, yet seeing anything pretty for too long becomes average, which is worse than ugly. The Bronco needed to rest soon, but I wanted to make the Rocky Mountains before we stopped. A speck appeared in the distance. It blended in with the purple clouds and fire engine earthquakes. The closer we got, the tighter I became. By the time we were on top of the speck, I was completely wound up. It was a man on a unicycle. I reached for my Polaroid camera while staring at the oddity, but never took a photo. I wondered where he could have been going out there in the middle of nowhere, probably on some spiritual journey, or trying to break a world record. I exhaled and became happy in the form of clarity. I turned around to see him going into the never-ending painting, mostly making sure he was actually there.

"What the fuck." I said. "Did you see that?"

"Ecc, how the hell would I have missed that?"

Sometimes I see things that aren't there so I have to ask. I turned around again, trying to get one more glimpse.

A Clapping Echo

I did all of the driving after Utah while Moll slept against the window. We found a campsite at the Colorado National Monument. It was the beginning of the Rockies, a little cliff dwelling that told foreigners to catch their breath while they could. We stepped out into the dusk heat, and were assaulted by thousands of bugs. There were mosquitoes, flies, gnats, beetles, and other annoying winged creatures that couldn't be swiped away. For some reason God created all these useless creatures that can't be swiped and these other useless creatures that can't invent a way to kill the ones that can't be swiped. There should be a Christian rock song about that.

One of God's winged creatures flew in Moll's ear and got stuck. It buzzed right beside her eardrum. She began to panic. She jumped up and down. She slapped the side of her head. I was being bitten all over while I looked for something to drag it out. Moll started to cry. I brought over a bottle of water and poured it into her ear canal. The buzzing stopped, but she still felt it. Then we tried to drag it out with a hairclip. After a few minutes of prodding, she was able to pull out some bug parts. She clung to me while crying and laughing out of shock. She could be hard as nails until something like a bug flew inside her ear.

We took a hike while there was still a little light. The park was basically a huge brown rock beside a valley of natural red dirt formations. We walked out to a cliff that was at least a thousand foot drop. Moll sat on the edge and swung her legs in the air. I couldn't get within five feet of the drop-off; my mind questioned jumping for no particular reason. She laughed at my fear of heights, fear of a falling death. I suppose that no matter how close one is to dying, they don't want to miss out on whatever shitty thing is next.

"That's fine, laugh all you want, but I'm not getting any closer."

"Would you cry if a bug flew in your ear?"

"I don't think so."

"What if I jumped?" She asked.

"Don't say shit like that. It's not funny."

Now this usually would be the end of the conversation with most people, but Moll isn't like most people.

"Seriously. What if I jumped? What would you do?"

"I'd jump after you." I said looking the other way. I didn't want to have this conversation, much less this conversation while she dangled her legs from what might as well be an infinite height.

"Yeah?" She said like she didn't believe me. "Would you cry?"

"Could we talk about this over here?"

"No. Why?" She did a fake head bob toward the open-air drop.

"Fuck! Quit that!" I started to walk away. "You can do what you want, but I'm leaving."

"Oh, quit being such a pussy. Just tell me if you would cry or not."

This has been a sore subject in our relationship, because I've never cried in front of her. If she had one wish in the world, it wouldn't be a billion dollars or world peace or crap like that, it would be to see me cry. And I would cry if she died. I would have cried right then if it was possible, but there's something physically wrong with me. If I was to put two and two together, I probably could come up with a relation between the knot in my brain and not ever shedding a tear when I was supposed to.

~

"Would you?" I asked Ecc again, my special torture move.

"Yes, of course I would cry."

"I don't think you would. You just give me the answer I want to hear."

"Oh Christ Moll, just get off the edge. I would cry. I would cry in some form. I would be devastated, I'd be beyond crying, I'd probably shit and piss all over myself if tears didn't come out."

My last boyfriend before Ecc was a very emotional guy. He fucking cried when his turtle died. At the time it wasn't that attractive, but now I'm in love with the Tin Man. I guess I prefer Ecc, because there's always been hope that he would get in touch with some of those feelings. With the last guy, there was only the prospect that he'd start crying when a bug flew in his ear or something silly like that.

I sat on the edge of a cliff that didn't seem too sturdy. I was scared, but I liked being scared. I liked jumping out of planes, I liked walking on thin ice, I liked when friends jumped out of hidden places and scared the shit out of me. This one time my friend back in high school, back when I was dating the emotional guy, jumped out of my closet and scared me so bad I farted. No kidding. It was so funny and embarrassing that we both just fell down laughing. Then I tried to get her back, so I hid and waited for her in her bedroom closet. The problem was that when I jumped out to scare her she was halfway in bed with my boyfriend. I suppose I did scare her though. You should have seen how emotional my boyfriend was after that, a real tearjerker.

~

"Alright." Moll said after a few seconds as if she was thinking about something serious. "As long as something comes out."

I've always been this way, reserved, in control, never trying to change out of fear of becoming normal, the kind of normal where humans stop contradicting themselves. For example, I always hope that others think of me as being intelligent, yet I go out of my way to do so many stupid things. I secretly always hope that others think of me as attractive, yet once again I go out of my way to look like I just rolled out of bed after a week bender. And the worst, especially in Moll's eyes, is how I try to seem to others very even-tempered and in control of my emotions, yet I get a hold of pen and paper, and become this blubbering-out-of-control-emotional-slob. God, I love her. And I hope I get to finish this journey, because she's right. I won't cry. I won't shit and piss on myself. Hopefully the words will count for something in the end.

Moll didn't respond to my last lie. She was off in another world, observing her big toe. She wiggled it up and down while staring at it in the manner of a caveman staring at a wheel. I also stared at it, but as if it was my own. She started to get up and I held my breath. One slip and off she would go. "I still don't believe you." She said as she wiped the dirt off her shorts. I went up to her and hugged her. We looked over the valley. "I promise you, if you ever died, that I would have no choice but to cry." I said and she buried her head in my chest. Down through the red dirt valley was a formation was called God's Hands. It appeared to be two hands in the position of praying. I said a little a prayer about keeping promises. Then the sun disappeared behind Earth.

A Religious Experiment

Our tent was like a mansion. It could comfortably fit seven people and you could stand up and walk around. I bought it with visions of Moll and me and about three or four runts in the forest, living off the land, eating veggie hotdogs, and roasting marshmallows, which incidentally aren't vegetarian. It's funny how things don't turn out to be what you expect, like animal parts in puffy white desserts, and empty mansion tents with not a single runt.

We stayed in this tent the whole night, because of the invasion of the bugs and because they didn't allow campfires. So we drank beers, listened to music, and embraced this freedom that one can only feel when they have a tank full of gas and no home to go lock up. There weren't any other campers beside our site, but apparently our conversation carried quite a distance. Later on, probably two or three in the morning, a beam of light shone through the tent's surface. It scared the crap out of us. I hid my pipe and reached for a weapon, which turned out to be my camera. Then we heard, "You guys are being so loud!" A woman's voice whispered angrily. We smiled at each other. I pulled the door's zipper halfway up and stuck one leg out. The rest of my body followed. She started to say something, but the flash from my camera muted her. The woman hurried off into the darkness.

"Sorry, it's for scientific purposes." I said as I stepped back into the tent and then kept talking to her since she obviously could hear me all the way across the camp. "You will be highly rewarded one day when we finally cure the disease of noise law absurdity. You will be held in high regard in the scientific community as the leader of lab rats! You will..."

"Shut up!" Moll cut me off. "We should be quiet."

"Yes mam."

She laughed with her mouth covered. I turned down whatever folk music we were listening to. Our wild party was over. All our rowdy friends had to go home.

"Did you get a picture?"

"Not sure. It flashed." I waved the picture, waiting for an image to appear.

"I'm going to get you a digital camera."

"Please don't, that would be an insult."

"That could be a classic picture that doesn't turn out. Half of your pictures don't ever turn out." She whispered.

"Half of my life hasn't turned out." I mumbled. "Taking pictures is like capturing moments in life. Imagine if something disagreeable happens to you in life, and all you had to do was hit pause, look at the moment, delete it, and then do it again. That's erasing beauty to replace with perceived perfection. Perfection is ugliness. Perfection is not life. That picture I just took is life, it's unpredicted, it's dark, it's light, it's a planned surprise, it's unknown how it will turn out."

"Fine, jeez, I won't get you a digital camera."

~

I just got the *perfection* speech from Ecc. He has several go-to philosophies that aren't so bad except the way he says it. He's a much better writer than a speaker. If he would just shut up and write everything down he could be cult leader or something awful like that. He used to be much quieter, like when I first met him in Amsterdam he hardly said a word. I liked a man of few words, a man of action if needed. I'm not sure who convinced him to start talking so much. People shouldn't ever talk unless it's funny or instructional.

He was waving the Polaroid picture, excited to prove me wrong. The image turned out to be a light explosion with a slight distinction of a woman's head and shoulders.

"Good enough." He claimed.

I got out the playing cards so we could do something in silence. It bothered me to bother people, even when it was ridiculous. I imagined that the woman had youngish kids and she was fed up with everything around her, but she still had the power, and this power was extended to the unwritten and written laws of the land. We were on that land and under those laws. I want to have kids, but I'm afraid I'll get tired of them. Everybody gets tired of everything, especially little annoying people that always want to be fed or they don't ever want to be fed, or they always want help with something stupid like a volcano project or a really easy math equation. Then one day the kid wouldn't be new any more and I would tell myself that I'm tired of her or maybe him. I've already decided that I would be tired of my little girl before my little boy, because my girl would be sweet and obedient and my boy would get in trouble in school for cursing and drawing pictures of naked women.

"Moll!" I sort of heard Ecc say.

~

"Hey!" I said for the second time to Moll. She was off inside her head, probably thinking about how she's going to run away from me the first chance she gets.

"What?"

I took a surprise picture of her sulking face. "What you thinking about?"

She flipped me the middle finger and said, "Life motherfucker."

People were always flipping me off, like they knew the shitty things I was thinking about.

An Arrogant Breath

The next morning Moll found a note on the Bronco that read: IT'S RUDE TO TALK AFTER MIDNIGHT AT A CAMPSITE! YOU BASTARD!

"I wonder why she just said bastard? Did she think I was talking to myself?" I said too tired to care, but it got under Moll's skin.

"This really pisses me off. Talking after midnight? Are we fucking Communists or something? I can't talk and fucking laugh!" She stormed off to go look for the lady.

"Everyone's gone man." I walked after her. "Don't sweat it. We got a great picture and great note. Look! When you put them together it's like some sort of proof or validation of our journey. Look?" I put the Polaroid photo underneath the note and imitated the woman's nasally voice. "You bastard!"

~

I gave Ecc a chance to talk me down. I had an Italian temper, which I've been told most of my life is the worst of all the tempers. Apparently Cubans and Koreans are also just as bad, but I never meet anyone like that, or at least I never get into arguments with anyone like that.

Ecc was right though; it was some sort of validation. What else were we going to do, collect rocks or magnets from every place we stopped? If we could somehow get a threatening handwritten note from every place we stopped, the journey would possess something special. It means we would have had a real effect on people.

~

It was nine in the morning and a hundred degrees out. We were trying to make Boulder, Colorado until something else came up. This was the one town in which we both pre-agreed on going back to. The last time we were there I left Moll right before she was about to leave me. She had always left me for the same reason, fear, love, fear of love, fear of forever. That time I beat her to the punch, only leaving behind a cryptic note and her cello fresh out of the music pawnshop. I couldn't believe we were going back to Boulder.

We packed everything up, took the top off, and got ready to get some wind in our faces.

"You said Communists." I said after we got on the road. Moll laughed and accidentally snorted. She could really crack herself up.

After driving through Grand Junction and getting past the brief desert plains there is a golden path that flows hand in hand with the Colorado River. There are surreal dirt sculptures made from the wind and rain that stick above neon green corn fields and giant toy silos. There are black hill frames that open up to a royal blue sky fighting with snow-capped pyramids. There are yellow streaks and a magic haze that start behind you and go off into the distance, saying, "Follow me, follow me!" and all the while your ears are being filled with a banjo and a bongo, and all the while your mouth is filled with a crisp, sharp, clean mountain air, and all the while your skin tingles to the beat of the moment. Little puffy cotton clouds wrestle to stay below Heaven and above the immortal stone. The last traces of ice melt down into a glistening pool that is cupped 10,000 feet in the air. And man and machine climb higher and higher along East I-70. Moll and I were completely silent, both staring out and above our topless vehicle. We got up to a peak of the mountain highway and watched an eagle hover in a content stream of consciousness. We went down in the valley to see the little fable of Vail, Colorado. We went back up to the sun to look down on this beautiful world like the Gods themselves. That's when the Great Divide gets wider and then thinner until leaving us behind the passing mountains. That's when we went around the speeding corners to dance with the choppy waters of the snow cold river. It all could have been a perpetual highway into nothingness and the smile would have never left my face. If given the chance to start over, there wouldn't be an answer, just wheels on the road. If given the chance a million times over, my ghost would rub elbows with this moment a million times over... If given the chance...

A Comfortable Mirror

We cruised over the last little hill before descending down into Boulder Valley. It looked so much smaller than that first time I took the same descent several years before.

Going down into Boulder was like entering a frozen time warp, the people who had been there since the 60's hadn't changed, the people who had been there since the 70's hadn't changed, the people who had been there since the 80's hadn't changed, and the people that came there in the 90's seemed to try and adapt to one of these past eras in one way or another.

As we got off the highway and down onto the streets, people started to appear on the corners, riding their bicycles, sitting cross-legged in the grass, blasting hippie rock from their convertibles, hitching on the sidewalk, showing their faces, their tribes. The young at heart came in every age and every size of skinny with long straggly hair, unshaven, wearing ragged t-shirts, wearing sandals all year through the snow and rain, and existing beyond the walls. It was a place where the people rarely stayed inside anything, their houses, their cars, and even their offices.

We drove across Pearl Street where the town clock still displayed 3:10. It had been stuck on 3:10 since before I had lived there. A town without time. I always wondered if it was 3:10am or 3:10pm. I pointed this out to Moll and she didn't seem to care, or most likely I had already pointed it out to her when we used to live here and she didn't want to mention it. I'm pretty sure I repeated myself a lot.

I parked the Bronco in the shade and we took a walk down by Boulder Creek. There were people inner-tubing down the mini river with big stoned grins, people having picnics, people throwing Frisbees and baseballs, people running and bicycling, and people sunbathing and breathing. We lay down in the grass and stared up at the endless blue. The big brown Flatirons jutted out of the mountain horizon. Moll played with a caterpillar on a stick.

"Why did we leave this place?" I asked rhetorically.

"You left me here jerk."

"Oh that's right, now it's coming back to me." I did leave her there, but she wasn't exactly innocent either. "Those were fun days, you never coming home."

"And you never caring if I came home."

"That's ridiculous. I just wrote a book for you, and you basically threw it away."

"You wrote a book for me called *I Don't Belong To Anything*. Not exactly wooing material."

"It was supposed to be romantic. If you would have really read it, then you would have been able to easily see that."

"Do you really want to get into this?"

"Why not? We've never talked about it, and since time is running out we should."

"What do you mean time is running out?"

It was like she really didn't know. "I just mean time flies by. Just four years ago I was chasing you around Europe, and now…"

~

When Ecc first brought up this road trip we were drunk and high of course. That was the only time we talked about anything important. We were at Bar Fly, a pseudo divey joint around the block from our Victorian house apartment.

"I miss my family."

He said, "You know what we ought to do?" A dangerous question.

"What's that?"

"Get out of here."

"Out of here?" I pointed at the ground.

"Not out of here." He spread his arms wide, "Out of here! Out of California."

"That's interesting. Out of here!"

"Like the song." Then he sang, "We got get out of this place. If it's the last thing we ever do!" He went to see if the jukebox had the song, and then put his hands in the air once he found it. We both knew the song was on the jukebox. He probably had played it a dozen times before. We both seemed to be highly attracted to songs about leaving; *Tangled up in Blue*, *Leaving on a Jet Plane*, *Ruby Tuesday*.

"Where we going to go?" I asked him.

"That's the beauty of my plan that I haven't planned yet, we don't pick a destination, we just go, we just get in the truck and go until we stop." Which sounded like a country song about leaving.

It was perfect timing to do such a journey. The bar I worked at had just closed down, Ecc hated his job and wanted to quit for a long time, our lease was almost up, and our closest friends had just moved away. There wasn't much reason to stay besides all the damn beautiful hills and houses.

"Sounds like our kind of plan." I said, and then went into the pros and cons of this lifestyle that we had gotten accustomed to, the one where we never settle anywhere, the one we never take the next life step, just a lateral move of spontaneous adventure. This was very ideal just a short time before, but now I get scared of life and its brevity.

"I promise, this will be the last time, the last big journey before taking the next step." He told me and I noticed he didn't mention what the next step might be, just leaving it open-ended as usual. "We can't stay here right? It's been great, but this isn't where we should end up? This isn't the end of our world?"

I couldn't put my finger on it, but besides all these perfectly timed reasons, there seemed to be something different about Ecc that was pressing this decision to leave, like maybe he had robbed a bank and needed to cool off somewhere else.

~

If Moll really didn't know then I wasn't going to bring it up. How do you tell someone that kind of information before it happens?

"I can't believe we left all those places."

"I think about that a lot these days. Leaving everywhere."

"What do you mean?"

"Everywhere, leaving everywhere in search of that one thing."

"One thing? What one thing are you searching for?"

"I knew you were going to ask that." I paused. "Moll, you know you're the one thing. No matter where I go or how the scenery and people change, you are always there. The one thing."

"God, that's depressing." She rolled her eyes and elbowed me.

"You're telling me."

We became silent. I was thinking about how *our* one thing could be change, and since we both were sharing a needle, it didn't occur to us that the drug was our bond and not each other. Moll probably was thinking about settling down somewhere in the world. This nomadic life was starting to wear on her. She wanted to move on to the next step, whatever that was. Whatever we were told, I suppose? It seems that we get tired, and want to find a place to die.

We watched the clouds a bit more, drifting off into our daydreams, of the next step, of the next meal, of the next set of stars we'd be under, and of the next moment we'd be inside.

A Devil In Disguise

"Boulder would be a great place to retire." This was a common phrase to overhear while walking down Pearl Street in the summer. A great place to die is what that meant. They saw it as amusement park beauty, a place where you could eat sushi, Italian, and vegan food in one day without the hassle of being in a big city. I sat out on a bench while Moll looked around in a bead store. Down the street was The Beat Book Shop in all its glory. I wanted to go in, but I couldn't bear to see Luce ever again in my life. He was the devil in some form, and no matter what I didn't believe in I wasn't ready to face that.

Outside of the book store, dirty little naked kids swarmed around a fountain, jumping in and out of the streaming water, while the panhandling teenage runaways gathered their change to buy apples and cigarettes, while several distant waves of music blended into the breeze, an acoustic guitar from the north, a saxophone from an alley in the east, and a rolling piano shooting up from the south, and then… and then that amazing universal feeling swept over me that this was all exclusively my moment, that my mind held this world together with melting glue, and then… and then the last musical note came blowing in from the west, there she came out of the glass doors as if floating on a cloud, stopping all that existed before us, putting the punctuation on that breath of air.

"Remember the rain storm?" Moll asked me.

"Of course."

We both remembered sitting out in the rain on Pearl Street a couple years before. We held each other's hands and promised that we would die for each other. It was something made more dramatic by the rain, more authentic. Saying things in the sun just isn't the same.

As it began to get dark, we walked toward the Sugar Magnolia Brewpub. We passed by the window of The Beat Book Store. I couldn't help but glance in to see if the owner Luce was there. Temptation. Luce's face appeared and then I saw flames rising from the floor. My feet stopped and I looked back in. The shop was empty and the CLOSED sign was displayed.

"What's wrong?" Moll asked me.

"Nothing, I thought I saw Luce."

She didn't respond.

When we walked in the pub Ned was sitting at the tiny bar sipping on a pint of beer. He stood up and I gave him big long hug. I'm sure it was more than he expected, but this is the part of the trip in which we would be seeing these people for the last time.

"Ned, what the fuck is that?" I pointed to his wristwatch.

"Ah man, I've got to wear this. There aren't any clocks in here so this is the only way I can manage this place." He said apologetically.

I just smirked and hummed.

"What'll you guys have?"

"Couple of pale ales." I looked around for Henry. "Where the hell is Henry?"

"Oh you know, it's summer time, he's up on his mountain retreat."

"Shit, I forgot about that." I said. "Maybe I'll go up there and bring him down."

"Good luck with that." Ned knew Henry better than anyone, and he knew that getting him off the mountain would take a small miracle.

"A Jesus miracle could get him down."

"Don't start that. No miracles today." Ned could play Jesus in a made-for-TV movie. And I don't mean just the scraggly long brown hair and beard. He had these sad prophetic eyes that if no one had ever seen a picture of Jesus, they would just assume his eye's felt like Ned's. "Plus we're not on the best terms right now. Don't even ask."

He turned to get us beers and I turned to see the bar that held many distorted memories. It was weird to look at something that was such a strong part of you for the last time. I guess it's always the last time without knowing it.

The illusion of permanence was the secret. The piles of board games were still there. The smell of jasmine incense was still there. All the same senses surrounded me, but I couldn't seem to make it a part of me. The room had left my mind. "Here Ecc!" Ned was slapping me on the arm. "You alright?"

"Yeah, just thinking."

We sipped on our pints and went into our own thoughts. It was a weird moment in which we all existed in each other's minds, but there were walls up. My mind was in the realization that I'd never see Boulder and Ned again after these days. Ned's eyes seemed to be on sadness, on a hesitant thought. And Moll perplexed me. Maybe she was just tired?

~

Some middle-aged man across the room winked at me as if we had some inside joke. Was there ever a time when winking was endearing or sexy or cool? It has never come off as anything but creepy to me. He did it again, and then I just thought that he probably didn't even know he did it, like it was a nervous habit. I felt obliged to tell him that his long dark ponytail was plenty of creep material, and that he didn't need to expand it further than that. Then I realized it was Luce. He had shaved his Satan-esque beard and mustache.

I wanted him to know that there was only one person in this world that I hated and he was the one, the one piece of conniving shit that existed without a single redeeming quality. I slyly mouthed out "fuck you" without the guys seeing. Ned and Ecc were catching up on their starving artist literary endeavors.

~

"So what are you working on these days?" Ned asked me.

"Well, I went through this existentialist phase in San Fran, and ended up working on a novel for about a year and after it was done, even I couldn't understand what it was about. Maybe the box it's in will understand why I wrote it, as apposed to what it's about."

Ned didn't seem to know how to respond to that, even though he was the champ of existentialist material.

"Um? Yeah." I said bashfully. "What about you?"

"I'm doing a screenplay for this director in LA. I've got a deadline and everything, which you know is a good thing for me."

"Ned goes Hollywood?" I kidded him.

"Man, I hope so. I'm tired of this artist bullshit, tired of hoping an audience will understand me, tired of trying to capture my generation. I don't know the first thing about my generation. All I know is that they spend money on crap Hollywood, so wouldn't it be wrong of me to not take advantage of the stupid."

"Absolutely." I put my pint glass in the air. "It would be completely dishonest of you not to."

Of course we were kidding in order to feel good about the inevitable, which, if lucky, would be a lifetime of rejection, of being misunderstood, of being happy.

Moll went to piss and Ned used that time to get something off his chest. "You want to know the truth?" He asked me. "The truth is I haven't written anything relevant since about six months ago when this stranger started talking to me about writing. He wanted writing advice from me of all people. But it was fine up until he asked me the question, 'How do you decide on which narrative to use?' And that seems like an easy enough question, and I started to answer him, but I just froze up. I didn't know how to answer that question, and not only could I not answer that question, but it sort of froze the creative side of my brain. I told him I don't know."

"The cursed question. Don't pass that curse on to me." I was joking, but not really.

"I'm not worried about you man. You'll always be able to spill out of that ball in your head."

"What does that mean?" How did he know about my head?

"What do you mean, what does that mean?"

"About the ball in my head?"

"The creative ball? I don't know? You just have that."

"Aw sorry, I thought you were talking about something else."

"So do you have an answer?" He pushed the question on me.

"For the cursed question?"

"Yeah."

"Seriously? You're trying to curse me?"

"Not trying. I just need to know if it's the question or just me."

"Fuck you Ned. Fuck you and the fucking jackass you rode in on."

"Like I said, you'll be alright."

"Fine, what's the question?" I was up for the challenge. What did I have to lose anyway?

"How do you decide on which narrative to use?"

For about three seconds I went blank and I thought he also cursed me, but then the ball spilled. "You decide whether you want to be mortal or immortal. Once you decide that, then the narrative presents itself."

Moll walked back up and we became silent like we were talking about a big secret.

"How's Sadie?" Moll asked about Ned's girlfriend.

He just gave the look of a man holding on to a cliff with one finger. Maybe that's where his thoughts were before.

"I see." She responded.

"I've got my own place now in North Boulder." He avoided the subject. "Are you guys crashing with me tonight or is it anywhere you land?"

"With you if all goes wrong."

"Cool, I talked to Kay, she's going to meet us in a few." Ned was desperately trying to get away from any talk about Sadie.

"Great. Is Kay still working here?"

"As you know, no one really ever leaves here. She does a shift every couple weeks, but she opened up a tailoring shop over by Arapahoe."

"What about the gas station dream?"

"Yeah, I don't know? That's just another crazy thing that comes out of her mouth when she's drunk."

"Drunken dreams, the best kind. Hopefully sobriety erases them."

"Speaking of drunken dreams, did you ever do anything with that book we started to write together?"

"You mean the book I started, and no, I just turned the first chapter into a short story with a mysterious ending. Which means no, I've done nothing with it." I took a slug of my ale. "Why? You got some ideas?"

"Nah, not really. I've got something though. I'll show you later."

"Another mysterious ending. Fantastic."

Sample in a Jar was playing over the speakers, there were groups of humans with these relaxed soft eyes that didn't wander, there was the smell of burnt onions and chocolate yeast, a waitress walked by me without any shoes, and I thought I was going to cry, but nothing came out.

"I got to take a leak." I said.

"What do you want, permission?" Moll said.

I tried to say something back, but nothing came out. Then I went to piss, but nothing came out. Nothing was coming out.

A Venice Stain

Out on the Boulder streets, under the stars, with the heat lifting up off the concrete, we hopped off arm-over-arm. Kay was waiting for us at an Irish Pub called Connor O'Neil's. The bar was packed with smiling faces, a bluegrass band thumped out foot-stomping melodies, the cocktail waitress laughed with a group coeds, shoulders and sloshing beers shuffled back and forth through the narrow walkways, the Irish bartender yelled out friendly sarcastic remarks to the hands waving money, and Kay stood in the back corner with a group of neo-hippies. She turned as we snuck up behind her. She gave Moll a big hug and then she attacked me with a hug, a push, and a punch to the chest. This was her version of being affectionate.

"Kay, you have your shop now, all you need is your gas station and you'll be set for life." I joked about her dream to own a gas station and to be the pump operator who filled the tanks. She always described herself with a little grease smudged across her face. You can't hate dreams like that.

After we downed a significant amount of whiskey and wine, we left the pub and walked up Pearl Street. There were still some straggling street performers working the late night crowd, a man on stilts that juggled fire, and a singer songwriter that Ned gave a couple of bucks to. We passed by microbreweries, bookstores, head shops, and record stores. Everything you'd ever need.

We hit all the old bars, drinking and remembering, drinking and forgetting, seeing all those old familiar faces that you can't quite recall the names of. Kay and Ned had some sort of flirting sexual energy happening. They seemed to go off into their own space, so it was just Moll and myself as usual.

~

I saw the Sundown Saloon and had to go in. Ecc and I had some good times there, but he also knew that it was a bar I would go to get away from us. He wrote a short story about that time, and after I read it, I realized how awful I had been. It was a romantic but ultimately sad story, and it made me think that I like to make people sad. It's nothing I would say I liked, but sometimes people don't know what they like until someone puts you in a song or a story or maybe until a therapist or someone disconnected tells you the fucked up things about yourself. Either way, it seemed to me that the Sundown Saloon was a hurdle that we needed to get over… or it was just me trying to make him sad again.

We went down the stone steps and into the long basement bar. All the smells forced hidden memories back into my head. The smell of stale beer, stale wood floors, cigarette smoke mixed with hints of marijuana, the smell of cocaine, the smell dirty hippy wannabes, and whatever the smell of mixing regret and sabotage is. There were a half-dozen old pool tables lined up, all full as usual. Playing pool was *the* way to pass the time between booze, drugs, and cigarettes in Boulder, and possibly every small town in the country. That was what America was to me: bourbon, jukeboxes, and pool tables.

We got beers and the bartender looked me over as if he knew me. He *did* know me, but I suppose trying to fuck someone at the end of the night for a couple months straight got so repetitive it was like brushing your teeth. He started to inquire about my identity, but I got away before he got the nerve. Of course, I never fucked him. He was a piece of shit, and I never wanted to make Ecc sad in that way.

Ned and Kay started up a game of pool while Ecc and I leaned against a wall silently. Finally, because I can't keep my stupid mouth shut, said, "I used to come here when I didn't want to go home." It was a selfish thing to say, but we needed to talk about it. We had never talked about the last few weeks in Boulder. "The bartenders and I would drink till the sun came up. Not the sundown, it seems that should have changed the name." It was a bad joke.

~

I got quiet. I hated those days. It was the most excruciating feeling waiting for her to come home. I would stay awake in bed shaking out of fear that something bad had happened to her, or even worse in my mind, that she was fucking someone else. Millions of horrible thoughts ran through my mind. Then I would hear the door open and it would all disappear. I would pretend to be asleep and she would sneak into bed.

"Nothing ever happened you know?" Moll told me proudly like she had done something right by not doing something completely wrong.

"No, I didn't know, I just hoped."

"We just drank and went home. Of course they would try, but that's just how you boys are. Nothing happened. As bad as I acted, I was still in love with you."

"Yeah, I just remember the time in Venice. That thought always came up when I waited for you." I was referring to when Moll was a junky in Venice, Italy, and I suppose I was too. I left her in some underground club while she fucked another girl on the couch beside me. We were slightly out of our minds and out of our morals back then, trying to convince ourselves we were a new type of free, a couple of brave kids testing the boundaries of regret.

"I know you don't believe me, but I did that for you. I didn't want you dead. I wanted me dead, not you."

"If you die, then we die. Remember that."

A Burning Castle

Ned's house was a wreck in the sense of unpacked boxes and ill placed furniture.

"How long have you been here?" Moll asked.

"Umm, like two months, three months, no, two."

"You'll get to this unpacking thing at some point I'm sure."

"Yeah, I've been busy doing stuff you know."

By the odd set up, I imagined him sitting in his living room taking pulls and staring at the walls, thinking of the *why* and the *how* and then the *why* some more. Walls give you answers if you stare at them long enough. I know this from personal experience. Ned grabbed us some beers and then his big glass piece. We all sat on the floor and shared stories of our recent past. The subject made its way toward Ned and Sadie.

Moll, who doesn't care if Ned didn't want to talk about it or not, told him, "I'm not going to leave you alone until you tell me what happened."

"Nothing happened! We just fought and she was demanding and I was undemanding and she cried and I was insensitive and she needed and I didn't. That's all, nothing crazy."

"God, are all you writers the same breed?" Moll said. "Ecc is exactly the same."

"Not exactly." I said. "Close, but not the same."

Kay was quiet and I knew why. But she broke silence after Ned crossed her territory.

"There were many times during the drama that I knew that I didn't need this ridiculous thing titled love. The concept is so mainstream in our day-to-day living that one forgets that it's not a day-to-day necessity. It's the same as basing your daily life to jealousy or panicking, just another emotion that is looked down upon."

"You're just a jaded motherfucker Ned!" Kay slapped him across the back of the head.

"Why do you insist on literally beating your point of view on me?" Ned grabbed his guitar lying on the brown carpet beside him. "You gonna finish that bonger?"

"What's the use?" Kay said, not referring to the bong.

"You see, this is what I have to live with," Moll said. "This is the same, I'm going to die tomorrow bullshit that I have to put up with!"

I smiled at Moll's pent up spite. "Ned, I'll take another beer if one is expendable."

"Expendable! Who the fuck says expendable?" Moll said.

I looked at her like a lunatic. "You're a lunatic."

"You're a stupid fucking writer." She and Kay laughed together.

I got another beer. "There's a time when that would have been a complement. Now it's just the truth."

We all took a moment of silence and listened to the little stereo push out a rock song I didn't recognize.

~

As smart as Ecc was, he could be equally as dumb, and I sometimes thought it was on purpose, like he was able to finally let go of all that pride, of all that need to be *right*. We were all smoking, probably thinking about our flaws. That was my go-to thought when nothing else was going on up there in the noggin. I would worry that my breath smelled bad, or that I was putting on weight that I would never be able to take off, or that I would end up alone. Ecc put up with a lot of bullshit from me in the past, and ultimately won me over, as they say. I wouldn't have put up with it, and it made me wonder if he had some bigger plan to really put one over on me. Maybe it was this trip? Maybe he was going to leave me in the middle of nowhere, without any money, or clothes, or anything? Just me. Naked and alone.

Then I felt his hand on my leg. I looked at him and he told me without words that he wasn't going to leave me naked and alone.

I looked around for the bathroom, making sure to know where to escape to if these thoughts came back. I could go there and turn on the sink until the worries disappeared. Ned's house was empty, hollow, like someone was moving out instead of already moved in.

I could see Ecc living in a place like this, with unpacked boxes of books, using them as tables and chairs, with some other girl, telling her all the things that he told me except they are better manipulated because he knows the parts to leave out from our experiences. It would seem romantic like it did when we first moved into our apartment here in Boulder. All we did was drink, smoke, listen to music, and fuck. Why did life have to change when it was so simple and perfect like that? He had to go and write a book about me, he had to show me a mirror, and I had to look.

~

"But you just can't sit there and not think about it," Ned started back after pausing for thought. "At the very least, think different than everyone else just for a few seconds. Love is chemical mixture of things like sexual desire, companionship, security, and other shit that really mixes up rational thought. And our bodies are designed in a way to conform to its environment, so like anything else, one can build a tolerance to love. All I'm saying is that I think I'm at a point where my mind and body do not need it, like, I could go the rest of my life without this advertised love."

Ned was playing my usual role as the drunken philosopher. It was nice to be off stage and watching the act. We *were* the same in the way we used alcohol to bring out an underlying confidence. Moll liked to challenge me in this state, just like Kay was challenging Ned. But Ned was like me in the way that our contradictions only made us stronger, because truth only lies in what happened.

"Ned, I would argue with you, but you sound just like Ecc, and I don't need two of you." Moll said. She got up and started looking through a box of pictures.

"You see… this is the hardest part to get over. It's an idealistic concept that is actually beyond anyone's doubt that it is ideal. We hear it in songs, we see it in movies, read about it in books, it is preached to us in almost every religion, we're supposed to teach it to our kids, there's a holiday in which we celebrate it, our most natural and animalistic ritual is called making love. But where is it? Reach out! Look around! Where is it? A world without it is visualized as chaotic and evil, but to me it's like any drug we take. It's just a diversion from reality." Ned took a long breath and then a long pull from the bong.

"The reality is that we're all going to die, so love gives some form of life after death in someone else's mind. It's easier to live with the inevitable when you know you'll be missed after you're gone." I said because the personal tension had worn off. "Or it's like eating potatoes instead of rice, a side-order substitution."

I got a laugh from Ned.

"You guys are both fucked!" Kay wanted love as much as she needed it.

"I was just making it out to be the simplicity of starches. Don't put me in the same category as the hater-hippy over there." I said. "I embrace all emotions no matter how they destroy me."

"So what is love to you?" Moll asked me.

"Love is a dog from hell." I quoted from Bukowski.

Then Ned actually paraphrased some of the poem. "There is a loneliness in this world so great that you can see it in the slow hands of the clock, that people are so tired and mutilated by either love or no love." We were an awful team, Ned, Bukowski, and me. The girls rolled their eyes while looking at each other as if they were exhausted of our types.

"Alright, here is what I really think." I said. "Love is a bond between two people that temporarily brings out the best... Wait, let me start over. Love is how another person can bring out the best qualities of a person that would be impossible before, or if they're alone. Does that make sense?"

"See, at least that makes some kind of sense, like two is better than one thing," Moll said.

"But! My little definition proves Ned's beliefs also." My contradictions. "What if other people only bring out the worst in the individual? Just because love can bring out the best, doesn't exactly mean that it's necessary for the whole human race."

"You see, Ecc knows that you can understand without believing it."

"I understand how fucked up the world would be if most people thought that love is a distraction or starch or anything that brought out the worst in people." Kay argued, but was losing momentum in her punch.

"The world is already fucked up," Moll muttered. "Hopefully it will really end when it turns the year 2000."

I looked at her like an alien, never hearing her talk like that before. She loved life more than just about anyone I'd ever met. Ned and Kay just looked down at the carpet.

Moll busted out laughing. "God guys, I was just kidding!"

"I thought I was a conversation killer," Ned said and strummed on his guitar.

"Just play a damn song would you." Moll told him like he didn't have a choice.

So Ned played the guitar until Kay mumbled out, "I just don't know what to do any more."

It sounded so sad that we all knew what she was talking about. I didn't know what to do either. "Ned are you going to be writer or a musician when you grow up?"

He shrugged and played what I thought was an Allman Brothers song. Kay was shooting Ned evil glances. She was dripping with a goal, not knowing what to do, but knowing that love was her temporary cure. She said, "I'm going to have a cigarette." But what she really said was, "Ned come outside."

They went out the back patio. I looked at Moll to see if she knew, but she had passed out on the couch. One of her talents was being able to fall asleep anywhere, anytime. I picked her up and took her into our little room. Our sleeping bags were set up on the floor and surrounded by Ned's numerous boxes of books. I tucked her in and she looked up at me with her crooked smile. I loved Moll, whatever it was. And for the first time since embracing my disease, I felt sorry for myself. Visions of my body floating away from the planet as my hands outstretched trying to touch Moll one last time. I wrapped my arms around her and squeezed her like there was no tomorrow.

I went back to the living room and stared at the wall. It said something, but it was hard to understand. It said something about grabbing another beer, so I did. Kay's cigarette pack was in the middle of the floor. There was a little bag of white in the pack. I grabbed both a cigarette and the mysterious yet not so mysterious bag and went out back. Ned and Kay were making out on the side of the little deck. I lit the smoke and looked up to the sky. The stars burned my brain. The air was crisp and warm. I saw Orion, the Little Dipper, and the Crux, but the Crux turned out to be just a bunch of jumbled suns in my hopes. I was like a kid sometimes, the way I never wanted to go to bed, the way I hated when the night ended.

A Man on the Mountain

I took the Bronco up the winding road to Nederland. The sun had just come up and I was still drunk, still high, Moll still passed out cold on the floor, and me still without any sleep. The one café in town served a big lumberjack breakfast that I engulfed, and then I took off on foot to find Henry. The path appeared easily enough, but the rest would take getting into the brilliantly insane mind of my friend on the mountain. It was getting hot and all the toxins were escaping from my body. I found the trees with

Henry's markers. I puked on one of them. I rested on another. Then the boulder formation finally appeared.

When I entered the rocks Henry was sitting on the ground wearing nothing but jean shorts and reading a book. He looked up at me slowly as if I was a ghost.

"Hello Henry."

"If I say hello back then that means I recognize that you exist, so I will refrain until you become a more solid image."

I could tell that he had been used to this scenario in the woods. I imagined that he talked to ghosts throughout the day.

"Then I will just sit until we know that we are real. We can see the truth in what happened."

"The immortal truth!" He exclaimed as proof of my reality. "Ecc, what are you doing here?"

"I've come to bring you down from the mountain. Just one night, for the last time."

"I see." He pondered. "If that must be, then there's no use fighting it."

~

When I woke Ecc wasn't beside me and I could tell that he hadn't been there the whole night. One day I won't be able to tell that he wasn't there and that made me sad. I crawled across the floor and peaked through the blinds. They were the kind of standard blinds that come with an apartment that would never get changed out for something nicer. The sun was high and it was at least past noon. I went out to the living room, and Ecc wasn't there either. Maybe he finally left me for good? Most likely he was writing in one of his old haunts, writing about leaving me.

Then I saw the empty bag on the coffee table with the remnants of white lines cut into the wood. We used to do this together, now we seemed to sneak around each other's judgments. I suppose I did pass out early though, another thing I didn't used to do. I felt over the stone dangling from my neck and made a wish to be a good person, a good woman. It was the least I could do.

Then I went looking for Ecc. I wanted to tell him about my wish, and see if he wished the same for himself. If we just would stick to the script everything would be just fine.

~

Henry stuck his head out the window like a dog on the way down to Boulder. He had been up in the mountain forest for three months and was far removed from being social. Then he finally said, "Ecc! This is the last time?"

"Yes, this is it."

"Let's not waste it on being sober. I don't want to remember it. I want to make it up as I go."

"Agreed."

An Astonishingly Useless Paintbrush

The sun went down and the demons of the night came out for one last hug in downtown Boulder. Henry was thawing out of his monk-like demeanor. You could tell he was almost back to normal when he stopped looking around in the wild wonderment. I told him about San Francisco, about how Moll and me found each other again, about how I found the perpetual moment. He told me how he and his gal had broken up and how it was the best thing for him, and how he had once again found himself in the woods and how he was ready now to really get deep into clarity of validity.

"This is stuff Ecc." He told me. "This is the stuff for water sharing." Water sharing was one of Henry's religions, a way of spiritually getting drunk and telling truths. It was more of an adult drinking game than anything, but whatever works was important in this case.

We went to Sugar Magnolia and Henry grabbed the bottle of elixir from his locker. The elixir was Henry's homemade moonshine of sorts that he called "water." I'm not sure what he actually called real water since I had never heard him use the word in the correct manner. Ned was going to meet us later, and Moll and Kay were still nursing hangovers, so it was just us two men sharing water, the way the gods did it before man was invented. We poured each other's waters in accordance to the specific laws. Henry had even made these special ceramic cups that were about the size and shape of a clementine. The shape was designed so the participant couldn't let the cup rest. It always had to be in one's hand, so the holder of the round cup usually drank more consistently than normal. We drank, making eye contact, no touching, no words, until the water was gone. When the water was done is when the words began. It was strange, but that was Henry.

~

Kay and I lounged around on her couches till the sun went down. Sometimes I loved being hung-over, when there was nothing to do but nothing. She passed me a spliff and asked if I wanted to do some Molly later.

"What's Molly?"

"Molly. MDMA. X."

"Oh X. Why do you call it Molly?"

"I don't know. I mean, I don't call it Molly. Drug dealers call it Molly. You know code. You can't go around asking people if they want ecstasy or X or MDMA."

"Oh." I didn't know if I wanted to do Molly. I mean I did, but I didn't. "Yeah, lets do it." I wanted to be a good person, yet I never tried outside my wishes. Ecc always listened to this song that said something like, my daydreams are just wishes. I daydreamed a lot.

"Sweet. Let's just chill for awhile and then go nuts."

"Where are we going to go?"

"There's this new bar that might be fun, it's at the end of Pearl."

"Cool." I hesitated to bring up the next subject. "By the way, sorry Ecc did your blow, he doesn't think straight when he's been drinking for ten hours."

"Yeah, I *know* Ecc."

133

The way she said that didn't sit well with me. It was an intimate statement. We had been away from people who really knew us for so long that I wasn't used to that kind of familiarity. I imagined someone else calling him sweetheart, or finishing his sentences, or explaining to a stranger how that's just how he is and you have to love him or hate him for it.

"He left me more money than it was worth anyway." Kay told me truthfully unconcerned. "I didn't really want it, so it worked out. Blow is never a good idea in hindsight, that's how you know not to do anything, but sometimes it's like the devil calling."

"Do you think it's bad that he was doing cocaine by himself?"

"Bad? No. He's fine. He's always fine."

"Yeah, I guess. Sometimes I worry that he's not fine though, like it's all a big ploy. How can someone always be fine?"

"Maybe he's not always fine, but I'm sure, I mean, I know that he has a solid grasp of his limits, and more importantly he knows why he has limits. He's fine."

~

"I think I'm close to dying Henry." I said as soon the last drop of the bottle was poured.

"Dying ain't much of a living son." Henry quoted my favorite line from Clint Eastwood.

"No, I suppose it ain't."

"Well, I'll miss you buddy, that's for sure, but to tell you the truth I wasn't so sure I'd ever see you again after you left last time."

"Funny how that works huh? How I might as well been dead in your mind, but since I was still theoretically out there in the universe it's not the same. No grief, just waiting for grief."

"That's right. And I'll see you again after this, you just have to tell me who you are."

"I'll do my best, you can count on my best." It was nice to talk to Henry. He was the kind of man that makes you open your own doors, but gives you hints to where the key is hidden.

I lit a cigarette, happy to have my hand back, my voice back, so happy that I took them both away again. Henry brooded as if he was back on the mountain.

"Are you okay with it?" He asked me.

"No, it's kind of getting to me. I'm thinking about it instead of breathing. My blood is thinking about it and it's trying to get out, get away. Once your blood knows it changes everything."

"Does Moll know?"

"Moll knows everything, she just chooses when to reveal it to herself. When she decides to reveal this we will become strangers, unable to hold on to the memories that make two people one."

"Like us right now, our bottle is done, it was us, and now we will fade away from each other until we get so far that we won't even recognize the other."

Ned showed up just as the angels were about to come down. He said hi to me and pretended as if Henry wasn't there.

"What's that about?" I asked Henry as Ned stood behind him, out of his line of sight.

"Fucking Ned won't talk to me ever since I got him in a little trouble at the golf course."

"You play golf?" I asked them both in a judgmental manner.

"Ecc. Golf is one of man's oldest games. In ancient Rome, golf was played to the death, in ancient Greece golf was the one game peasants and kings were allowed to play together, in the Aztec culture the-"

"Okay, okay, I get it. I just asked if *you* played golf?"

"No, I guess I don't. But I tried."

Ned didn't want to talk about it. He started to walk away.

"What happened Ned?"

"What happened is Henry is a psychopath, that's what happened." He said.

"Oh Ecc, we were just having a little fun in the golf cart, and this son-of-a-bitch from the clubhouse decides to bring us in his little fucking office to scold us. So, I told this motherfucker that I'm a grown man and I don't need to be brought into an office like a fucking kid. If he wants to say something to me, say it like a fucking man talking to a man, so I have this guy fucking shaking in his golf shoes. He thought he was going to be some kind of big-shot Ecc, but you know me, and now that guy knows me."

"Yeah, and now I'm banned from that golf course."

"Yeah, that piece of shit golf course, who fucking cares?" Henry said. "I tell you another thing."

"I just can't believe you guys played golf together. Ned?"

"What?"

"Writers don't play golf. That shit is for bankers and retired government workers."

"That would make sense, because I'm not a writer." Ned had always insisted that he was a waste of a scribe.

"And I tell you another thing Ecc. Ned didn't say a fucking word. He was embarrassed of me. He didn't say a word the rest of the ride home and I haven't talked to him since, like four months."

"You left for your mountain retreat right after that, of course I haven't talked to you!"

"You guys should hug." I said sarcastically, and Henry attacked Ned with a bear-hug. Ned just put his arms up in the air and gave into the moment. "See, don't you feel better?"

"Henry, you know I love you, you're just so damn embarrassing." Ned wore a giant grin.

"Now give him some water." I said to Henry.

"Yes! I have another bottle in the back."

"No, no, no water sharing for me tonight."

"It's the flow of life Ned. It's not a choice."

"Oh yeah dip-shit? Watch how it doesn't flow through me tonight."

"I'm so glad I could sweep through town and reunite enemies. It's my special ability apparently."

"Yeah, thanks for nothing. Ned and I work better as enemies."

"By the way, I have something for you." Ned said. "I wasn't going to give it to you, but now, I don't know, it feels like the only way."

"What is it?"

"You'll see."

A Cosmic Resolve

We went around town to more of the old haunts while running into all the old ghosts. They mostly asked all the same questions. How was California? Where you going? What are you doing? You still writing? Which was the strangest question of them all, like I would just stop writing, like it was a phase or a job or a mistake. It probably was a mistake, a lifelong mistake that I wouldn't just stop doing.

We ended up at an underground bar called the Catacombs and after putting back tequila shots I felt a presence around me that I hadn't felt since I left. Luce was standing in one of the many dark corners staring at me. I didn't recognize him at first because he had shaved his facial hair. He came slowly strutting over in true form. "Smoke?" He asked with a cigarette out.

"Sure." I took it and he lit it with the flick of his zippo.

"So how's California?"

"California is dead."

He just tilted his head in some sort of agreement. "So it wasn't good for writing?"

"Everything is good for my writing. Even you Luce."

"I'm not *good* for writing, I'm necessary."

"If you say so. How's the bookstore? Still refusing to sell anything?" I said because Luce owned a bookstore that was filled from floor to ceiling of the best collection books I'd ever come across, but he had insanely strict rules of whom he would sell to. He never would sell me a book, but he did let me borrow a couple of Bukowski novels.

"It's not refusing Ecc, it's carefully picking. Hardly anyone respects the word any more. I'm just rightfully protecting it."

"It's a nice position to be in, Heaven's leftovers."

"Saw your little lady earlier. She's looking good."

"I suppose I could say thanks, but I suppose I'll just say fuck you instead. Where was she?"

"If you still can't keep up with her, I'm not going to help."

"You never did Luce. I don't expect it now."

"The greater good Ecc. I'm here to help the greater good. You will soon come to a desert, and in that desert you will become so thirsty any old piece of blank paper will do. Then the mirage will be the gods looking down upon you laughing, laughing at your thirst, and you will remember this moment, and you will see the greater good, and your thirst will disappear, because Ecc... the gods can't help you, only I can."

~

I was trying to carry two beers back to the pool table where Kay and I were playing when that asshole Luce ran into me. I spilled part of the beer on me and he laughed in his evil laugh. "Sorry about that little lady. May I buy you another?"

"Go to hell Luce."

"Been there and back. Let's make better use of me."

I could feel his stare on me as I walked away. Even when I got to the next room it felt as if he was right behind me, right on top of me. Then I realized that it was the MDMA coming in paranoiac waves. "Is he behind me?" I whispered to Kay.

"Who?"

"Anybody."

"No, I mean there are some people far behind you if that's what you mean."

I slowly turned around and he was gone, but the feeling never went away. The feeling went on for hours before I thought to check the time. It was late, or early, early in the morning. We were at a house party of this trust fund guy Ecc used to work with. He owned one of the many mansions in Boulder, and it was known as a place you could just go to do drugs and party till dawn if not longer. There were some familiar faces there, mostly just faces I remembered without names. A girl that recognized my face and my name approached me as we were cutting up lines in the kitchen.

"Moll. How the heck are you? Thought I'd never see *you* again!"

"Oh hi, how are you?" I think her name was Mary, but that just seemed too plain and easy, so I just kept it to myself.

We talked about all the small things that people talk about while they wait for their turn to do blow. But then she struck a cord.

"Are you still playing the cello?" She asked, and I was surprised that this person who I barely knew remembered that I played the cello.

"Not really." Which meant no. "I drag it around with me like a dead limb that used to be a part of me." At one point it was my identity. People would refer to me as a cello player, the girl who plays the cello, the girl who got a scholarship to every top music school in the world. But now, I'm just the girl who used to play the cello, now I'm the girl who travels the world with her boyfriend, the guy who people have a hard time remembering his name so they just call him my boyfriend. I'm now half of a whole something, so now I'm half of something that doesn't play the cello.

"Well, you could always start playing again." She said as she wiped the debris of cocaine around her nose.

"Yeah, I could, maybe I will." Even if I did, I still would never be called the cello player again. "I just want to be a good person." I accidentally said out loud, or maybe it wasn't an accident.

~

Moll still hadn't come back. I waited by the phone like the old days, hoping that she would call to just let me know she was fine. Ned went to his room to pass out. I went to get my toothbrush from my backpack. Lying on my sleeping bag was a thin manuscript with the title: *Ending to the Ecc-Ned Endeavor.* Ecc-Ned was the name of our two-man writing team that incidentally never wrote anything together. Well, at least I thought we never wrote anything together. But, he pulled this out of his hat.

After finishing the dozen or so pages I realized why Ned never gave the ending to me. It was the perfect frightening conclusion that defies any future. One in which the human has to accept that when a world ends, the individual is born, and when the individual ends, the world also ends. I fell asleep that night by myself, letting all the worlds around me disappear.

2

THE ILLUSIONS

An Untimely Death

I have given up on trying. All of my words fall short of the depression that tried to invade my mind. All of my thoughts fell short of the illusions that predict them. I am a coward. I want to leave this world. I want to see what is next.

An Attempt To Build Mountains Beside Mountains

There's a large hump that divides Boulder Valley from the rest of the world. We were on top of that hump when I looked in the Bronco's rearview mirror down into the crater. Then on the other side we dropped into another American puddle. The vast land of style and hope lied in front of us, waiting for us like ghosts holding hands and pointing fingers. We cruised along I-25 South with the musky warm wind tangling up our hair. Denver moaned from a short distance. It was as confused as any other city. They tried to build mountains beside the mountains. Then they gave up and built chain foothills, tar fields of lost dreams, and plastic pine trees. We were flying past a city asking to be burned, flying past humans that wanted to burn, but decided to wait for the next day, flying over the hungry, the starving, the people full of misdirected lust, our people, a nine to five society of dreamers, a vast army of cultures that come together in the same sock store, a million people eating mashed potatoes and going to bed cold with blankets, saying it over and over until it becomes a billboard, screaming it in the streets until the gutters are clean by Wednesday, shouting it into the sky until the air is filtered by Sunday. These cities are the humans who build and destroy them, these humans are the cities who build and destroy them, committing mass suicide, committing mass sewage thoughts, separating the brick from the dirt, the blood from the sidewalk, the anger from the dinner table.

~

Ecc had changed since we left Boulder. It was probably Henry and his water sharing shit. That always threw him into an over the top philosophical phase, looking at people like he was them, like he could see inside them, like he knew all of their fears. But at least this time we were leaving the town together, and we were still a team.

Maybe we should have never met anyone, gotten close to anyone, snuck out the back door whenever someone suggested any further interaction past what we had in the moment. I imagined us by ourselves in the desert, content but still wondering what other people were doing, still bleeding, but breathing also, breathing mostly.

I turned on the radio and Prince's song *1999* was playing. The song had appropriately made a resurgence with the matching year. "I never noticed that he says 'two thousand zero zero, party over, oops out of time.' So even Prince predicted the end of the world at the millennium." I told Ecc while he was attempting to change lanes. He hated when I talked to him while he was doing simple driving things like changing lanes or making a right at a red light. "But now it's obvious, Prince is the modern day Nostradamus. He's saying goodbye to the 20th century and everything around it."

He made it over to the left lane before responding. "It never made any sense to me because he says, we're going to party like it's 1999, not party like it's the year 2000. There's still a whole year left before the turn of the century."

"Yeah, but he probably means that it's the last day of 1999, otherwise that's a good point, it doesn't make any sense. Plus it wouldn't rhyme or flow, so you have to respect that first."

"Rhyme and flow?"

"Yeah, the rhyme and flow." I crossed my arms like they used to do in rap videos. Now they don't cross them anymore. I'm not sure what they do now. Maybe they throw them up in the air?

We were creeping along in Denver traffic, on our way to southern Colorado. There were mountain sand dunes that we were going to to look for answers. Ecc still had that distant look, as if he couldn't quite catch whatever he was chasing.

~

I gazed into the hundreds of brake lights in front of me and knew that I was holding hands with these people in the most modern way. We're not going to get it right, but we're going to keep on trying. We're going to get it wrong a billion times and then turn into dust, leaving behind our glass mountains, leaving behind roadside graves, leaving behind all of our hopes for a better world. We will keep on moving, keep on trying. That thumping in my head kept on reminding me.

A Two-Way Mirror

On the wide flat horizon sat little brown surreal lumps of sugar. We were heading into an 80-mile dead end where the Great Sand Dunes of Colorado were getting greater by the second.

"Last store! Last store!" Moll mimicked the road sign while slapping me on the shoulder. The Bronco abided her request. She went in to use the bathroom. I sat in the car watching dozens of chunky Midwest legs go in and out of the glass doors. I got a little nauseous keeping track of all the hotdogs, the ice cream cones, the sodas, the magazines, and all of the consumption coming out of the store. Ever since the water sharing I couldn't shake this feeling of overzealous wonderment. Only the other side could tell me the answers, so I popped a stem and a cap from the bag of shrooms we brought along. Moll didn't need to know. It wasn't her time to go to the other side. Sometimes you need to be the only one behind the two-way mirror.

We pulled into the little sandy parking lot where groups of blank-eyed people sat around eating sandwiches out of plastic bags, brushing off their feet, and staring at the new faces that had yet to see the Great Dunes. An older man smoking a cigar gave us a disgusted look as we parked beside his RV, but then he kept the look so I guess it was just his normal expression. He had his blue jeans rolled up to his calves and a Colorado Rockies cap on. We got out and stretched. There was a line for the vending machine. I quickly turned away.

"California heh?" The old man sort of asked with contempt.

"Yeah, that's right. That's where my license plate is from. I see your hat is from Colorado?" I tried joking around, but sometimes I wasn't funny at all. He chose not to hear me, because he had something more important to tell me.

"You know, there's this town in California where they say you have to have a tattoo and smoke reefer to be a citizen." He started to go into a long newspaper article rumor, but I cut him off. "That's right, those towns are all over California. It's where I found her."

~

Ecc was pointing me out to the man by the RV as I was walking up. I had just gone to the bathroom again. I tried going at a store before we got to the dunes, but the hand-washing sink was outside the toilet area. There were people waiting, so I couldn't go. Since I had to waste time to make it seem like I had a raging pee, I just read the graffiti on the dirty tile walls. My favorite tag was: RIGHT NOW IS GOING TO BE GREAT! It was what Ecc and me were trying to catch, and it was nice for someone to try and remind us. We all need reminding, because forgetting never stops.

Then of course someone had to tag about the millennium: REPENT NOW, FOR THE END IS NEAR. HAPPY NEW YEAR. At least they made it rhyme. It just didn't have flow.

Ecc was trying to get me to come over to talk, but I acted like I didn't hear him. I wanted to make it to the top of the dunes before the distant storm reached us. We had read that they were the biggest sand dunes in North America, that the mountain pattern had formed a trap for the desert sands blowing through, and after centuries had formed this out-of-place natural oddity. I always liked that saying about how there are more stars in the sky than grains of sand on the beach. But I'm not sure if they meant just the beach I was on at the time or all the beaches, and I wonder if they thought about all the sand including the sand that's in the middle of Colorado. That seems implausible to me, but I suppose that's the point, to make you feel small. I already felt small, insignificant enough. I didn't need to be reminded that we are all the equivalent of a grain of sand in the universe.

~

The old man rubbed his chin and looked at Moll like I was looking at those people at the last store. We all had these stupid things called brains that couldn't help but to think ugly thoughts about our differences.

"I had to complete a series of tasks in order to free her from that evil Californian town." I said loud enough for Moll to hear me. She interpreted a dance of being set loose from chains, and then ran away from us.

"No kidding?"

"Nope, no kidding." Then I took off running before he could respond. That should give him another good story to tell the next foreigner from California.

———

Before reaching the sand, there was a sign: DO NOT OCCUPY THE DUNES WHEN LIGHTNING IS VISIBLE. I wondered what humans did before signs were invented. In this case I suppose some were struck by lightning.

Moll was just ahead of me. The sand mountains flowed over one another. They seemed so close, but we must have run for five minutes before going into a jog. When shrooms take over my brain, I can read minds, or at least that's what I think. When I got to the top of the first smallest dune I locked eyes with this man. He held hands with his lady friend. He was thinking how I was confused and frightened, looking for an easy way out, and that I should turn around. I mentally thanked him, but I don't think the message was completed because Moll ran up and took my legs out. We fell into the sand and the couple left. Moll jumped on top of me like a maniac. Maybe that's what the man was trying to tell me? Watch out behind you! I rolled her off, but she clung to my leg.

"Who's the champ?" She seriously asked me and I went into an uncontrollable mushroom laugh. "What's so funny?"

"You're so funny."

"I'm not funny!" She jumped up and tried to get me in the headlock. I barely slid away from her. She pounced toward me like a cat and wrapped her arms around my waist. "Who's the champ?"

"You! You're the damn champ!" Then I pushed her off and ran to the next dune. I had to stop because the fungus was really kicking in. The dunes looked like waves rolling over one another. A thunderstorm was growing in the distance. Lightning struck down over the horizon. All the two-legged animals began to run back toward their cars. A sign? The sign? Apparently quite a few people had been killed from the fire of the sky, but what did I really have to lose. It would be kind of romantic if Moll and I were struck down together. So we climbed higher as the clouds got closer and darker. It began to drizzle. We looked down on the scurrying people below. They looked like roaches scrambling for a hiding place. We climbed higher. I thought about warning signs, because they were supposed to be a part of an idea for the *End of the World* novel. I was going to put in a chapter about the government of the fictional city that put up all of these absurd warning signs like: WARNING: Cracked sidewalk ahead. WARNING: Sidewalk smooth ahead. WARNING: These bananas may contain more potassium than one's RDA. WARNING: This building is made of wood and possibly could catch fire. Stupid stuff like that, but that's how I thought about the lightning warning sign. Words on sheet metal took away responsibility.

We finally made it to the top dune and we both flopped down from exhaustion. I asked the gods to strike me down. The thought of a million watts of electricity shooting through my brain intrigued the hell out of me. Something cool would have to happen like figuring out the key to the universe or you meet Him and his voice whispers, "Two plus two actually equals three." Something mind-blowing like that.

After catching my breath, I stood up and held my keys in the air like a modern day Benjamin Franklin. "Come and get me motherfucker! Take me now you son of a bitch!"

The wind blew a whirling tornado of sand around us. It hovered around us for a few seconds, and then it started to drift away down the hill. I ran and jumped as far as I could, trying to get right in the middle of the eye of the storm. As I was in the air going down, my body jerked still for a second and then I came crashing down into the sand. I looked up the hill at the girl smiling like a kid. "You're fucking nuts." She said with the smile of a lunatic. We both had issues.

I began jumping all the way down the dunes. There was a Park Ranger down at the bottom flashing a light at us and blowing a whistle like he was a lifeguard. By this time there was a full-on storm. The rain was coming down in buckets. The Ranger was a warning sign in the human form. If we died on his shift, he'd be held accountable. "I won't let you down!" I yelled, but he couldn't hear me. Moll attempted to cartwheel her way down. We were covered with wet sand. She caught up with me, grabbed me, and kissed me. It was a blissful gritty moment, and it seemed to heal my temporary disease. She was the cure almost all the time. "Come on! We can't let Him down!" We ran backwards so we could watch the bolts strike the top of the dunes. "I won't let you down!" I kept shouting at the waiting Park Ranger.

He directed the flashlight in our eyes as we ran past him.

"Hurry Mister!" Moll said. "There's no time to lose!"

He began to jog behind us.

"Don't worry, we'll meet you there." I yelled behind me.

When we got to the shelter in the parking lot, he asked us, "Didn't you two read the sign?"

"Don't worry." I repeated. "We're going to meet you there."

He stopped and looked into my drug-induced pupils. "Meet me where?"

"At the end of the signs of course."

He shook his head and walked off without answering.

We stripped off most of our clothes and stayed out in the rain until we were mostly rinsed off. The old man stared out at us from the window of his RV. Moll was only in her bra and shorts. He could see the willow tree tattoo that covered most of her back. It was decorated with beads of rain, some still, some stringing along, and some evaporating into the atmosphere. I ran my fingers along the tree and the rain, and thought about how she couldn't see them. She would never be able to see them.

A Chosen One

"Don't you think getting struck by lightning would be one of the best ways to die?" I asked Moll as we drove out of the parking lot. She thought about it. She dried her feet off. "It would be like getting this crazy half-a-second rush, and then you're just gone." We got to a stop sign. Moll threw the towel in the back and propped her feet up.

"Just like being in an electric chair except there's probably no one staring at you, or wishing you were dead, or hoping that it hurts really badly."

I was still at the stop sign, staring off in the distant, thinking about a giant electric chair in the sky.

"Buster? You going to go?"

Then the sound of a car horn woke me out of the trance. I looked in my rear-view mirror and it was the RV from the parking lot.

"Maybe you should drive?" I told Moll.

~

Ecc thought I didn't know he was shrooming, but his pupils were like black holes and then when he forgot that we were at a stop sign I knew for sure. He pulled the Bronco over to the side and that RV from the dunes pulled off to the side. It was the perfect setup for one of those horror road trip movies. I imagined the old man asking us if we needed any help with one of those friendly serial killer smiles, and then cutting Ecc's head off so he could keep me prisoner in the back of his RV. He would then take me to some extremist Christian compound and they would put me on display in a cage for the members to throw rocks at.

Ecc and I switched positions. The old man stuck his head out the window and asked us if we needed any help. It was just as I thought! I just smiled and shook my head, not believing his sincerity to help us. People just help other people on the road to make themselves feel better. I wasn't falling for it. I wasn't going to be put on display in a cage. I got in the driver's seat and hit the gas.

~

I looked out the back window at the thunderstorm chasing us. My eyes were full moons reflecting the light into the car. We passed over the rolling hills of Colorado, through the jagged humps of New Mexico, and into the oil fields of Texas. The day was surreal and forever. The oil painting clouds made it seem like a perpetual dusk. All across the plains, lightning crashed down and disappeared. It made me realize the dissatisfaction of nature and how it would defeat man one day. Lightning came from the meeting of two charged entities in the atmosphere. The only resolve to equalize each other is through a bolt of energy, a lighting strike. I crept my hand over to Moll's arm, attempting to barely touch her, attempting to resolve the lingering unrest. To my complete surprise I shocked us, a tiny spark just big enough to know we weren't dreaming.

"What the hell are you doing?" She yelled at me.

"Resolving the storm."

"You're the only one in the storm jackass. You don't think I know?" She pointed two fingers at her eyes and then at mine like special ops do in the military when they are ready to move. I went into an uncontrollable chuckle, telling myself that I just made lightning. I have to imagine it sounded like an evil chuckle.

Right before sunset we had outrun the storm and made it to Abilene, Texas. The air and the sidewalks were empty like a ghost town. It was a sad brown city that probably had never thought about building a dead-end street. Every turn led to another deserted street that held lost pages of quality. It seemed that there were people once there that were concerned about progress, but progress never came. Only a song and a few thousand tears kept the buildings from crumbling, only a country of explorers could find a spot of beauty in the desertion of life. I loved Abilene. It had an assumed warning sign that reminded Americans that life doesn't have to be demolished in order to disappear. A single human passed in front of the Bronco. He glanced at us suspiciously, as if we were there to destroy something. I wanted jump out of the car and show him that we could make lightning together.

A Collect Call

We circled back to the highway and stopped at the Royal Inn and Lounge. They boasted a ridiculously tall sign that read: $25 SINGLE. LOUNG with the E missing, or maybe that's how they spelled lounge in Texas. Our room was a dirty little box with 1970's matted brown carpet, a broken television, a dorm room refrigerator that smelled like eggs, an air-conditioner that sounded like a 747, and a bathroom that I wouldn't go in without shoes. But it was poolside, so we had that going for us. Moll brought in our sleeping bags and put them over the bed covers. I watched her eyes. She saw what she wanted to see until it built up into disaster.

"Close your eyes." I told her.

"Why?"

"You don't need to know everything." The shrooms had me feeling slightly more spiritual than usual.

"You think you know everything."

"Just close your goddamn eyes, and I'll give you something."

"Ok!" She would always be a child at heart.

"What are you thinking?" I was trying to create lightning.

"Are you going to give me something or what?"

"I'm trying! Hold on!"

"You aren't doing a good job trying."

"I'll show you." I went over and began taking off her clothes. She started to take off my shorts like she had been waiting for me to do this forever. Once we were naked and on the bed, I went inside her. She started to move quickly, but my hands kept her down on top of me.

I was trying to show her that we were one entity in one moment, and that's all there is, just a piece of electricity between us. I held her tightly on top of me while she moved her hips around.

"What are we doing?" She whispered.

"Just be."

"Would you just fuck me for Pete's sake."

I didn't like when women mention other men's names during sex. All I could think about was Pete, whoever he was. Either way I held her tightly against me. She held her breath. After several minutes I could feel the inside of her clinch up. The layer of sweat joined our skin instead of the electricity.

"What was that all about?" Moll asked while panting.

"Nothing, it's stupid, I was trying to make lightning. I thought I did it earlier."

"Well, do it more often."

Moll faded off into a nap as I lay staring at the ceiling. I still had a reserve tank of energy, so I slipped out of bed and went out to explore around the motel, hotel, Inn, or whatever it was.

~

I woke up from a nap and Ecc was gone. I looked around the room and it seemed like I shouldn't have been there, like it was somewhere I was abducted and I was waiting for the police to come break down the door at any moment. I thought for a second that the old man from the

RV had captured me then I slowly came back to reality. The reality was that Ecc loved these shitty little motor lodges that housed criminals and perverts. He would probably eventually be both, but not any time soon.

I put on my sandals and went outside to the Bronco. It was parked right in front of our room, literally three feet away. The sun had gone down but it was probably still around 90 degrees. There was an Indian family, or maybe a Bangladeshi family cooking out in the parking lot. I could never tell the difference, but I did know that both cultures disliked being called the other. It was like how Americans and Canadians didn't like being confused, except it was on the other side of the world and it just didn't seem to matter that much. There was a kid around five years old that waved at me. I waved back while wondering if he had been raised in shitty hotels like this. Their elaborate setup looked as if they had been here for a long time. There was a sign in the lobby that read ASK ABOUT OUR MONTHLY RATES so that seemed to be the case with them. They probably asked about the monthly rate and had never left.

I grabbed a handful of quarters out of the Bronco's console and found the payphone. Then I ended up making the call collect instead, just because I hated guessing how many quarters it would take to call New York. My little brother answered the phone and the operator asked if he would accept the charges. His young boyish voice sounded like an older lady's voice and the operator called him "Mam." He was 16, but much younger in reality.

"Joey, it's me, Moll. Just say yes you will take the charges."

"Oh hi Moll, let me ask mom." He said without any shock that we hadn't talked in 2 years.

"No, don't ask mom, just say yes. They need to know now."

"I don't know, I think I'll ask mom."

"For Christ sake Joey it's not a big deal, just tell the nice lady yes!"

"Hold on." Joey went away, and the operator told me I would have to try again. She told me to have a nice day and then hung up. I stood there with the phone still against my ear. A man and woman walked past me and I wondered whether they were criminals or perverts. The woman gave me a nasty look and the man peeped back at me trying to catch my eye. I assumed they were perverts.

~

I went through the lobby and followed the signs to the lounge or LOUNG or what turned out to be something far from either. It was a large cafeteria looking room with dozens of little round tables and those stacking convention chairs spread out in an organized mess. There were three people sitting at three different tables. I could hardly make out their faces because the room was so dark. The only recognition of humans was the cherry of the cigarettes glowing in the shadows. There was a disco ball with half of the mirrored squares missing and below it the tables had been pushed away for a makeshift dance floor. I found a table that seemed to be at the consistent distance that everyone else chose. One of the men got up and walked out. There must have been a three-person maximum. That left me, a chunky lady trucker that had probably never wore a skirt, and a skinny trucker man that had probably never seen a French movie.

"You mind if I get one of those cigarettes from you?" I asked the man.

He got up, gave me a smoke, and said, "No reason sitting around here being healthy. The two don't go together." He kind of laughed. I made an agreeable noise and he lit for me.

"Where'd you get the beer?"

"The reservation desk." He said.

I went to the reservation desk and came back with three Buds and handed them out. The lady took it and gave me a suspicious look like I was going to try and screw her. I took the last draw from the cigarette and my nose began to bleed. I used my white shirt to stop it. "I guess these things really are bad for you." I put out my smoking butt. The man grabbed some paper towels for me. "Thanks, it'll stop in a second. Something in there just needs to get out."

"You know, my nose hasn't bled, hell, probably twenty years or so." He said. "And you know what else? If I cut myself right now, even a good size cut, by two days, it'll be all healed up. No kidding."

The trucker lady rolled her eyes and looked away.

"Yeah, the body is a self-fixing machine." I said with a wad of paper towels under my nostrils.

"Until it isn't." The lady morbidly replied. I liked her. Maybe I would try to screw her.

"I think it depends on one's blood and brain connection, of how fast it wants to be fixed."

"Yep." He proudly replied, because he was under the impression that I was complementing him, like I was saying that his brain is quick. But that wasn't it.

I took out my notebook and pen, because I had come there to specifically drink beer and write. Despite the two other people in the lounge being a part of the atmosphere I was still able to vomit out all the thoughts built up in my head. I had to stop the bleeding.

"What you writing down there?" The man asked me, but I ignored him until all of the words and the blood were out. So instead of talking with him, I talked into my notebook:

I think everyone's blood is full of ideas, thoughts, opinions, and stuff that we think of only being from the brain. While the brain is stable, the blood is transporting these things around the body to control actions. When the blood is content it clots easily and hence the man beside me heals very quickly. It may be a ludicrous idea, but it helps me to understand something. Most people I meet are content in their lives, but they all have this tiny natural voice that questions their life, and doesn't understand why they are content. Humans are the only animals that do exactly the opposite of their instincts. The double-edge sword of this situation is that the drive of being content always beats the tiny questioning voice because it is its own invention. Its purpose is to create satisfaction, so when it questions itself the purpose is breaking. Just like a cut across one's arm, the body fixes and makes the host more comfortable. The comfort creates the content. The ideas, thoughts, and opinions become content.

Of course, I can't express this to my new friend, otherwise he would think I was nuts. "I'm just making a list of things to do." I lied. "If I didn't get them down now I'll forever forget."

We had about seven more beers in the lounge. My trucker lady got pissed off and left, maybe because we stopped showing the slightest signs of wanting to screw her. The man reminded me of my dad, at least what I remembered as a boy. I told him this and he seemed to get a little emotional, because he also had a wife and son at home.

"Is he still on the road?" He asked me.

"Yeah, something like that." Both of my parents had been dead for a long time now, maybe a dozen years, maybe longer. I suppose they are still on the road.

We had one more beer in silence and then I headed back to the room.

Moll woke up when I came in. She saw my bloody shirt. "What happened?"

"I got in a bar fight, I mean a lounge fight?"

"Did you win?"

"Who's blood do you think this is?"

She laughed before getting serious. "Was it your nose again?"

"Yeah, it's weird huh?"

"You should see a doctor."

"Yeah, maybe... Hey! Do you know the difference between a hotel, motel, and an inn?"

She sadly smiled. "Come to bed drunk boy."

A Preferred Balloon

"It wasn't your face in my dream." I told the person without a face in my dream. It was one of those times in which I realized I was in a dream, and it was up to me to take control. The faceless person was looking inside me, as if I was turned inside out for the entire world to see. The big phony was found out, the scared boy was on display for the brave men that had sacrificed before him.

~

Ecc was tossing and turning all over the bed, maybe in a nightmare, maybe just a regular dream. His shorts were on the floor and his little pocket notebook had fallen out. I picked it up with intention of putting it back in his pocket so he didn't think I was looking through it, but then I wanted to look in it, I needed to see what was in it. The notebook was what was in his mind and I needed to see inside, needed for once to get a glimpse of what was going on.

I turned it to the last passages. He wrote about the validation of life, how he has found it in the only immortal truth he'd ever known, in what he called the fleeting present. He wrote about doing something to give his life meaning, to give *our* life together meaning. I'm surprised that out of all the dissatisfied people in the world, that he felt this way. He left his home when he was 18, traveled the world, and probably has written hundreds of stories about all of those times. He's probably done more than any other 23 year old that I had met. This is exactly one of the reasons we probably weren't going to make it together. He doesn't tell me any of his fears, he just tells his notebooks, he turns his fears into stories and forgets about them, turns his loves into muses and forgets about them.

Ecc grunted out a snore that temporarily woke him up, but he just turned over and went back to sleep. I shoved

172

the notebook back into his pocket, and went to find a vending machine. I all of a sudden felt like being bad, like my new version of being bad, like eating Doritos and drinking a Coke.

~

I woke up to Moll washing the blood out of my shirt. I tried to say something about my dream, but broken gibberish came out instead.

"What did you say?"

"It wasn't your face in my dream."

"It wasn't? What do you think that means?" She asked me like she was mad. I must have done something stupid last light. The last moments were a blur.

"I think I was looking for help, and I wanted you to be the one, but the person who was there was faceless."

"You? Looking for help? It was definitely a dream then."

I rinsed some generic headache powder down with a cup of coffee, took a bong hit, popped a stem, and chugged a dirty glass of water. The hotel room looked even more disgusting in the morning sunlight. Moll was outside waiting for me in the driver's seat. Before going out I found the Bible and turned to Ecclesiastes. ALL STREAMS FLOW INTO THE SEA, YET THE SEA IS NEVER FULL. TO THE PLACE THE STREAMS COME FROM, THERE THEY RETURN AGAIN.

I went out and stretched into the Abilene air. There were several Indian families that set up their kitchen in the parking lot. I watched the kids run around, the women talk in a circle, and the men smoke and cook. It was their home, it was their life, their family, in the middle of Texas, so many highways and waterways from their homeland, yet they fit. America is so weird. It made me want to stay. Just sleep and die with Moll in my arms beside the 747 air conditioner. I'm sure there was a country song about this.

An Unfinished Moment

After several hours on the road, we stopped at a gas station. It was over a hundred degrees and I wanted to rest the Bronco in the shade. We sat under two trees in our camping chairs. There was nothing out there. One day it will be a shopping mall, or condominiums, or a water park, but now it was just two trees, a path, a rinky-dink gas station, and a small worn down billboard informing us that LIFE STARTS AT CONCEPTION.

"Did Ned give you a book he wrote?" Moll asked.

"Nah, he gave me the ending to the book we were going to write together."

"I thought he never wrote anything for that."

"Me too man, me too."

"So what's it like?"

"Oh, it's good, it's pretty damn good. It's as if a prophet wrote it. I mean, the language is like a prophet speaking." I said, knowing the next question.

"Can I read it?"

"Mmmm..."

"God, I hate you." She had her pouting face on.

"You hate God?" That was my attempt at avoiding the subject, but the pouting face wasn't going away. "You haven't even read the beginning."

"Because you haven't let me."

"Yes, this is true, but we just can't harp on the facts all the time."

She gave me the old stink eye.

"What? It's unfinished! There's only been the beginning up until now, and now there's no middle. You know my rule." I said sheepishly. "There's no point in reading something that's unfinished, and a novel isn't finished until the last word is put down."

"Well, at least tell me what it's about." Moll is very good at this, getting her way that is. If she would have started by asking me to tell her about the book, there wouldn't be a chance in Hell. But since she went for the big guns first, she has the leverage.

"What is it about?" I pondered out loud. "That's tough to say." I thought about it, took out my notebook, and silently read:

It's about every moment that makes up one's life. About how every moment is passing by in a constant invisible machine. How every moment is now the past. How every moment trusts you to not abuse it as it is a disposable, consumable, repairable item. It is a blessing waiting to become your enemy, hoping to create beauty, holding it's breath, destroying an idea, framing your misery, putting a sheet over the world's distractions, waking you from the dream you've never had, pushing you to your next mistake, painting scenes of that never-ending train in the mind that burns, fights, and laughs...

I looked up to give Moll an answer but she had walked away.

~

I went to the gas station to take a pee. In the middle of our conversation, Ecc decided to pull out his notebook and forget that I was there. It was typical. I didn't feel so bad for stealing a look into his notebook now. The man working inside seemed like a very nice person, not like what I expected. The movies always portrayed the people in these places as sociopaths or just normal creepy men. He told me to let him know if anything was wrong with the women's bathroom. He said his wife took care of the maintenance in there, but she went to town today. I loved the idea of going to town. Just saying it out loud made me happy. In the exceptionally clean bathroom I looked in the mirror and said, "Be back later honey, I'm going into town. Do you need anything from town?" I turned on the sink and sat down on the toilet. There was no graffiti on the walls and it made me want to write on them, ruin something perfect. Outside was an anti-abortion billboard that inspired my vandalism. I found a pen in my bag and wrote LIFE STOPS AT PENETRATION. Ecc wrote in one of his books how there's so much fatality in sex. How its purpose is to create, and its side effects to destroy. It was one of his few philosophies I sort of agreed with.

There was no key to the bathroom, so I didn't have to face the nice man again. He would have been able to see right away that I did something wrong. I was the worst liar ever. People didn't even have to ask me a question; it was all over my face. I imagined when his wife came back from town and saw the graffiti, he would tell her that there was only a nice girl that went in there and that she couldn't have possibly done it. It made me feel bad, but feeling bad sometimes made me feel good. We were mostly an awful species. I'm not sure why people would want to keep every single live conception available? As far as I'm concerned, conception shouldn't be limited to the sperm and the egg. The act of conceiving has no beginning or end, it just is.

There was something about that moment that struck me as very important despite it being one of the more bland parts of the journey. I snuck the Polaroid camera from the truck to take a shot of Ecc writing and smoking in his blue folding chair under the trees. The abortion billboard was in the background. It all seemed to fit perfectly into a square photo, like that was the only way it would ever work together. I tried to capture the moment, but the button wouldn't go down, and when I looked up and saw him creating a world that couldn't ever be produced on less than a million photo albums, I blinked and made it disappear.

~

I saw Moll out of the corner of my eye trying to take a photo of me. I closed my notebook. "*It's about* finding that universal moment of clarity in life, a search for the search, a realization of life, instead of an acceptance. Something like that?" I told her the answer to her question that she had walked away from.

"Deep thoughts." She moaned out.

"See, that's why I don't tell you anything."

"Are you still talking about what Ned wrote? Because if you're trying to answer the question that I asked ten minutes ago I'm over it."

"Yeah, I just wanted to get it right, to say it right, you know?"

"Ecc, it's okay to not be perfect every single time. It's actually more attractive to fuck up sometimes." The camera clicked accidentally. Moll pulled the photo out, waved it until a picture formed, and then handed it to me. "See, this is what you were just saying."

I looked over the photo and she was right, all those useless words I had been spitting out were all right there, laminated and forever. "Dammit, I hate when you're right." I leaned over to kiss her, but she pushed me back.

"I don't think so Buster."

I thought how I would one day give her this incomplete book, so imperfect, so ready to be brought to life. Maybe it would be the validation we were searching for?

A Spontaneous Combustion

We drove into Luckenbach, Texas. I looked around for Cowboy heroes, but saw no one. Not only was there no Willie or Waylon, there was no one at all. The town closed down on Wednesdays. I asked Moll if it was Wednesday and she confirmed. The only business open was a gas station with a gift shop. Just beyond the gas pumps was a sign claiming a population of 16. Now the song named after the town made a lot more sense. They needed to get back to nothing. I was starting to feel like I needed a day to close down, close down the madness. We could just stop in a field in the middle of nowhere, lay out a blanket, and stare up at the sun without talking, eating, or even thinking.

That dream ended as quickly as our scenery changed from the nothingness of the desert into a cloud of progress. Big banana destruction machines began to appear on both sides of the highway. The dust of a newer better America surrounded the Bronco. All the usual suspects began showing up, the blue of Wal-Mart, the yellow of McDonald's, the green of BP, the décor for the mediocre. Designer shopping bags and maze parking lots shouted out catchy slogans. These were times in which we still had a chance to be original, but most declined to do so. Being original doesn't pay so well. Having conviction is a minimum wage lifestyle.

The construction dust thinned out as we entered downtown Austin. We got a hotel room across the street from the State Capitol building. I hung out on the balcony while Moll showered. There was a boy's baseball tournament in town, and half of the hotel was full of rowdy 13-year old kids running around the breezeways and perfecting cannonballs in the pool. Other than that, there didn't seem to be many people out on the streets. The furnace-like heat didn't help. It was the kind of temperatures that they tell old people and northerners to stay inside.

I grabbed a beer from the cooler.

"Already eh?" Moll was putting on deodorant, which was rare for her.

"Yep, want one?"

"It's too hot to…" She put a comb in her mouth while fixing her long brown hair.

I didn't care. Those melting faces needed to be forgotten. I looked over at Moll. She was staring at a wall with nothing on it.

"What?"

Her eyes turned slowly toward mine, and the change was even deeper. "What?" She mimicked.

"I just asked you that."

"You did?"

"I think I did. Maybe I just thought it?" I had lost my moment. Death was preoccupying my subconscious. Or maybe it was something else, maybe I was spreading it out. I chugged the first beer, and then opened another as Moll got ready to get sweaty. She sadly glanced at me in the mirror while playing with the raindrop on her necklace.

"I'll be out here whenever you're ready." All I needed sometimes was shelter at my back and view of anything else in the distance.

~

Ecc and I walked out of the hotel, not really knowing where we were going, but that seemed to be our theme anyway. Most of the time, I try to not call it indecision. I read this book last year about getting anything you want in life just by doing a few specific things. One of them had to do with being decisive in every situation and accepting whatever fate came of it because you made it happen. I didn't finish the book, because I made the decisive decision to not listen to the author. Indecision seemed so much more like living to me. I saw some homeless guys outside of the Capitol building and thought they were probably all indecisive also. The white ones were really tan, like tropical island tan, and it made me happy that they didn't need to worry about blankets and coats.

"Why are homeless people always hanging outside the Capitol buildings?" I asked Ecc, because it was the same in Denver, and the same in Albany. I couldn't think of anymore at the time, but I'm sure it's the same everywhere, even somewhere like Juneau, Alaska.

"Maybe they want their state leaders to get a good look at how they haven't succeeded?"

"How the homeless hasn't succeeded?"

"No, the government. As long as there are citizens living without proper shelter then it means the people running the government are failures."

"Do you really think that?"

"Not sure, it just popped in my head. What I actually think the reason is, is that there are probably government services for the homeless near the capitol buildings, so it's probably just a case of proximity."

"Did you see how tan they were?"

"Yeah, they fucking look good." He joked.

Sometimes I loved talking to Ecc. It must be difficult for him to talk while always thinking about what to say before it comes out, so I appreciate the times when it seemed natural.

~

By the time we made it to around the university area, our clothes were soaked in sweat. The air went from a musky dead heat to a swooping gust of wind that stopped us in our tracks. Then it went away. People passed by us in a quiet slumber, sweaty Texas hippies, rockabilly activists, business cowboys, wall-eyed students, post-punk fashion slaves, and everyone else in between. They all seemed drained, waiting for the sun to go down, so they could howl at the moon. Another gust of wind roared around us. This time it actually made me step back. I got the strange feeling that Austin was trying was trying to tell me something, like the Texas gods had decided my time was up.

A Blinding Wager

We ended up in a downtown pool hall after getting lost in those oily waves of dusk, and after making a bet that I might not ever be able to pay off. Ever since Moll and I met, we had been absurdly betting on pool. I had been thinking about this bet since we checked into our hotel room. When I was standing out on the balcony, I couldn't help but think how I could easily jump into the pool.

~

It was best out of five games. The loser had to jump naked off our hotel room balcony into the pool. It was only one floor, but I don't think I would be able to jump far enough out. Ecc could make it, so I had to beat him. After he started the break and didn't pocket anything, I practically ran the table.

In the beginning of our relationship I had played better than ever, because I wanted to impress this new guy in my life. Then after that phase had passed, I began to play mediocre unless we were playing against strangers. Once again I was showing-off to the new. Then we brought in the wagers, starting off with sexual bets, moving on to dinner and bar tabs, and then taking it to our current double-dare stage. I suppose it's like this in many phases in life.

After I beat him, he said he needed some inspiration and went over to the jukebox. I noticed the bouncer was eyeing us since we had entered the bar. He wasn't at the door when we got there, so maybe he thought we were underage or something. Then when Ecc walked away the lanky bouncer honed in on him and not me.

~

The bar was pretty quiet save a barely audible noise from the television, the cracking of the pool balls, and the cackling of two girls in the corner booth. After Moll beat me in the first game, I went over to check out the jukebox. I needed some game-time music. It was the kind with 100 compact disks with the covers laid flat. There were a couple of bars in San Francisco that had just put in these digital jukeboxes. The selection was too immense and it gave no identity to the bar. There was nothing more American than a jukebox, not apple pie or hotdogs or baseball. It was the one unapologetic concept we could hold above our head anywhere in the world. I flipped through the pages and it wasn't too bad. I found Dylan's *Desire* at disk 92. My fingers punched in 9202 and a thump came from the back of my head. Then the front of my head hit the clear plastic cover of the jukebox and as the floor came toward me, I faded out.

A Remarkably Tall Hat

My head was in a tailspin as I looked up at the ceiling. There were a few faces staring down at me. The closest was a guy with lightning bolt tattoos where his eyebrows used to be. This seemed to be thematic. Moll was beside him. She looked upset.

"Ecc! Are you okay?" She said desperately.

"Yeah, sure." And I was okay, except that I was on the nasty bar floor, dizzy and confused. Moll slapped the lightning bolt guy across his temple, but it seemed to hurt her more than him. I asked what was going on, but no one answered. Bolt eyebrows grabbed my hand and pulled me up. I got a head rush for a few seconds. He helped me over to a stool at the bar. I watched all the people in the room watch me. With their eyes they asked me what I did, and with my eyes I asked them what I did. The guy with the lighting bolts was a lanky rockabilly doofus type, tall, probably six and half feet. The people staring at me began to disperse in a disappointed fashion. The bartender put a glass of water in front of me. I was afraid to speak because apparently my voice wasn't working with my brain at the moment. The doofus explained as Moll attempted to keep me stable on the stool. "Man, I can't tell you how sorry I am. I just reacted because I was certain that you were the dude that pepper-sprayed me last night, and I would still swear by it, but your girlfriend said you just got into town today, so shit man, I don't know what to do, I'm just sorry."

"Did you hit me?" I asked.

"Yeah." He made a cringing face. "And then your head hit the jukebox and then it also hit the floor."

I started laughing, but then it turned into more of an uncontrollable cough.

"I'm glad you think it's funny." Moll said. "Are you going to be okay here? I really have to go to the bathroom."

"Sure, as long as this guy doesn't punch me again." I laughed again. The doofus half-smiled, unsure of what the right thing to do was.

"I'm really sorry. You can punch me back, no kidding, as soon as you're ready just sock me."

"I think my girlfriend already took care of that. Thanks though."

Moll scurried off while giving the doofus the stink-eye. I'd never seen her so tough before.

~

The worst thing about hitting someone is that it hurts you also. I felt like I had broken one of the little bones in the palm of my hand. I had never punched anyone before, and even though I technically slapped him, it felt good, like maybe a punch would. I had never seen Ecc get punched either, even though he's thrown a few defending me. I've seen him grab men by the throat. I've seen him throw men up against walls, a pool table once, a bar-top once. Even though he isn't a big guy, he had rage.

I wanted to go back out there and give that guy a real punch, get the bar all riled up again. They'd probably all start fighting each other like in those cowboy movies from the 70's, chairs would be thrown, bottles busting, women breaking glasses over the back of men's heads. But that guy actually seemed kind of nice. He just wanted revenge for an unjust act.

I felt over my hand and realized it wasn't a broken bone, but a burst blood vessel. It was a weak war wound, but a war wound all the same. Maybe I would get a tattoo there just to always remember my first and only real face slap.

A girl had come into the bathroom and gone into the stall.

"What was that all about?" She asked from her squatting position.

"You talking to me?"

"Yeah, you're the only one in here ain't ya?"

"Yeah, but sometimes people talk to themselves while they pee. I mean I do."

She laughed at me, maybe with me. The mirror had a crack in it with someone's initials scratched across it. There was also an unfinished heart, like whoever was etching it, was interrupted by another pisser. It needed to be finished.

"I used to date the tall guy." I decided to make the story interesting. "But he cheated on me, so I brought my new boyfriend here to piss him off. I didn't think he would sucker punch him, well… I probably could have guessed it, he was the kind of asshole that wouldn't just stand up to a man face to face."

"What a jerk." The girl said after flushing the toilet.

"You said it. But I suppose I'm kind of a bitch for bringing my new boyfriend here."

"Yeah, that's kind of bitchy. What are you going to do?"

"I'm going to leave them both here. They seem to be getting along now. Who needs men right?"

"I need a fucking man, but good for you."

I left her at the mirror as she applied dark purple lipstick.

~

"I'm Sham." He put his hand out. "I'm the bouncer here." I shook his hand. "I was blinded by this little punk last night, for like three hours, after I kicked him out." Sham wasn't comfortable talking to me yet. "I just don't know what to say. Get anything you want, on the house, beer, pool... you still have some credits in the jukebox."

I laughed again. It's the only reaction that made sense to me. "Um, don't worry, don't worry about it dude, it wasn't my time yet. It was supposed to happen this way."

"That's cool. I dig it. Like this was all supposed to happen for a bigger purpose." He was trying to erase some guilt, which was fine with me. He was the kind of guy that had never accidentally kicked someone's ass. It was a first for both of us.

"Maybe not a bigger purpose, just the purpose of the moment." I chugged the glass of water and I could feel the knot on the back of my head and the knot in the front of my brain.

"So why do you think you're here, you know your purpose?" He asked like it was leading up to something personal.

"You mean right now or in general?"

"Well, I was talking about right now, but in general is fine, or both, or whatever." He stuttered out.

I told him an answer that I've told several people. It's from some science fiction book. "I'm here to observe, to spy for a higher being. And when I die, those beings will drain everything from my brain, then send me back in another empty body." It sounds as good as any other theory.

"Did I knock something loose?" He finally smiled.

"Maybe." I looked around like I really was a spy. "Hey, I'm going to tell you something that no one knows, and I mean no one, so you can't say anything and if my girlfriend comes back, zip it up. Okay?"

"Yeah man."

"I have something fucked up in my head, a lump, something swollen in my brain." I told him like it was a cool thing to have.

"Huh?"

"You heard me right. If you would have hit me the right way, or even the wrong way, you could have killed me back there." This was just for shock. "That's something to think about huh?"

"Listen man, I'm sorry I punched you, but you have to stop talking so weird. You're freaking me out." He thought I was messing with him.

"I'm serious man. I wouldn't fuck with anyone like that, not even someone who almost killed me."

"That's enough alright, you proved whatever point you're trying to make." Of course, the first person I tell about dying doesn't believe me. We sat there, kind of looking at nothing. I wasn't sure what point I'd be making by telling him that. It would make a good story for the rest of them.

"Why did you want to know my purpose of being here?" I asked him, because it was the reason he asked me, reciprocation.

"I just wanted a stranger's point of view, because I think I'm here to deliver a message through my music."

"That's cool man. It's good to have something to say. Is it a basic theme or... ?" I couldn't really phrase the question correctly.

"Yeah, it's like, that, our society is shameful, and we need to fight together, like, rise up and break free, you know, rock and roll man." He was having a hard time expressing his plight. Sham was dead serious, yet I was the one who was crazy.

Moll came back over and I gave him the hush-hush look. He thought I was a nutcase. "Let's get some air." I told Moll.

"Let me go out first, and then come out like a minute later." Moll whispered in my ear. I nodded and then watched her walk toward the door, hesitating to wave goodbye to one of the girls in the corner booth.

"We might come back later and take you up on the free beer." I told Sham. "You can have my jukebox credits, just don't play any greatest hits."

"Yeah man, take care of that head."

"And you keep saving the world. Rock and roll!" I sarcastically said, and waved myself out the door.

A Severing Of Rhythm

Out on 6th Street the sidewalks were getting full, so full that people had to walk in the road by the gutters. Moll and I got separated and then came back together and then separated again. We were busy looking in at the never-ending string of bars, looking out for all the drunken bodies, and dragging ourselves away from the auction voices of the barkers. "Two dollar Kamikaze's! One dollar beers! Live music! Freak show! Beautiful women! Five dollar pitchers!" Moll and I were both the kind of people that had never made an immediate decision in our lives. Sometimes it worked out, actually, it always worked out. I mean, we were still together and alive.

After the crowded air thinned out we found a saloon with a band about to start. We figured it would be some sort of sin if we didn't see live music in Austin. The narrow bar was packed with what seemed like a college crowd. Everyone stood in little groups, but they all looked outside their inner circles to find something else.

Moll went up to the bar and got two bottles of beer and two whiskeys, portable boilermakers. We pushed the whiskey back. Moll didn't even blink, but I washed it down with half of my beer. I let out a tedious burp and Moll followed with a crowd-stopper that made several heads turn in amusement. She could really make me proud sometimes.

We stood by the front of the stage in anticipation of the music, but I started to get the feeling that the band was actually performance artists. It seemed as if they were about to begin for about half-an-hour. There were five of them, all a different ethnicity, and all with something wacky going on. The real act seemed to be each faux musician coming up to the stage one at a time, giving their instrument a pop, pull, or blow, and then saying "Test-testing-one-two." The performance was titled *Setting Up*.

And then an Indian guy who was testing out his trumpet, began to blow like mad. I looked around at the lackadaisical and judgmental crowd. They stood against the walls drinking their Shiner's, they stared at one another's neo-punk-cowboy outfits, they talked about their new tattoos, and finally their eyes made it up to the Bay of Bengal's Roy Eldridge. Then a white guy with a tambourine jumped on stage, grabbed the microphone, and began to shake. Next was a black guy complete with a parted afro and electric bass. He thumped and twitched while an Asian drummer came from behind the backstage curtains and began to play standing up. The last addition to the quintet was having a drink and a chat down below the stage. The band continued to jerk into their intro while the Latina gal finished her booze and pointed to the ceiling. Then she crawled on stage, grabbed her six-string, and began jumping up and down. By now, all of the distracted audience had focused in on the shaking, twitching, jumping, and jerking machine. The music was purposely off, the rhythm went from East to North, and the first words from the tambourine man were, "Your TV eats donuts on Mars!" I thought about that ghost of a TV from Ely, Nevada. That TV eats donuts on Mars. Moll woke me out of my daydream by slamming into my chest. "I'll take another Tex!" So I went to grab some more drinks. I found that the awkwardness of the music had made its way into the crowd. All of the young bodies were twisting and exploding. The off-rhythm formed a path to the bar. If the music was tight and melodious, the crowd would have been in a sway that would have made it impossible to get through.

"Two PBR's please." I told the bar man. He handed me two 20-ounce cans. "Three dollars please." Doing our part for the upcoming revolution. They were red, white, and blue with deodorant and dreams of bad haircuts, always ready to be a little more clever than needed.

I bounced my way back to the stage where Moll had chosen the jump. I was more of a twitcher. The tambourine man broke out a harmonica, blew three notes, and then attempted a stage-dive into the crowd. The offbeat audience barely caught him. The rest of the band went nuts like the music would bring the jingle-jangle man back. They went dud-duh-dud, screech, bam, tid-dee-don, straight hard power chords, then boom! It was like Batman and Robin in a fight with The MC-5. The loosey-goose crowd joined in the mayhem. I was drenched in sweat. The saloon was packed with life. I got dizzy. Moll fake punched me. Flashbacks. Tambourine man crawled back on stage and tackled the afro-bass man. The guitar goddess straddled the two boys and played some power AC/DC riff, and the band played on, and then we moved on, a little more a part of the clouds than before. I held my arms up in the air and tried to grab the moment. Moll pushed me from behind until we were back out in the blanket air.

We sat down on the sidewalk and caught our breath while figuring out where to go next. An old skinny man in a neon green thong, bunny ears, and flip-flops walked past us. He was our Alice in Wonderland rabbit, so we followed it. There were so many noises decorating the streets. Little nuances of inhibitions dropped, shredded, and forgotten forever. At the end of the block our fearless bunny leader just disappeared. Moll looked at me wondering if he really was there. I told her that if we sensed it then it's always there. "There is nothing but what is in our minds!" I shouted with my arms out wide like I was waiting for a group of rabbits to come and embrace me.

Two good-old-boys in pick-up truck cruised by and gave us a whoop and holler. Moll yelled, "Hold on!" So they did. We ran up and jumped in the back of the flatbed. "Go, go, go!" She told the boys and slapped the back window. The driver burned down the tires and took off. The short shot of warm wind was like taking a cold shower. Two blocks later we jumped out at the stoplight. The boys didn't understand, but also didn't care too much.

There was a piano bar on 6th street right in front of us. Moll went to dance to Billy Joel while I went for more drinks. The bar was packed, so I just waited patiently behind a few UT girls. I was so drunk that I didn't realize for a few minutes that they weren't waiting for drinks. The bartender, an adorable Tex-Mexican gal waved me over to the side. I stumbled down to the end by the wall to an empty space. "Hey, I don't think I should serve you another." She smiled.

"It's ok, it's my last night on Earth." I said surprisingly straight.

"So, I'd be the last girl to serve you."

"So to speak, yes."

"Well, then we better make it a good one." She went away to get me something. I think she was flirting with me, and I may have been flirting back. "Here you go sweetie." She put down a pint glass of a mixed drink.

"What is it?"

"Just drink it and hang out here." She went to help out the other bartender. So I drank it and hung out there. The drink was big and strong, very Texas, the last thing I needed. I wondered why she wanted me to stay there. Maybe she didn't say that at all? It was extremely loud in there. I looked around at the room and it all seemed to be one organism, nothing existing on its own. Suddenly everything was happening without me, as if I had just disappeared without a history, or any ideas, or goals, or mistakes. Before I could ask myself any more questions, it seemed I was out on the sidewalk again. I had to find Moll. Where was she? The streetlights were so blurry. Those noises that were once decorations turned into molecules of oxygen telling me to go this way and fall that way and lay down over there…

~

When I went up to the piano man he was playing the song *Piano Man*. I put two dollars in his bucket and wrote down a request for *Scarlet Begonias*. He took it and looked at it while singing and playing. It was very impressive, reading, singing, and playing the piano at the same time. When I played the cello I could rarely do anything except fall into that world of only hearing the notes of what came from my instrument. He smiled at me to convey that he would play my song.

I watched Ecc down at the busy bar. He was being ignored by the bartenders, standing behind a group of girls, which meant he was to the point of drunkenness of being passive. He might have been on something else. I wasn't sure what he was doing behind my back. The piano player went into my song, so I obliged by acting as if it was the greatest thing that had ever happened to me. I went to dance with Ecc, but he was nowhere to be found. I assumed he went to the bathroom, so I got a beer and waited. When he didn't show I went to check the men's room, but he wasn't in there. Then I went outside to see if he was smoking. Then I went back inside to check past the stage area; maybe we crossed paths without seeing each other. When I had exhausted all options I had to assume he had made it to that dangerous drunken side that he went to sometimes. Like a sleepwalker, he would just wander off without telling anyone. Sometimes he would run away from whatever group he was hanging with, almost daring the others to try and catch him. Of course no one did, he was like a track star when he was that drunk, twice as slow when sober though.

I walked up and down 6th Street figuring I'd find him sitting on the sidewalk, chain-smoking cigarettes, but once again came up empty. It was as if he had just disappeared. There was no other choice but to go back to the hotel and hope that he went there. When I got back I could tell before even entering the room that he wasn't there, but I wasn't too worried. We always found each other, and we always left each other, never knowing the outcome, but taking those chances was a part of our system.

I took a bong hit and hung out on the balcony, waiting to see a silhouette of his body wobbling up the road. After awhile of standing out there I assumed that he was probably arrested for public drunkenness or something like that. I looked down at the swimming pool and thought about our bet earlier. It didn't seem so impossible at that moment. So I pulled up a chair to the railing, assessed the distance, probably a five-foot outward jump and twenty feet down. There must have been harder jumps that I had taken in my life before this?

~

When my eyes opened, it seemed I had passed out in an alley. I was assuredly confused and still inebriated. My will alone got me to my feet. There was just a little blood coming from my nose. An unfortunate taxi stopped for me, so I mumbled out the name of the hotel and we took a small tour of Austin. It seems my hotel name was also a street that the driver took me to. Without even looking around, I started to pay the fare. It was twenty-one dollars, and I only had eleven. As I searched for more money and spread the eleven dollar-bills in my hands I noticed that there wasn't a hotel outside my window. The driver was silently angry. He took my eleven dollars and I stayed in the cab, unsure of what to do. There wasn't a choice. I got out, slurring a thank you. He burned down the tires, angry with the idiot.

The neighborhood seemed harmless, little wooden houses, big stucco mansions, thirsty trees swaying in the high breeze. I could hear a highway not too far in the distance, so that's the way I headed. After the confusing journey, I just settled into a concentrated stumble. My bladder turned to stone. I had to piss since I woke up in the alley, but had been putting it off for the hotel room. There was a dark area on the side of one those little wooden houses. I stumbled over the dry lawn and released on a chain-linked fence. A dog barked from inside the house, but I couldn't stop. The barking got louder. I pushed to get it out quicker, but there was so much stored up. Before I could even finish, a voice came from behind me, "Hold it." A man with a shotgun to my head told me in an unnerved Texas accent. I zipped up, and started to explain my situation, but only drunken mumbling came out. He put the barrel of the gun to my forehead. He asked me, "You live round here?" I couldn't answer. All I could sense was that cold steel against my warm skin. "This way." He told me. "How'd you like it if I came to where you lived and pissed on your house, woke you up in the middle of the night?" Even though he wasn't really asking, I attempted to answer and said something like, "You piss, I live, I at Capitol... sorry." I just remember how the words wouldn't form sentences. The thing is, I wasn't really thinking about dying, what I remember thinking about is the smell of sulfur from gunpowder. It reminded me of a time when I was a kid and my neighbor killed a snake with a shotgun. After that, sulfur was the only thing I'd been able to smell in my nightmares.

The man kept backing me up with his gun until we were in the street. He asked me, "Where you going?"

"Don't know."

"Go that way." He used the gun as a pointer. So I did. I waved goodbye to my new friend. He seemed like a good guy, they just let him have a gun. I have to imagine if they didn't let him have a gun then he would just have peeked through his blinds until I went away, same result without the threat of murder.

After he gave me a direction to go in, my feet started to gain some composure. I walked through the neighborhood, breathing the heavy air that still had hints of sulfur. I came upon a large open green space where the tree line stood way back in the distance. Over the trees, the sun was shooting a few preliminary rays into my sky. There was just enough light to see the point of the State Capitol. For some reason a Grateful Dead song was stuck in my head, and I kept singing the lyrics from it, "Once in a while you get shown the light, in the strangest of places if you look at it right."

A Responsibility of Souls

The phone was ringing. It was an hour past the noon checkout time. Moll started laughing about the night before. My head was killing me, so I couldn't laugh out loud. She curled up into my body. "Quit trying to kill yourself." She whispered in my ear. I didn't respond. "I love you." She said, trying to dig deeper into my torso.

"I love you too."

The phone kept ringing. It could only be the front desk trying to kick us out.

"Let's just stay in bed all day and night." Moll said.

"Aren't we supposed to meet your buddy Herman today." I said in an exaggerated jealous tone. We were supposed to go to Houston, which was only a couple hours away. Moll's college friend Herman lived there, but he was leaving the next day for vacation.

"Oh shit, I don't care that much. We would just have to talk about what we have been doing since school, and probably how successful he is, and how unsuccessful I am."

"You mean you will have to talk about how boring he is, and how awesome you are?" I said and she gave me a look that meant we were not going to Houston. She jumped on me, kissing me, showing me how awesome she could be despite all the unsuccessful endeavors she had not attempted.

The phone kept ringing. I would have loved to just lie in the bed and do nothing, go nowhere, think only about Moll's skin, and just *be* for once, just be. But, the phone kept ringing.

"Hello?" Moll answered like a receptionist. "Oh I'm so sorry. My husband has come down with a stomach thing, and if all possible we would like to stay one more night?" She covered the receiver with her hand and whispered, "Is that okay?"

I shrugged. "Are you asking me or your husband?"

"It sounds better, people for some reason give more respect to married couples than homeless couples." She took her hand away. "Yes, yes, sorry. Yes, just one more night, thank you." She listened to the person on the line intensely. "I'm sorry, I don't know what you're referring to? Say that again. Someone jumped from their room to the swimming pool. Wow. How could that even be possible?"

~

Ecc looked at me like I was the nutcase, but I didn't break, I had to play the part with the hotel operator. "It was a girl? That's crazy. Was anyone hurt? Oh good, well thanks for understanding about the extra night. My husband will be very thankful."

I hung up the phone. Ecc was still giving me the stare. "What? I'm not the one who passed out in an alley, took a cab to nowhere, and got a gun pointed at them."

"How did you make it?"

"I got skills son. Hops."

"Did anyone see?"

"I guess so, but I didn't see anyone see me. I jumped right out of the water and ran back up the stairs. It was still dark out so if anyone saw they apparently just saw that I had tits."

Ecc went right back to sleep, so I went to look for a bead shop I had seen the day before. The heat hadn't changed, just as hot, draining, one degree from being unbearable. I walked through the middle of the University of Texas campus. I remembered seeing a TV show about the guy in the 60's who shot students from a tower in the main building. It was still there. For some reason I expected it to have been demolished after the murders, like it represented evil and it was reasonable that evil should be out of sight-out of mind, but I guess that doesn't make any sense. I distinctly remembered in the documentary that the shooter guy bought a can of Spam before going on the killings and in his last note he referred to himself as an "average reasonable and intelligent young man." Both of these facts were the scariest part of humans, first; Spam would be one's last meal, and second; An average reasonable and intelligent man would kill his wife, mother, and random people because he wasn't satisfied with how life was going so far. I imagine being average must be tougher than it sounds.

I bought some beads for a road necklace I was making. I was trying to get beads and such from all the places we were travelling through. It was more for memories than to actually wear. My raindrop necklace was the only piece of magic I needed around my neck at the time. Whenever I needed some sort of reassurance about myself, Ecc, life, I just held onto the drop and rubbed it till providence appeared. Maybe that guy with the Spam should have just had raindrop necklace and history would have been different.

~

I ended up getting my Luckenbach, Texas day. I slept all afternoon until Moll got back, and then we just stayed in bed watching TV and eating delivered pizza. It was the break I needed. Moll called her friend in Houston to tell him that we weren't going to make it that night. He was going to South America for two weeks and told us we could stay at his apartment if we wanted.

"He said he'd leave the key with his doorman. Said we could stay there the whole time." She told me.

"Doorman? Sounds too fancy for us."

"We can pretend to be fancy. We pretend to be all the other things don't we?"

"I'm pretending to be lazy right now. But tomorrow I need to start to pretend to be a writer again."

The next morning Moll took a shower while I made shroom, peanut butter, and jelly sandwiches for our lunch. I lay back down on the bed, closed my eyes, took in the lemon mothball smell that most hotel rooms kept, and tried to take in the sober moment of the journey. It was what we had, the reality and the escape of reality constantly battling against each other.

A Cloudy Boundary

The two-hour trip in between Austin and Houston was a big construction dust cloud with strip malls and dried up swamps in the cracks of semi-gloss air. It was the kind of highway that would never see a piece of innocent shade, a 20th century trail of tears on the edge of the second millennium. In one of the short spans of deserted highway, I spotted a hitchhiker. He held up a small cardboard sign that read, THAT WAY. I have a thing about picking up strangers. For some reason I always think that they're going to reveal something beyond profound that no one else would ever know except a lost highwayman. But unfortunately, they were always just nut-jobs or just as brainwashed as the rest of us. They talk about the news, the weather, movies, and sports. Sometimes they talk about missing whatever they were running from. Either way, I pulled over on the shoulder to give it one more try.

The Bukowski looking man walked over to the Bronco like he could have cared less if we stopped or not. Moll opened her door and I told him, "There's not much room, just try to squeeze in."

He climbed over the back, wedged his lumpy body in between the cooler and the back of Moll's seat, and looked off to the side like a dog would.

"We're just going into Houston, is that good for you?"

"Hell no." He said without any angst or sadness. "Have, have you ever b-b-been to Houston?" He had a stutter that made him seem dangerous.

"No, first time, why?"

He just grinned and nodded at the seat. It seemed we had a real loose one on our hands.

"Well, we have a friend we're meeting there, so it's kind of in the cards… unless you plan to kill us or something."

Moll put her head down into her fingers. "You're not are you? Going to kill us?"

"You, you sh-should see it at least once." He said, completely ignoring our jokes.

"So where should I take you?"

"That way." He pointed toward the windshield.

"Good enough."

"By the way, I'm Moll." She said like I was being rude to not introduce my long lost friend to her. Or maybe it was something else I did. I tend to do many wrong things that I'm not aware of.

"And I'm Ecc."

He just gave us a half-nod. "This car, this car, it's doing you, you good?"

"It gets us there and sometimes back." I said unsure if that was the right answer.

"That's good, good, real good." He contemplated. "You, you s-see, my thumb and my ass are my c-car, my freedom, but ya'll, ya'll got this p-piece of machinery. Four wheels of freedom!" He was all of a sudden grinning from ear to ear. "Four f-fucking wheels of freedom!" Maybe he did have something to say?

"Well, it's a vehicle. If one is going to be free, then there needs to be a vehicle, whether it's a car or a state of mind." I told him, but it's not spontaneous mind you. This is something I've thought about a hundred times before.

"Ah ha! Hmmm... Ah ha! So my thumb is just the means to my state of mind?"

"Sure."

"Ah ha!" He began to laugh, and then just stopped abruptly. "Wh-What's your vehicle sweetheart? Wh-What do you, you do to be free?"

Moll didn't like the sweetheart comment, but she played along anyway. "I don't know, I suppose a journey like this, I used to do yoga, and-"

"Yes, yes, yes." He interrupted her, and she shot me a look that indicated his inevitable drop off. "And you?" He asked me. I thought we had already covered me, but I made up an answer anyway.

"I write, make up worlds, stuff like that."

"It's good to make up worlds. Th-This is all make-believe anyway. And I, I, I... I can make up a story better than you because I am real. You, you, drive around like a big shot, going to your job, going home to your beautiful wife here, just go-go-going nowhere."

"Well, first of all, she is not my wife, she is someone else's beautiful wife." I said and Moll punched me.

"You, you're not real man, you just going through the motions, but I, I can make up my world better than you! Do-do you know why?" He asked me.

He was right so I gave the right answer. "Because you're probably insane, so you're able to go outside of the boundaries that I'm trapped in."

He put his head down and grabbed the sides of Moll's seat. Then he started to slightly shake it. He wasn't as crazy as he wanted us to believe. "Who the hell knows?" He said. Moll leaned up and braced against the dashboard. I slammed on the brakes and his head bounced off the back of the seat. He chuckled. Up ahead, at the next exit was a sign as high the clouds that advertised LOW GAS PRICES. I pulled off and stopped below the sign. "Okay, we're here."

Moll opened the door and he crawled out the back. Before we rolled away, he told us to watch out for something in Houston, but it was hard to hear him.

~

"Did he say watch out for ants?" I asked Ecc. I swore that's what he said. I was just about to lose it on Ecc. He always had to fucking pick up hitchhikers, and they were always dipshits. Why can't we just meet people in a normal fashion, in bars, at church, AA meetings, ballroom dances. Those places were just too normal for his palate. He asked me one time, "Do you think we've met every important person we ever will in life?"

I told him that was ridiculous, but who the hell knows. Picking up hitchhikers was his way of playing the interesting person lottery. Also, I know he has always wanted to be a hitchhiker, or to say, hitchhike for an extended period of time. I don't think anyone can just be labeled a hitchhiker.

I could see the wavy skyline of Houston over the horizon. We hit bumper-to-bumper traffic, no wind coming in the Bronco. I'm surprised that it hadn't broken down yet. It was old and despite all the love we gave it, we hadn't given it much else. I hesitantly turned on the radio with this in mind, thinking that any other power source used might just make all mechanics stop on the spot. There was a radio program on about the year's latest technology and how it would change how the everyday person interacts. Something called a Blue Tooth and a Blackberry and a Napster. Why couldn't they just say what it is instead naming things after fruit? The radio announcer said that for the first time there would be mass marketed cell phones. The studies showed that over half of Americans would own one of these personal digital assistants in the next five years. I saw Ecc roll his eyes. He didn't want to be a part of this innovative era we were going into. One time after I asked him if we should buy a computer he said something highbrowed like; 'Technology dilutes creation with speed of information so that we don't have to be a part of it. As apposed to giving us more time to experience life, technology has given us more time to experience technology. Life is a form that one can't make more efficient. There is only the present moment and it is immortal, one moment happening forever all over the universe.'

I asked him, "So wouldn't we still be experiencing life while using the computer? I mean it would still be the present moment."

He shook his head because he knew I would never *not* argue with him and then said, "It's a slippery slope Moll, a slippery slope."

~

"Did he say watch out for the ants?" Moll asked me.

"I think so."

He obviously didn't tell us anything profound, but at least he didn't tell us that it was hot out. We drove back into the dust cloud and eventually into the line of traffic that led into Houston. We hadn't turned the air-condition on the whole trip. I couldn't even remember if it worked. The last thing any car needed in San Francisco was air condition, and on top of that I believe the Bronco would just keel over and die if I turned it on. Moll and I were sweaters, willing to take uncomfortable to the next level.

The top above our seats came off, so we usually took the wind from that and our windows, and dealt with what the gods gave us beyond that. The other people in their cool cars looked at us like we were lunatics. We were covered in sweat. There wasn't a drop of wind. Carbon monoxide drifted all around us.

"Sorry about picking up crazy Larry back there. I won't do it again."

"It's okay, you will do it again."

"Not today I won't. By the way, I made us sandwiches for lunch." She looked over at me with a sweaty nose and smiled.

An Unused Coat Rack

We pulled into a parking lot of the downtown high-rise. The Bronco was third in line behind a Lexus SUV and a Mercedes convertible that had its top up. We preferred one-star motels and three-star tents, but this uptown joint would have to do. Moll rummaged through our crap, trying to figure out what we should take with us to the apartment.

Little heat waves rose from the concrete up past our sweaty foreheads. The valet hurried up to us with tickets in his hand.

"Hello sir. How are you?" The clean-cut young man asked me.

"Hey man. I'm pretty good. You?"

"Fine sir. How may I assist you?"

"Um, we're staying in a friend's apartment here, we've got a bunch of crap, so we might need to keep coming down and grabbing stuff, and I hope we won't be a hassle asking for the truck a couple of times, I mean I'm just saying that I don't won't to be a bother."

Moll finally hit me to shut my babbling up. I was embarrassed to be using a valet. I didn't know much past doing anything and everything for myself, so having someone park my car was weird.

"There's not a such thing sir. I'm here to take care of the hassles."

"Um, okay. I'm Ecc and this is Moll." I said.

"We're driving around the country." Moll informed him of our state. "That's why we have so much shit. We're not homeless or anything, well, technically we are homeless but not that way."

"That's great. I'm Brian." He loosened up. "If you'd like to grab what you need for now. I'd be glad to bring your car down and you can just let me know when you need to grab other… shit out of it."

"Thanks Brian. We needed someone to take control of this situation."

"How far ya'll going?"

~

The valet dude asked us how far we were going and me Ecc looked at each other, waiting for the other to answer. What was the answer? How far were we going to take this? Maybe ten years from now we would be in a van with kids and a dog going through Houston again, stopping in to see what Brian is doing with his life. He would ask us how far you going again and we still wouldn't have an answer.

~

"All the way Brian, all the way." I told him after Moll was stumped for an answer.

I got the ridiculous idea to give him a five-dollar bill wrapped around a bud of weed as a tip. He didn't even look at it, just thanked me and stuffed it in his pocket.

So we left everything with Brian, and decided to take a walk instead of checking out the apartment first. I looked back and saw the filthy blue truck going up the ramp. I took Moll's hand and smiled at her.

"What?" She asked.

"Nothing." For once in my life I was elated with an overbearing pride, with my gal, my vehicle, and my life. There wasn't anyone in this city that could see through the dirt and grime that shaded our moment, this moment that hid a lifetime's worth of beauty.

"I'm not sure if should have given him that tip."

"Why?" She asked.

"Because, he was cool and all, but what if he's like anti-drug and he reports it to his boss?"

"Oh shut up, that's crazy-talk." Moll said.

"Yes, it is crazy-talk, but, not impossible." I felt a weird twinge in my head, and then in my legs. "Oh, speaking of crazy-talk, if you couldn't tell, I put shredded up shrooms in our peanut butter and jelly sandwiches."

An Invisible Exhibition

Downtown Houston was the future prototype of the United States. There were already many of these nice cities under development, not to say all of them. It was a time in history in which culture and character were being destroyed for the sake of cleanliness, safety, and ambiguity. There were plain white vans driving all over the streets. There were hundreds of buildings without doors. All we wanted was water, but it seemed the corner store had been abolished in all these paint-store plans. The plastic chain streets came pouring down. "I want soft serve ice cream, no, no, a chocolate milkshake." I said out of nowhere as if I couldn't stop my mouth from gushing out my thoughts.

The shrooms were powerful. We were already in a strange new land, but on top of that, we were in a strange new mind.

We walked another seven or eight blocks before coming to this bar called Area 51.

"Beer?" Moll asked me.

"Well, it's no chocolate milkshake."

It must have been fifty degrees inside. At first I didn't really pay attention to the surroundings. There was a search for the ultimate seats that occupied my moment. There was a big plush couch across the room. We began walking over and I noticed it wasn't a normal bar, because the atmosphere was so contrived to be unique. Everything was made out to be spontaneous and random, but so obviously done on purpose, I wondered whom it was fooling. Then I remembered how we all secretly liked to be fooled. I looked over the people and watched them systematically line up behind each other while taking their beers and splitting off into other lines. They lined up at the bar, then lined up to get to the big German style tables, then lined up at the window booths, and then lined up outside the bathrooms. At the very least, it was orderly.

"Do you see this?" I asked Moll.

"Yeah, crazy huh."

The cocktail waitress came over. "You guys ready?"

"Sure, two waters and two beers please." I said, unable to think in detail. Detail surrounded me and drained the room.

"What number?"

"Excuse me?"

"What number beers?" She pointed to the menu that had symbols and numbers to help in one's ordering process. There were probably a hundred beers to choose from.

"Umm, how about, number 3 and number 46." I didn't even look.

She grabbed the paid check from the previous patrons. As she walked away counting her tip, she muttered, "Fucking cheap ants."

"Did she say cheap ants?"

"That's what it sounded like. Maybe it's a specific Houston accent or some strange esoteric saying?"

We sat back with wide-eyes, wanting to do something and at the same time we didn't want to do anything. Moll pretended to look at the menu, but was really just staring over it at the anomaly of order. I just stared outright, unabashed interest. There was this noise that hummed over the conversations and music that sounded like squirrels eating nuts. I had to ask myself if this situation was strange.

"I have to go to the bathroom, but… I don't know?" Moll gritted her teeth together. "Okay." She said to herself. "I'm going."

A woman in a pink business suit followed behind her, directly behind her. In the meantime I was sinking into the couch, having the overwhelming feeling of being weighted down by the mushrooms. I was able to reach into my pocket to grab a couple of uppers to hopefully balance me out. Between breathing and eating, it was a constant world of balancing.

~

The bathroom had a dozen stalls, a dozen sinks, a little couch for resting before peeing, and the toilets had these automatic flushers and automatic toilet paper dispensers that I'd never seen before. Was this the future?

After peeing and going to the sink to wash my hands I saw myself in the mirror for the first time since the mushrooms kicked in. I couldn't look at myself, so I stuck my hands under the automatic water dispenser and tried to focus on something besides my image. There was something two sinks down from me in a pink suit. She adjusted her wig; I think she was adjusting her wig.

"I love your hair." I heard her say; I think she was talking to me; I think I heard her talking to me. I slowly turned toward her image in the mirror and for half a second saw this giant ant in pink suit with her wig in her hands, but then it turned into an over-tanned woman with pronounced overbite.

"Me?"

"Yes, I love your hair. It's so silky. Are you a Native American, or part?"

No one ever knew my ethnicity, but they always tried to guess. I'm just an American mutt, nothing special. "Yes, part Cherokee." I lied, using the most badass sounding tribe I could think of, even though I probably did have one of those tribes in me. She adjusted her hair, an ant with a wig, a human with tentacles. I wasn't sure which one.

"You see what you want to see, then everyone else manipulates it."

I thought I heard her say that, but I didn't turn to confirm. The sink water was running full blast. I felt over my abdomen, not necessarily a pain, but just a feeling.

"You alright sweetheart?" She said to me, and I turned to ask what she said.

"I said, Sioux is in my family, but then everyone else exaggerates it."

"Exaggerates what?"

"You know, how they are part of the original America."

"Oh right." I didn't know. Her words were turning into steam.

"But you actually look like a Cherokee."

I turned the water off and finally, maybe, saw that she was a black woman, not an ant, not a Sioux Indian. Her suit was pink though, that had to be true.

~

The waitress brought over the drinks and I over-tipped her. For some reason I felt like I should make up for the table before us. Saving the world two dollars at a time.

"Hey, thanks a bunch." She said. "These ants are driving me crazy."

"Did you say ants?"

"Did I say what?"

"…Ants?"

"I'm sorry, it's so loud I can't understand you."

"Never mind. May I get one of those giant pretzels also?"

"No problem."

Good, I thought, no problem. I became more relaxed with a beer in my hand. No problem. It was like my bottle of milk, a pacifier dipped in whiskey. No problem. I scanned around the room and noticed that everyone had on wristwatches and most had on suits. Maybe that's why they kept it so cold?

Moll came walking back with a grin.

"What?" I asked.

"There was this woman in the bathroom. She had this pink outfit on, and, well... she started, like, complementing my hair. She wanted to know what I was and I couldn't figure out what she was, and then she wanted to know how, I mean, she wanted to know where I got my hair done, and... how much it cost, who did it, and there was, and all kinds of things." Moll was having trouble forming sentences. She wore a big confused grin.

"So what's so funny?"

"I don't know? I think she thought I had fake hair and she was testing me, that I had it put in. I don't know? You had to be there."

"Cool."

"Oh, I know! I think she was bald."

"What do you mean, you think?"

"Well, I think *she* had on a wig, and maybe she thought I did too. I don't know?"

"I don't know if that's funny either." I said with a laugh.

"Yeah, that's not funny. It's not ha-ha funny, it's like, it's funny in a way in which someone asks you a question that doesn't matter, like a bald woman asking someone where they got their hair. You know what I mean?"

"Yeah, I do know what you mean?"

We sank back into the big black couch.

"This place is weird." Moll said slowly.

The waitress brought over our pretzel. Moll spurted out a laugh. "Man, that's a big fucking pretzel!"

The waitress gave her the old stink eye, but smiled at me. Then it hit me. *We* were the weirdo's in the bar. They always say if you can't find the weirdo on the bus, then it's probably you. That was us.

Two ants sat down at the couch beside ours, one in a grey pinstriped suit and the other in a black suit. The grey suit talked really loud and cocky. The waitress went over to them after the cocky ant whistled her over. "Hey hun. Me and this gentleman here want the best champagne in the house, I don't care what it costs, as long as it's the best."

She cut him off. "Are you aware we are beer only?"

"Beer?" His lip curled.

"But we do have a very rare Belgium beer that's called, West, Westen… I can't remember, but it costs like fifty dollars a bottle."

"If it's the best you got, then I guess we will have to settle for it. Bring us two." He flashed his wallet. "Amex Gold good?"

She snatched one of the cards away from him and went to the bar. I could tell he bothered Moll. His friend stayed silent while he kept on rambling. "Steve, I have to make a call. You make sure you like whatever they bring out. I'll send it back if it's not phenomenal. We aren't getting anything less than the best. You hear me. I'll be back." He walked outside while yelling into his cell phone. This cell phone culture was getting obnoxious. It was mostly just businessmen talking loudly about useless crap like real estate and stocks and golf tee times. Hopefully they will discover later on that it gives you brain cancer, a slight redeeming possibility.

Moll and I were too enthralled by the scene to talk to each other. It got more and more crowded by the minute. It was just after five, so it must have been the after-work crowd. They formed these perfect lines in between the spaces of the bar and the tables. One after the other they moved in unison. The contrast of this bar and the one in Austin really blew my mind, a tale of two cities, so close together yet so different.

Poor Steve sat by himself on that big couch with a hundred-dollars worth of beer. The more I secretly stared at him the more he began to take on human features. Every once in awhile I'd see his cocky friend outside the window, yelling into his phone.

"Let's get out of here." Moll told me.

We left behind the giant pretzel untouched.

Outside a man had been run over by a street train. Cops and rubbernecks gathered around, but inside the ants kept chattering away. I remembered what the hitchhiker said. "I guess that's what that hitchhiker was warning us about?" I said.

"About getting run over?"

"No, about the ants."

"What?" She gave me dumbfounded look.

"He warned us about the ants."

"So, what's that got do with anything?"

"I'm not sure?" I said.

"Are you alright?"

For some reason I thought that we were in the same mind state, but...I needed to get my head straight. I needed to find that balance.

A Bloody River

We went back to the apartment to regroup. I was glad her friend from school wasn't there. It would once again remind her that she left the future behind, and there were only two people to blame, and one of them she couldn't get away from.

A couple of hours after taking a nightmare-filled nap, I got up and grabbed a cold beer out of the cooler. I held it against my cheek until gathering reality. Moll was staring at the wall.

"I dreamed that these crazy chickens were trying to hunt me down and eat me." Moll said in a half-asleep voice.

"I dreamed we lived inside a peach."

"Oh?"

"You want a beer?"

"Just put it in front of me. I'll take it to the shower with me."

I felt the blood running from my nose. "Me first." I went to the bathroom with my beer.

"What are you trying to do?" Moll asked me as if she was angry.

I yawned.

She had a hold of her glass rain drop.

~

I hated how that apartment building looked so big from the outside, but it was just a bunch of small apartments stacked together. It was like a moment, from the outside this life looked so big, but it was just a bunch of small moments stacked together.

I had this professor at the university during my freshman year that had just given us back our first graded exam. It was a large class, at least a hundred students, and the class was something generic like music history. We went over the questions and answers. Many students raised their hands to inquire about the ones they got wrong. The professor at some point told the class to save their questions till the end of the semester. He told us if for some reason the question hadn't been answered on its own by then and if we thought the incorrect answer was still correct, and if we thought that by changing it to be correct would affect our overall grade for the whole semester then please come see him then. Everyone put down his or her hands and I think it would be safe to say that no one went to his office at the end of the term to dispute a question.

You blink and it will be tomorrow, and then you blink again and you will be old, and then you blink again and you will be taking your last breath. I couldn't help but think if I would want to dispute any questions at my last breath.

The mushrooms had me thinking too much. It was much easier to be drunk, to be numb. That's why booze is legal, for the same reason religion is legal. I went to the bathroom and banged on the door. Ecc had been in there forever.

~

I told Moll once that as long as you don't believe in the future it makes this life a lot easier, and it's true until you have to be a part of the future. Like if you have to plan for a meal or you have to think about your next step, that's when it gets hard. The mushrooms helped, but one couldn't go around tripping all the damn time. You start to see the worms and the clouds, your ears take in the crickets and the rumbling 18-wheelers, you begin to breathe in the magnolia and the carbon monoxide, you talk to the ant, the hitcher, the farmer, businessman, the American, the foreigner, and like it or not something from the past has to eventually come out.

A thin gush of vomit sprayed from my mouth into the toilet. On my knees, I leaned backwards and put my head against the wall. It was a big beautiful bathroom complete with wall dispensers that had soap, lotion, shaving cream, and sanitizer. The room spun. It was easy to know this world wasn't real. It was easy to give up on this fuzzy pink bath mat.

After an involuntary nap on the floor, and after getting back some balance, I chugged the last half of my beer, turned on the shower, and then sat down in the tub. My only energy was my exhaustion and it was at a level beyond panic. The warm water splattered over my chest. A jagged stream of blood trickled down my neck until getting to the pounding drops of Houston sewage. I hoped that my overflow would form its own little river and make it into the Gulf of Mexico, make it somewhere more validating than here, than the present, somewhere just out of reach. That was my only solace, my blood just out of reach.

Someone was banging on the door. Moll was banging on the door.

A Punchline Existence

"Give us three tequilas." I told the shirtless bartender.

"I can't have tequila." Julio waved his hand at the shots.

Moll was dancing her hippie-twirl beside a couple of guys dressed in leather. I stood across the room in awe. "I have to." I whispered in a mimicking tone.

"What?" Julio asked.

I downed his shot and then mine. I took Moll's over to her. Her eyebrows were arching with intrigue. She spilled half of it on her hand and then licked it off. One of the leather boys caught the glass out of the air. She grabbed my hand and pulled me into her. Our feet became tangled and we fell onto the sticky floor together. We got up and danced hand in hand as awkwardly as we always had. I let Moll spin off and dance on her own. I stood there by myself, drunk, high, everything. It had come to fruition, the possibility of everything.

"How about a beer?" Julio had a goatee and smelled like a new umbrella. He was tall; he stood over me. I think the umbrella smell was coming from his hair gel

"Yes, let's drink!"

We got beers.

"This is as good as it gets." He told me.

"Always was."

Every new man that came in kissed the bartender, some with tongue, and some just an excited peck. I watched the dance floor. Moll acted like the wind. It was an impossible task to dance with Moll. One just had to be near her and watch out for the floor, understand what was behind them, what was in the absurd air. I was so in love with this entity. Nothing else existed. She was this hazy window that I saw everything through.

Julio and I talked about all of the places that Moll and I had briefly lived. He never gave me his name, but I liked the sound of Julio. "I'm going to kill myself if I don't get out of here soon. I want to go to San Francisco, New York, fucking anywhere!" He seemed like he wanted me to ask him to come with us. It must be hard for most humans to just take off, start over completely, reinvent themselves, kill their former selves off. It had always come easy for Moll and me, easier than staying somewhere, easier than dying somewhere. Julio kept on his rant about leaving, but I got a strong feeling that he would stay right where he was. "This whole shit about being different in Houston has gotten old as hell honey. I need to be with my people!"

"Well, at least you're not an ant."

"Hmm?" He politely questioned.

"Nothing. It's nice to be around people who understand you."

He stared at me for a few seconds. "Do you like boys?"

"I like her."

He followed my stare onto the dance floor.

~

How we ended up in probably Houston's only gay bar is hilarious to me. We were taking a taxi to an area that was supposed to be the nightlife district when Ecc spotted a wall with a huge mural of cartoonish trannies on it. "What's that?" He asked the cab driver, and the driver told us that we don't want to go there. "It's for weirdoes and faggots." He told us.

"Well turn around! She's a weirdo and I'm the faggot!" Ecc laughed out. We spent most of our time in gay bars in San Francisco, which is easier than most cities. My best friend cried when we left. He was in love with me, and in lust with Ecc. I told Ecc that he was going to really miss all the attention and groping that he had become accustomed to in San Francisco. At that moment he was talking to a tall Latino at the bar, while others swarmed around, waiting for their chance for fresh meat in Houston. "It's so nice to have new faces in here." One of the men I was dancing with told me. "It's always the same old fags in the same old tired chaps." Then the inevitable question of, "Do you and your man swing? I think it's hot to watch. Do you like to watch him with other men?" He barely gave me a chance to answer. All of his thoughts just spilled out on the dance floor. I told him that we just liked the company in the bars, not the bedroom. "Well then let's just party our faces off and see where the night leads us!"

I could feel Ecc staring at me. When I turned toward him he was giving me that awful look that tells me he loves me more than anything he's ever known. It's not a good look for him. Most of the time his look is his unconditional love for writing, for writing books, writing stories, writing, writing, writing… Then he fools himself every so often into thinking that he loves me more than writing, that he loves me more than living in this writer's life, but he doesn't. I've accepted that.

~

Moll caught me staring.

I wondered what Julio saw, what anyone in that bar saw, if anyone in that bar really existed, if me and Moll existed. What if we were just a part of someone else's dream, a god's nightmare, an evil genius' painting. I don't know? I just remember the song playing over the stereo said something about how life was a countdown. I kept my focus on Moll. She flowed backwards as if she was able to defy time.

A Clear Static

There had been seven roadside gravesites since California. The Bronco rolled along on East I-10. The eighth grave came as we passed over the Texas-Louisiana

border, the ninth after Beaumont, the tenth around
Lafayette, and the eleventh was somewhere outside of
Baton Rouge. Along with the graves there were also
multiple broken down automobiles. Signs of the highway
were becoming apparent. Vultures glided above us and the
worms wiggled through the nitrogen filled soil below us.
My time was running out, but I couldn't grasp what was
running out. Sometimes I think so hard that nothing but a
void is displayed in my head. That's when I have to move
on. The only release from the void is to keep on running.
There was the outline of three fingers in the dust on the
dashboard. I matched my fingers up to the three and
pressed the other two down to complete the ghostly hand.
We passed the twelfth grave. It hadn't been visited in a
while. The flowers were fake, but still withered.

~

"Where you want to go?" Ecc asked. I wanted to go to
water. It felt like we had been trapped inland since we left.
Ecc was in the driver's seat, holding the steering wheel for
balance. He wasn't doing anything out of the ordinary,
besides steadying a large moving piece of metal, besides
keeping our world moving, keeping the edge of the sword
at our throats. We were both hung-over, but in a good way,

probably still drunk. We stood still in the heat at a gas station outside of Baton Rouge.

"I suppose we have to go back?"

"Back where?" We'd both seen all the signs. They were everywhere; they were every few miles at that point. We would have to make the decision now or never go back.

"You know where."

"New Orleans?"

"Yep."

"Revisit the demons?"

"Or we could go to a beach?"

"Beach? It's all swamp around here. We'd have to make it to Florida."

"Or we could go north?"

"Yeah we should go north. Why the hell do we keep going south in this heat?"

"Got me Buster."

"But to be fair, it's fucking hot everywhere. Saw the weather at the apartment. Global warming they're blaming it on. It's over 90 degrees in Canada. The Canadians are melting!"

He was still drunk. "Should I drive?"

"Oh Moll, do you really think you can outrun the melting polar ice caps? It's going to be like Noah's Ark again, except this time we will have to build a spaceship."

"So we should just go to New Orleans?"

"Yeah, we can't avoid it."

~

All of the places we'd tried to make work, just never worked. New Orleans was no exception. We were making freedom work for us, but we were young, and as difficult as it might seem at any age, young works better than any of the others. You can still convince yourself that there will be so many more chances, so many more immortal moments.

A Blinding Perception

The sun was behind the clouds as the Bronco cut off the highway, and just when I thought all that ambiguity and reckless goal for monotony was going to kill me or at least keep me alive in a coma, we drove into New Orleans. The black and gray layer over the sky would stay there our whole time, and I understood why. Henry always used to say, "Kill your idols!" But sometimes your idols have to kill themselves. Truth lies in violence, but no one wants to hear the truth. Apparently, it's why suicide seems so tragic, because it's too truthful, it's too symbolically violent. Anyway, my idol, my God, my sun killed itself for the days we were in America's drunken jazz painting.

We drove over the tattered streets of the French Quarter. I nervously stared at the rotted out balcony bolts, the shadowed pagan slums, the pages of saxophone sidewalks, the school of dying black poets, and all the joyful misery and reality in between. It was the kind of emotion that came up from the gutters and disappeared south into the nowhere ocean. We rode around for a while without a destination. Then we came across an old broken-down mansion that had a twitching VACANCY sign. It was about four blocks from Bourbon Street going the *other* way. Hustlers, druggies, and drunks floated down the salty streets. They weren't ghosts yet, but you could tell that they wouldn't mind one way or the other.

"You want to check it out? I'm going to have a smoke." I asked Moll because we always get treated differently and get better rates when she asks about rooms.

245

~

I went inside the big leaning house, into the foyer that had an empty desk with an oscillating fan that barely moved the air around the room. There were two dogs sleeping on the floor and an old man sleeping in an antique chair. There was a bell at the front desk, so I gave it a couple rings until one of the dogs came up to be petted. The man just kept on snoring. Then a woman came from the back, sweating and friendly. She took my money and gave me a key without any questions about identification, or deposit, or other guests. That was becoming a rarity very quickly those days.

"You have a car?"

"Yes mam."

"Moses!" She yelled at the sleeping man.

"Uh huh?"

"Help this girl park her car! And help her with her bags!"

"Oh that's okay, thank you, we have a place out on the street."

"That's up to you. But if you want to keep your car, you let Moses put it in our locked gate. If you don't want to keep it, just leave it on the street." She smiled in a way that backed her statement up.

~

I was approached immediately after getting out of the truck.

"Excuse me brother, I'm just an old alcoholic looking for some change. I need my bottle, you know?" It was a large man with a gentle voice that had probably never seen an apple tree without a snake.

"Yeah, I do know." I gave him about thirty-five cents.

"You from around here?"

"Nah." I looked around. "I guess not? Used to live here once, but I left for the same reason I came."

"The same reason heh? Sounds like a riddle."

"I suppose it is." I told the air and we both just stood there. "Smoke?" I asked him.

"Sure, sure, trying to quit but that's how it goes right?"

"So it does."

Moll came back out with a key, and an old man behind her. He went to the gate beside the house and waved us over. Moll shot me a look that meant victory. We were winning. Despite all our failures we were winning.

"Now that girl definitely from New Orleans. Look at her! A Creole if I ever saw one."

Once again someone got her ethnicity wrong, but at least it was an accurate guess since Creole is a mix between Spanish, French, Native American, and African.

"Not born here, maybe born again here."

"Hm..." He looked over at Moll and then in my eyes. "You'll see. You not from here right now, but you'll see." Then he limped off. I'm not sure what that meant. Maybe it was his version of a riddle.

Moll came up to kiss me, but then stopped. "Your nose?"

I felt my nose. It had a little trickle of blood coming out. I guess I was getting used to the wet feeling under my nostrils.

"Has it been bleeding much?"

I guess I had to lie. I don't know? If she really knew, then it wouldn't be her and I anymore. It would be just me, about me, about my time. The real truth is that my time is just as long as anyone else's. I just have the advantage of realizing it every day, every hour, every second, every time the stench of a clock seeps from my head. Henry also always told me, "It's all about the WE." So there had to be secrets in order to keep the Moll and Ecc dynamic intact, in order to keep the WE. So I lied.

"No, hardly at all."

A Silhouette Of A Nose

The Bible in the room was pocket-sized and looked as if it had been in a lot of pockets. The passage read: I TRIED CHEERING MYSELF WITH WINE, AND EMBRACING FOLLY – MY MIND STILL GUIDING ME WITH WISDOM. I WANTED TO SEE WHAT WAS GOOD FOR PEOPLE TO DO UNDER THE HEAVENS DURING THE FEW DAYS OF THEIR LIVES.

I opened a beer and stood on our balcony that overlooked the hotel's courtyard. There was an ashtray full of butts and ash. I gazed into it, mesmerized by the little speck of red that survived my sight despite all of the used cigarettes. Two couples splashed around the swimming pool while little drops of rain sprinkled over their heads.

They looked up at me like I was invading their fun. I've never been able to control my facial expressions, so who knows what they saw. If I had to guess, they saw a man who just saw an angel inside an ashtray. I took a deep breath and looked away. The air was heavy with a dank mossy smell. It was invigorating to have that odor around me, after being in the carbon-monoxide-window-cleaner air of Houston. I stood above the audience even though it seemed as if they were the actors. I was just creepy. Moll walked out with her feet sliding along the uneven wooden planks, her body slumped, her eyes squinting with that comfortable child-like smile.

We headed through the dirty little side streets and then down the narrow Bourbon Street. I breathed the city air in and out like it was my last breath. Shots of musky old shoes wafted by my nose. Then there was stale beer, then the salty ocean, then cotton candy mixed with burnt shrimp, then a hundred different perfumes and deodorants, then wine and hangovers and rain and wood soaked in urine and a thousand other things that my nose couldn't catch in time.

Repeating these lives made me think of this book I read once. It was all about how life was a form that couldn't be made more efficient. How technology was in competition with creation, and how it could never compete because life was just one moment happening forever all over the universe. We had already done this, but there we were again as if no time had passed, as if a century had passed. All we had were these denominations called years to let us know something had happened. We were about six months away from the millennium, a thousand years, the second one, two thousand years we have been keeping track.

~

Coming back to New Orleans made me sad, like reading a book over that you once loved, that once made you feel so alive, but then after reading a second time makes you feel dead inside. It was time to move on, time to create something new in my life that wasn't this, time to read another book.

I went into a store that I used to know the artist owner. Her paintings were up everywhere, but she was nowhere to be found. When I came out Ecc was missing as usual. It took awhile, but I just went looking around in the closest bars and found him. He might as well have been building a cathedral as far as I could tell, leaning against the bar top, empty whisky glass, an ash as long as the burning cigarette, a dying junked-out pen, and a stack of napkins full of naive revolutionary gibberish. It was going to be hard to start another book.

~

Without saying anything about Doris or Bound Souls Bookstore our feet took us that way. About every third storefront in the French Quarter was closed. It was ridiculous that this could happen to the most unique city in the country. I suppose they would turn it into Houston if they could. We got to the dilapidated building where I used to live. The downstairs windows were boarded up. The paint chipped all around the edges. My old bedroom window up top still had that weird excuse for a curtain dangling behind the filthy glass.

Behind that dangling curtain held a short lifetime of memories, so much hope to survive and once that was solidified, so much hope to be the greatest writer that had ever existed. I lived and worked in a bookstore, breathed in millions of pages and trillions of words and thousands of stories and essentially the history of humans. I remember being in that room with Moll on one of the many smoky wet hot nights of the French Quarter. I was writing and drinking, and she was plucking at her cello and drinking.

"Do you ever write about me?" She asked me. I told her that all I did was write about her. "Will you do me a favor?" She was looking out the window, not at me when she asked, "Will you kill me off in whatever you write about me? I don't mind being in one of your books, I just don't want to stay in one of your books." That's how we talked back then. Everything was temporary, so it didn't bother me at the time.

Doris, my saint of New Orleans and keeper of the former bookstore was no longer alive. I said a little prayer for her and put a daisy in front of the door.

A Camouflaged Perception

The night brought out the sick looking for a cure. It was the stage before the show. The empty-headed actors and stagehands all came together to do their best not to be themselves. As we dove into the pool of drunken debauchery, the cheesy comfortable sing-along music got louder and more frequent. The cover band bars were a dime a dozen and it created such an idiotic magic that one could not fight it. So I stopped looking at the audience for once and delved into the illusion, into the illusions.

"You ready to find John?" Moll asked me about our friend who lived with me for a few months in San Francisco. John Bigsby had moved back to New Orleans after giving up on the west coast. He told me, "This has been a great experience, but I believe that sometimes people just belong somewhere specific, and sometimes people don't belong anywhere at all." He obviously belonged in New Orleans, disasters and poverty would not dissuade him.

"Yeah, let's do it." I said. "It shouldn't be too hard."

We went to the Unicorn Club where John and me had emptied several hundred bottles of whiskey. My regular bartender Lloyd didn't recognize me with my rapidly growing beard. I was finally becoming a man, something that comes with facial hair and accepting death. Moll and I grabbed the one available bar stool. It was a busy night, but there was no John Bigsby.

Lloyd put us at last priority because he most likely thought we were a confused tourist couple that didn't know we were in a gay bar. He finally came over and before he could say anything I leaned over the bar, grabbed his head, and planted a big kiss on his lips. "Hello Lloyd."

"Holy farts! Ecc? Is that you?"

"Yes sir. Lloyd this Moll, the girl I left New Orleans to chase across the country."

"Pleasure Moll, how did you do all that and he still turned out a fag?"

"It's a special ability I have, to confuse and destroy."

"Sounds like someone with a vagina." He laughed out while pouring us beers and large glasses of whiskey.

"So where is our boyfriend at?"

"Bigsby? Haven't seen him tonight, but I imagine he'll be in before too long."

~

"I'm going to go outside and smoke while you guys catch up." I had gotten accustomed to going outside the bars to smoke cigarettes. California had banned smoking inside public businesses, and after a brief time of rebellion I eventually preferred it. Plus my stomach was feeling weird, sharp pains coming and going.

Outside was muggy with spurts of yelling and laughter coming from passing groups up on Bourbon Street. I wondered what they were in New Orleans for, probably a bachelor party, a wedding, a bachelorette party, a 21st birthday, a 50th birthday, all the usual occasions that signify getting fucked up with friends. I was tired of getting fucked up. Ecc seemed to be just getting started. When I first met him in Amsterdam he was so naïve, so innocent. Our friend Jouet was teaching him how to drink, how to smoke pot, and then I came along to teach him the more advanced persuasions. Something was growing in me and I couldn't explain what, but it definitely had something to do with trying another life.

I lit a second cigarette and held my stomach. A gang of dudes came wobbling down the street, obviously looking for another bar to conquer. "Hey honey! Let's see them!" One of them held up a rope of beads in hopes to see my breasts.

"There's plenty to see inside there." I motioned inside the Unicorn.

They groaned and went inside the gay bar. It took them longer than the average dumbass to figure out where they were. They came stumbling out giggling like teenagers. "How did it go?" I asked them as I went back inside. "Get a good teabag for your beads?"

"Fuck you!" One of them yelled out after figuring out what I meant. I didn't see where Ecc at first. I scanned the room thinking how it really needed some updates from this tired 1980's gay look. There was a poster of Cher pinned up that was from that aircraft carrier music video. Then out of the corner of my eye, I saw him, saw him for what he truly was. He walked across the bar just as anyone else would, one foot after another, one breath after another, with eyes fixated on something that wasn't in between those walls, seeing gods where half full ashtrays took up space. Being with someone for so long could blind you to what they really are at their core, and that was Ecc, someone who saw gods in the most inconspicuous places. It made me forget about the guilt of getting wasted all the time.

~

After three more beers and shots we told Lloyd we would try to come back later. We ventured out into the street circus. There were old couples with cameras, bachelor parties with meat-heads whooping it up and clinging to each other's shoulders, bachelorette parties with grinding teeth and penis lollipops, shifty-eyed hustlers sucking on cigarettes, weekend warriors with their ties and slacks half-way off, sloppy teenagers cashing in on lax drinking laws, and us, whatever we were.

A piece of newspaper blew by my feet and down the sidewalk past very few others, so we followed it until getting to Molly's Bar.

I ordered more whiskey and Moll let out a long sigh that was supposed to get my attention.

"What?"

"I think I'm tired of drinking. Why do we have to get so drunk every night? Why can't we just be?"

"It's our infected spirit." I plainly said.

"Oh, here we go."

"Here we go where?"

"Give me a break Ecc, you know you're setting up for a rant."

"Maybe, but all I'm saying is that there is a spirit that lives on from the pages of the life-book that no one will ever be able to kill. It infects one's mind. It gives another world, another way of thinking, but without saying, 'this is how you should think' because it's just a story to read, take in, and then take the parts that have infected you and change your life for the better."

"What does that have to do with us? And me not wanting to get fucked up every night?"

"The infected spirit goes hand in hand with the page, with the moment, there are plenty of times in which we can just sit and stare over the universe, take it in, and take it for what it is worth, exactly what it is, but the infected spirit is a whole other moment. It's all that's left, and what was there before was a challenge to forge through without giving in to complacency, soberness, delusions, illusions."

"You are such a contradiction. Every day you have a new theory that discounts the one from before. Your living in the moment before was the sobering reality of the mountain, how it is the mountain, how the stone on the mountain is the epitome of time…" I faded out from Moll's voice because I couldn't believe she was preaching to me my own words. I wasn't ever sure if she ever heard me or not. I leaned over and kissed her while she was still talking. "Hell no, you can't get out of this!" She said feigning anger. "We're going to finish this Buster!"

"Alright, alright, take it easy." I said with my forehead against hers.

"What was that?" She said all of a sudden while staring at my forehead. "It was weird, like a heartbeat in your head."

"It was probably your own heartbeat." I said, but knew it was definitely from my head. She tried to put her hand over it, but I tilted away from her. "Can we stop talking all serious?"

"Classic Ecc. Avoiding anything serious until it's conveniently placed in your philosophy lectures."

"That's true, but! You know what we need?" This just popped in my head. "Voodoo!"

"What are you talking about?"

I felt the heartbeat in my head again, and put my hand over it. "Voodoo. That's why we're here. That's why we came back." The head heartbeat happened again. I tried to drown it with whiskey, tried to forget it was there. Moll wanted to stop getting fucked up, but there was no other way for me. There was the beating, or there was forgetting the beating.

A Gun To My Head

My eyes squinted open to the doormat room, closed, opened, and then soothed back into the darkness. The sound of the world ending rumbled from the window, the walls, the beating in my head. It was the greatest thunderstorm I can ever remember. It was the greatest headache that a living soul could take. The bed shook.

I recalled the night before, going back to the Unicorn Club. I recalled taking two shots of a secret liquid supplied by Lloyd and distributed via the lips of Moll, two vixens in cahoots, test-tubes turned upside down, fingers grabbing the back of my head, and with the force of a girl destroying a boy, she sensually put the secret liquid into my stomach. The liquid burned my mouth and throat, seeming to be a high-powered fuel, poison, something dangerous. My lungs were on fire. I tried to catch my breath. I asked myself *why* and then I woke up in the rumbling bed without Moll beside me.

I vaguely remembered seeing John Bigsby at the bar. It was crowded and I was dizzy, daring life to end there. It seemed he had changed in the way that someone never changes. To say, before he wasn't changing, but he at least had the desire. I missed John Bigsby; I will always miss him. Maybe it was John who gave me the poison? I wanted to get out of bed and go get the answers. I wanted to get out into the French Quarter, run through the drops of rain, through the vibrations of the sky, but the night had crippled me. My Juliet was supposed to take half the poison. What happened? We could have gone to Heaven together, became ghosts in an old New Orleans mansion. The thunder became angrier than before, the wind swayed the ceiling, and every few seconds the air would light up with God's fury. I tossed and turned in the bed, I tried to play tricks on myself, on the spirits. I was delusional with my eyes closed. Sharp imploding pains stabbed my mind. This was it, this was the death that had followed me, the disease coming to the top of the mountain. Oh, life! Spawning little embryos filled with viruses, spawning viruses called embryos, fucking life. I became dizzy and then dozed off again. Maybe Moll was right?

~

I went down to the corner of St Philip and Chartres where I used to busk for change with my cello. The building was still condemned as it had been years ago when I had nothing to lose, and only quarters and dollars to gain. It was in between thunderstorms, giant drops of rain with space to run between, so I sat up underneath the awning and tried to get a grip on this journey that seemed to be getting out of control.

The night before was mad, manic, a lunatics nightmare. It was as if Ecc was trying to drink himself to death. Just mentioning that I was tired of drinking seemed to fuel his fire of self-destruction. Luckily I was able to get him in bed before those last drinks hit him. He had shot girls coming at him from all the shadows, 18 year old sluts holding the back of his head and pushing test-tubes of liquor down his throat. I thought he was fine until he started calling one of them that resembled me my name, and when he tried to kiss her I dragged him out of there.

It would be easy to be mad except I haven't been without my own indiscretions in the past. I'm sure I've called other men Ecc when I was blackout drunk. There was little I didn't do to get rid of him in the beginning, get rid of love and commitment that is. Now that was all I wanted, and it seemed he has turned into what I used to be. That's how it goes I suppose.

Even John Bigsby asked me what was wrong with him. "I've never seen him this bad, even when you were gone."

"I think he thinks he's dying." I told him. "He wrote it in one of his notebooks, but you never know with that, because it might just be one of his characters, he might be using a first person character as someone else."

"You read one of his notebooks?" John asked in shock, because he knew that was the worst thing that anyone could do to Ecc. It was like cheating on him and stealing from him at the same time.

"I couldn't help it, I had to find out what was going on. But it honestly just confused me more."

~

I woke at least once to the sound of thunder, and then a knock at my door woke me again. My boxers were soaking wet from sweat. I was lying on top of a dozen or so open notebooks. I had red spiral imprints all over my skin. There were more pages, more words, letters than one could ever read, or want to.

There was another knock at the door, so I prepared for the worst as my pulled it open. On the wooden deck floor sat a television. I held my forehead and wished for the dream to end. "So there you are, nothing to do huh?"

"Hey, who you talking to?" A boy who worked for the hotel came up the side stairs.

"God."

"Sure." He shook his head. "I've got to replace the TV in your room."

I looked down suspiciously.

"Yours don't work." He wiped the sweat from his face with a red bandana.

"It's better that way." We stared at each other. I was still dazed. "Would you mind doing it when we're gone. We're sleeping, really exhausted." I'm not sure why I said *we're*. Maybe neither one of us existed without being *we*? There were so many maybes that day.

"Sure." He propped the TV up on his right shoulder.

"Be careful, I've seen bigger men killed by those devices."

"Sure." He didn't believe me. I don't blame him. When I went back inside and saw my reflection in the mirror, I was looking at a crazy man. I looked like an old California bum looking for a mountaintop. I threw some cold water over my face and I seemed to wake up for the first time, I seemed to be young again.

An Inevitable Rise

The air out in the French Quarter streets could really make your brain giggle. The moving sidewalk locked my feet in and we went for a ride. Life could really blow your mind if you stopped and let the earth move you. I was in a state of delirium, in a state of grateful melancholy. This sad old city was waiting to be gobbled up by the gulf or by the hovering mediocrity, a race that no one wins. All the broken concrete cried loose stones, staying drunk till noon, waiting to get beaten with a brush and a sailor's stompers. "Wait for the ocean!" I yelled to the spirits, and all the tourists moved to the other side of the street. I stopped at every corner and stared down the alleys and at the wonderful broken down terraces with the thousands of flowers and weeds clinging to the stone-like fungus. The cameras flashed. I walked right in front of one of the explosions that would come out like a painting or a mosaic window. The map in my head led me to the deserted streets where sleeping junky artists pretended the stars were out. The thunder's claws were being cut, but the sky was still filled with jet-black clouds. I found Café Du Monde. It was crawling with all the other clowns of the circus tent afternoon. I ordered their famous beignets and two chocolate milks. The unconcerned waitress brought me a pile of heated dough covered with powdered sugar. My teeth sunk into the sweet French donuts and occurred to me that it was a trick. They covered us clowns in white powder and picked our pockets, and picked our hate, and picked our decency. Oh what glorious concept! I laughed at my thoughts, "Picked our decency!" No one paid attention to the insane, for the sane in New Orleans was outnumbered. I washed down the drugged powder with my chocolate milk, embracing it as it ran through my beard. Those black clouds finally got together and released their anger on the Quarter. Legs scrambled from everywhere to get under the circus tent. The rain came down in wheelbarrows. There was so much conflict between God and Satan, beautiful evil music making us dance like morons. Heaven and Hell battling for the spies of Earth. My head swiveled around to see the trained hobgoblins panicking. The joy it brought to my heart I can't explain. They all had this white residue dripping from their lips. I finished off my chocolate milk and walked out into the shower. The streets were flooded. It was a perfect day.

I stood at the crosswalk letting the rain rinse the powder out of my thin beard. After a half an hour of pouring, the sky opened up to a smoky haze. The streets glistened with Heaven's own steam. The painters and performers dashed out from the awnings to claim their stage. Location was everything. I weaved in and out of the released prisoners, until coming to my own heavenly sight.

~

I ducked into a photo artist's shop near Jackson Square as a rainstorm erupted. There were dozens of photo-series decorating the walls complete with the stories written below the frames. Everything has a story. Everyone has a story. I sometimes forgot that, and I had already forgotten it since we had left California. There was a series of photos displaying a very old couple that hadn't seen each other in decades, but seemed to pick right up as if it had been just days. I could see my face in the woman's face; I could see Ecc's face in the old man's face. I wanted to save him. I wanted to see him decades later and it be just like today.

I all of a sudden remembered Sean and Lauren from Ely, Nevada, remembered that they had a story, and I needed to send them a postcard. I needed to complete the story. There were some gift shops up on Decatur, so I headed that way as the rain tapered off. I got to the corner of Jackson Square and saw a soaking wet man across the street. He looked confused, but committed to the feeling.

~

Then out of thick air turning thin, a slice of sun came piercing down upon retracting umbrellas. Through a small crowd looking at street artist's paintings, I saw Moll staring at me. Now this may seem like a coincidence, but this happened all the time. We have become one in the way we explore the veins of the Earth. From Amsterdam to Venice to San Francisco to Decatur Street, there was no way we couldn't find each other. We just smiled as if we knew it would happen at some point. She was soaked just like me.

"You look like shit." She kissed me.

"Yeah, you should see the inside of me."

We walked along the hazy streets that were attempting to dry up, holding hands, holding tightly.

"We need to get a postcard."

"What for?"

"Remember Sean, how much he wanted to get a postcard."

"You mean the guy from Ely, the one who shoots cats?"

"Yeah, the cat killer." She surprisingly laughed. We picked out a typical card with a scenic view of a French Quarter buildings.

Hey Sean – We had a great time in Ely. Hope you guys got home safe that night. Ha ha. Now we're on our way to Florida and who knows after that. Take care. Your friends. Moll and Ecc.

"What should we put as a return address?" Moll said, and it stumped us.

"We have no return address, nowhere to return to…"

Moll grabbed the postcard and put the address of her childhood home in New York without talking about it.

A Star's Instinct

The next night after a series of heat naps, we went back
to walking through the black angel alleys. Lloyd told us to
go down Magazine Street, "until the slums after the
mansions turned back into mansions." He said the divider
would be a church, and that's where we needed to go. The
woman of the church was supposed to be the
granddaughter of Marie Laveau, the most famous of all the
Voodoo queens. But Lloyd made sure to point out, "I just
know what I know." Which meant he could only give
directions, not promises. Even though Moll really wanted
to know why I needed to see this Voodoo queen, she
refrained from asking, which is a big deal. She rarely
refrained from anything.

So we headed that way, under the crescent moon,
through the downtown, through the second-hand shops,
and then through an area with boarded up and broken
down houses before getting to a church. Just beyond the
church was a string of old southern mansions sitting
nervously. The church was wrapped around the corner of

the block, seemingly yellowish in the moonlight, and rickety, not to say on the verge of falling at that moment. We went up to the front doors and I knocked once as directed. Moll is shooting these goofy looks to make fun of the mysterious situation. I played along with her, but was still quite serious in my mind. I needed to believe in something.

The door opened. A skinny black woman with a thin layer of hair gave us the once-over. She wore a plain white t-shirt, ragged brown skirt, and no shoes. She shut the door and came back within seconds with a mug. "I'm Valier, drink this before you come in." She specifically handed me the mug. I got closer to Moll and looked up at the stars. The liquid was bitter like spoiled mint. "Ok, come in." She told me. We started to walk in, but she held up her hand to Moll. "Not you, this isn't for you."

Moll gave me a pouting face, but it didn't detour me. "I'll be right out, if not, wait another minute." I told her, and she hated me for the second, but mostly just hated being left behind.

~

I was surprised that Ecc wanted to see a Voodoo queen. He rarely believed in anything that had an ounce of questionable practices. I had done this before, and I really wanted to believe in its authenticity. I always wanted to believe everyone. It seemed useless to just go around questioning what seemed questionable. What would it really change if it weren't authentic? People would just find something else ridiculous to believe in, or I'm assuming chaos would ensue.

This one time I went to a voodoo doctor because I was having these severe stomach pains and he tried to get me to kill a chicken, just like you would see in a movie or something. He told me I was a vegetarian, which was true, but not that difficult to guess. Then he told me that I needed death, all humans need death, and that without it in me or on me or around me that life is obsolete. When I first met Ecc and found out his parents had both died when he was a kid, I told him my parents were also dead. For whatever fucked up reason I wanted to feel what he felt, maybe because I wanted some identity that hadn't ever come natural, maybe it was all the drugs I was taking, maybe I wanted to feel closer to him, to his innocence. I was the furthest thing from innocent, but I had never had anyone close to me die, and it seemed like this innocent and naïve boy was surrounded by death. I can't explain the correlation between the two, but they somehow worked together in my mind. So in the time it took me to recall these events while the voodoo doctor handed me a bowie knife and brought the chicken over, there was never a single moment in which I had any defying thoughts. He brought me the chicken and I took its neck and slashed it until the blood flowed over my fingers. I killed the chicken and the pain went away. Maybe it was entirely psychological? But I killed something and the pain went away.

~

I followed Valier in, and in my mind I already had my preconceived thoughts of what a voodoo parlor would look like. There would be lots of bones hanging from the walls, everything draped in red velvet, a shelf with potion bottles only recognized by their shape, and of course headless chickens and varieties of voodoo dolls stashed in a wicker basket. This wasn't the case though. It seemed to be more of a rundown flophouse for women. Each room I passed held sad eyes of a woman or a child. I caught each one with unwanted precision. There was a heavy smell of mildew and sage. There was a heavy glare of darkness. Everything seemed so weighted down. We went down a long hallway that curved to a dead end of double doors. They seemed at first glance, wood carvings of an apocalyptic scene. We went inside a room just to the left of those doors. As she closed the door behind us, I became paranoid that it was a brothel, that once again in my life I had been fooled by the combination of sex and money. Valier sat me on a stool. "The tea you drank will clear your thoughts, will clear your paranoia and misconceptions." She lit a blue candle and moved it several times around a table. There were also two books on the table that she opened and closed more for a pattern's sake than to get information from. After a few minutes of this, she stopped in a satisfactory mood, and my mind went blank. I could only think about how I couldn't think about anything. Valier put her hands over my head. I could feel her heartbeat in rhythm with the pulsating in my brain. She said, "It is okay to be afraid. Embrace it, because the world you're entering is a long test of what it is to be afraid, and how to use it." She kept her grip steady. After a minute or so, she continued, "You will follow a path upward without an end. There will be a fateful disturbance of the medium, of the flow, the winds will change in the universe's favor. Your fears will disappear with the joining of the stars. This will happen, your comfort will be born above the sign of Aries, below the golden horses, and under the river of life and death. Your home is your destiny, but your destiny isn't home. Your past will remind you of the goal and show you the beginning of this path."

She took her hands away and looked deep past my eyes. My normal thoughts started to gather. She opened the door and stood waiting.

"Is that it?" I said regrettably condescending.

"It's what you came to find out." She said calmly. "There's nothing else to tell until you need to find out something else. You are a human of constant searching, which you already knew. Just be aware of the signs and you can't go wrong."

It sounded right. I wanted to ask her if I was dying, but of course I already knew the answer to that. I reached into my pockets for money. "Thank you very much. I didn't mean that you didn't help, I just, it seemed short, everything seems so short." Before I could get my wad of cash out she put her hand up.

"Accepting money would make this all untrue."

I felt stupid for having such a consumer mentality.

"If you'd like, there is a root, it is for a price." She retrieved a tiny jar containing twisted brown sticks. "These will help you next time you need to know something. It will tell you when you need to know this. The roots are twenty dollars."

I gave her the twenty and left the room. "Thank you again." I said, and she just responded with an empathizing look. She shut her door behind me and I was in the hallway alone. The double doors upon closer inspection were actually carvings of intertwining women all giving birth. I went back outside. Moll was sitting on the steps, still pouting. She had a flower in her hand

"What happened?"

"Turns out it's a brothel, so I felt obligated to have sex with her, I mean, otherwise it could have gotten really embarrassing."

"C'mon, tell me Buster."

"She felt my head and told me the winds were going to change with a disturbance of the medium."

"What the hell does that mean?"

"Not sure? Guess it'll have to be revealed in time."

"Sounds like a rip-off. How much was it?"

"Free." I didn't mention the root.

"Like I said, a real rip-off." She laughed at herself and hugged my waist.

"Wasn't it cool though? How she knew that only I was here to see her."

"Yeah, real cool... real stupid."

We walked back down Magazine Street toward the French Quarter. John Bigsby was waiting for us at the Unicorn Club.

"What's that?" I asked about her flower.

"I don't know, found it on the church steps." She showed it to me. "It's like a rose made out of dried palm leaves." I tried to take it from her, but she unintentionally moved it away. It wasn't that big of a deal. The air was thicker than it had been. I could feel it flowing through my head and sticking to the inside of my lungs. I kept that with me.

A Wall Leading To Nothingness

I suppose I didn't think about what Valier said too much, but now writing about it, I suppose it was with me no matter what after that, just as that hangover will always be with me, just like the rain that soaked me and my clothes will always be with me, just as Moll will always be with me, and so on, and so on… As we got closer to the French Quarter, the smell of booze made me nauseous.

Moll felt the same. We were becoming one person, taking in the same ankle breeze and the same pulsating walk. I pulled out the shrooms, and put one up to her mouth. She gave me an exhausted look. "Let's just finish them." I told her and she opened her mouth.

There was music coming from all over, but a distinctive sound caught our attention. It wasn't the usual jazz, blues, or rock cover band. We went inside the bar where a Salsa band was playing. There was a table in the back that reminded me of this painting we saw earlier. It was of a man boxing with his shadow. The waitress must have hated coming back to the corner, because it was an obstacle course of feet and other tables. We ordered two ridiculous fruity martini concoctions from her while chuckling, but she didn't get our joke.

"Isn't John Bigsby waiting for us?"

"Probably, maybe." I almost didn't want to see John, just because I didn't want to say goodbye to him.

"Shouldn't we go check?"

"Probably, maybe. If we go to the Unicorn it's just going to be a repeat of the other night." I told Moll, but she could tell I was lying.

"See, that could be us up there." Moll pointed out. There were two couples dancing in front of the stage. She always wanted to dance like that, not the way that I punch in the air.

"We dance in our minds." I whispered to her. She rolled her eyes.

"But I want to sweat and be flipped, and be twirled, and shake my booty."

The blonde gal brought over our fruity martinis, still not concerned with the joke. The shrooms seemed to be kicking in. I paid her and then put more money in a passing hat for the band. It felt right to be back into consumerism, a horrible confession of expectations. I tried to pass the hat to the next table. They froze up and wouldn't take it. "It's just a hat to tip the band." I said, but they still refused it. I gave it to Moll and she passed it back the way it came.

The seconds went by with much more absurdity than before. The detail of the room heightened. There was a conversation about getting up to dance, there was a girl staring at the floor with a cigarette in her mouth, there was a table laughing so loud that it was another instrument in the band, there was a man at the front door who was contemplating how much roses cost, there was a sidewalk full of trash and half-empty trashcans on the corner, there were thousands of bodies on a street to forget, there was a black telescopic side-street that held tragedies in it's broken concrete, there were humans who have lost their way many times but have always made it back to the path, there was a white cracked wall with a land of ghosts on the other side, and there was a thin layer of soft green mud that our shoes sunk into. The ghosts spoke all at once as if they had been waiting for visitors for centuries. The ears of midnight have so much to hear from the voice of the world. There's so much to misunderstand, but there by those gravestones, there was only a true understanding that nothing is there any longer. You seek for those walls to wail, you tear out the hearts of man, you cry for this one time to make sense, but we all end up sitting in a cemetery that must have been at least a few hundred years gone. And it burns in you, the questions, the words that limit our minds to never find out, and then we have to go to past letters and numbers and all of the brilliant phrases just to find a rip in the air, just a slit wide enough to put an ear through. Then, and maybe only then the ticking in your head will make sense.

"Ecc!" Moll hit me in the arm.

"Huh?" I woke out of my daydream.

"You're in crazy world." She said.

"I had a vision." I stood up from the table. "Come on! Pay the lady! Let's go!"

We ran until we had to catch our breath, and then ran again until we got to the St. Louis Cemetery. I lifted Moll over the concrete wall and then she pulled me up. We were enabling our super powers. We stepped lightly over the sinking ground, keeping afloat by pushing off the gravestones. "Did you hear that?"

"Hear what?"

"A voice."

"No, what voice?"

"Nothing, I guess it wasn't a voice." She hated when I did this, but it never stopped me. The graveyard became a maze. Some of the passages in between the stones were just inches wide. We found a good spot to sit near the middle of the yard. It was a high and flat aboveground tomb. We were silent for a while, looking over the vast land of graves. Moll spoke up, "What about death are you afraid of?"

"I'm afraid there won't be beer on the other side." I joked, but would still be disappointed if it were true.

"Be serious."

"Ok then, I'm afraid *you* won't be on the other side."

She didn't respond.

"I said I'm afraid you won't be on the other side!"

"I heard you Buster. It's just sad and I don't want to think about it anymore."

"I don't know, I'm freaking tripping my balls off here." I felt that hollow feeling of uncertainty that comes with hallucinogenic drugs. "I just mean that, well, my question proposed is, if we died together, do you think that we would be on the other side together?" I caught her eyes for half a second, and she saw something, she saw my fear of going away without her.

"Don't worry, we'll find each other on the other side no matter what."

I tried to believe her, but I couldn't help thinking that she said it because of the fear she saw. "Well, what about death, are you afraid of then?"

"I don't know if I could give you a quick answer. You sounded as if you'd already thought about the question before." Moll was very sincere in the sense that she doesn't ask questions that she secretly wants to give answers to.

"I probably have. I always think about death, always have. Not sure why, but I think I'm obsessed with it to a fault."

We stared off across the dark horizon into the faint lights of the city. Above us the highway sporadically roared with lumps of eighteen-wheelers.

"I'd say I'm afraid of being buried in a place like this. That scares me." She said.

My eyes scanned the model town of graves. "Yeah…"

"I don't know if I'm afraid of that as much as depressed though." Moll took out a cigarette. "When I think about Hell, that sometimes still scares me, like, what if there's a place your soul goes and is tortured forever?"

"That's life. Hell is the illusion of life." I took a lighter from my pocket and lit her smoke.

"Huh?"

"Exactly. Our souls are continuously being tortured as living humans, so there's no Hell to go to."

"So you think we automatically go to Heaven when we die?"

"Maybe. Heaven in my mind means walking on clouds. So, where we go, I don't have a theory." I laughed for no particular reason.

Moll laughed also. There was nothing funny, but we were spaced out.

"I just call it the next great adventure, to make myself feel better about dying. It's like a novel, a beginning, middle, and an end. Right now in life we are in the middle and when the book is finished we start another. Maybe that's what I should call it, the next great novel."

We both got silent again. I'm thinking about the next great novel. I know in general what Moll is thinking. She's thinking of the next great question. If I didn't have her in my life, I would be like the meditating Buddha on the mountaintop, keeping my thoughts confined for inner peace.

"You know what I'm really afraid of? Nothingness." She answered her own question. "What if death is just nothing? We just die and disappear."

~

I had been keeping a secret notebook, writing in secret, mostly in bathrooms with the sink running. Ecc has no idea. It makes me feel better about dying, about disappearing, about the end, about not existing. Maybe that's why he does it?

~

A beam from a flashlight scanned over us. We humorously hid behind the tomb. The flashlight and sound of squishing feet got closer. We moved in and out of the gravestones like we were playing a game. "To the wall." Moll whispered loudly. As we crouched through the yard I thought I saw my full name on one of the graves: ECCLESIASTES. Moll kept going. I went back to look again, but before I got there, the flashlight beam found me. "Alright buddy, let's go." An old dark man said slightly unconcerned. "Where's the other one?"

"Waiting for me in Heaven."

"You want to be funny, you can tell jokes in jail, if you want to find your friend, you can walk out of here with me."

Moll popped up with a smile. "Got me. Don't shoot!"

The security guard actually laughed at her. His name was Leon and he believed in Heaven.

"What about death are you afraid of Leon?" Moll asked him as we walked toward the gates.

"Death?" He pondered. "I've always been taught that if we ask for forgiveness, God will absolve us, but it mostly doesn't feel that way, so, I suppose I'm afraid that we won't be able to leave the regret we've collected on Earth when we go to Heaven."

"That doesn't sound like Heaven at all." I meant in the way that Heaven is supposed to be the perfect place.

"Sure don't. Maybe I'll just stay here instead." Leon said in jest.

I started to say that that would be nice, but then I just thought about how we are always wanting the things we can't have. There would never be a more perfect place than that.

3

THE FUNERALS

A Remarkable Fire

I woke to Moll shaking me. Her little brown eyes were set on me as if we were taking our last breaths. "Hey! Wake up!" She said loudly in a panic. "Are you okay?"

"Yeah." It took me a second to gather myself. "Why? What's wrong?" Before she could answer I figured out why. I could feel the drying moisture in my beard. My chin and neck were covered with paths of blood. Moll wanted to say something as I jumped out of bed and went to the bathroom, but she just sat there shaking. It was rare for Moll not to ask everything that popped in her head, so I figured she had to know something was very wrong.

As the water washed over me in the shower and the dried flakes of blood shot down the drain, I tried to think of some excuse to tell her, like I just developed a bad sinus infection, or something to do with the heat, I don't know. She was packing up the bag when I came back in. I began to help her without mentioning anything. She wept silently and focused on folding clothes. I started to say something about it, but the words wouldn't come out. I noticed that she started crying randomly after that for no reason, or to say the reason was so subtle and at such a slow progression that it was tough to put a finger on it. When we were back in San Francisco, she would catch wind of reality when I'd least suspect it, usually when our relationship seemed to be going perfect. Most times people are suspicious of perfect and it just feels better to be flawed. I remember just a few months ago as we were taking a walk down Fulton Street, she was looking at me like I was her disease. She wanted me to see it, but I was pretending to study the curving branches of this lone tree in Alamo Square. Behind it, up the grassy hill were many other trees with regular old limbs.

"I don't know what I'm doing. This isn't working, whatever I'm doing." She waited for me to respond. I didn't. "There's no validation. Whatever is happening here has no validation."

She had given up playing the cello and I had given her much grief about it. It seemed she was much more satisfied when she was playing it. I didn't mention it anymore.

"I'm floundering Ecc, we're floundering."

I didn't think I was floundering. I thought I was living. I thought I was not dying. This is when the beating in my head started, and then shortly after that the lump grew and the nosebleeds started.

~

I didn't want answers from Ecc. Sometimes I wish he would just shut his mouth and listen. These thoughts come and go like any ache or pain I get. The ironic part being that the only cure for this pain that is caused by time moving too quickly is time itself.

~

She let go of my hand.

"Your greatest quality that will help you on your search, and don't go taking this the wrong way or get upset at the ambiguity, but your greatest quality is your conviction of not giving in to the first pat on your back that you got in high school." I told her and regretted it right away because the high school reference accidentally slipped out. Moll was a romantic despite her tough interior; she turned everything into a dream, an unreachable dream. Her high school senior class quote was from a Rolling Stones song, "Go catch your dreams before they slip away… Lose your dreams and you will lose your mind." Funny how stuff like that can influence one's whole life. She claims someone else put it in the yearbook without telling her, but I'm not sure which way is better or worse, letting someone else dictate your convictions or sabotaging yourself for a lifetime of disappointments.

There was a long silence. We sat on a stone wall and looked out over the San Francisco skyline. I convinced myself that I was wrong again, which made me keep blabbing out handshake philosophies. "You have to be patient and once the little spark comes, you just build the best goddamn fire in the world." It was great advice for someone who could be patient. It was awful advice for Moll. I used to be so naïve and quiet, and I wish I could get back there.

"What gets me is you always have some answer for everything, yet you're always looking for the answer. Do you ever think about something like, maybe you don't have any true answers and you might not ever find the one answer?" She was relentless.

"Yes. I am fully aware that I could be wrong every time I open my stupid mouth, but the point is that the answer is the search, I mean, contradictions will always be a part of the human tragedy, but as long as we keep on searching for whatever it is, then the destiny is being fulfilled."

"Are you sure about that?" She was trying to set me up.

"Of course not, not about anything."

Moll kissed me. "That's enough Buster." She felt better, but she still wasn't there. It was a cyclical conversation with a temporary cure for us, but like I said before, she was changing. It was in a way that I think if we had this discussion driving through the bottom of America, then maybe she'd kiss me and it would always be alright, maybe she'd be there with bleeding wrists, looking back at herself through my eyes. I honestly thought she would always be that girl in Paris that didn't give a fuck about anything. She had been my inspiration. At some point that I don't remember, we crossed paths, we became the same person, and then we traded places.

We drove through Gulfport, Mississippi silently. I knew she was deep in thought with images of my blood on the pillow. We got lunch and gas in Mobile, Alabama. We crashed in a cheap hotel in Florida. There was some small talk. No talk about the blood.

A Costly Duty

We were trying to make Savannah, Georgia before mid-afternoon. It's funny when you don't have a timeline or a real destination, how the small daily goals seem so much more important than they really are. It all of a sudden is the only thing you have.

The temperature was already ninety degrees out, time to start heading north in hopes of a little break from the heat. My sweat felt thick, felt as if I were bleeding in a different way. Whatever Podunk town we were leaving was so quiet that it made me want to unpack my life right there, play a game of basketball, mow the lawn, and eat a bag of popcorn while falling asleep to my favorite TV show. What else is there really to see? The Pyramids? The Himalayan Mountains? The bottom of the Atlantic Ocean? I don't know? I was being a coward, wanting to just fall down in a ditch and go to Leon's regretless Heaven, wanting to not have to say goodbye to anyone else. I looked over at Moll to see if she felt the same. She was reading a magazine about the fifty most beautiful people in the world. We roared past Tallahassee and Jacksonville, and then up 95 until we threw our beat up old bags by another questionable hotel bed.

I loved the feeling of walking out a hotel room door into a strange town. Every little space on Earth kept a different smell, a different madman, a different sadness, and a different breath of air. We found a bar down by the quiet Savannah River where only lackadaisical waves filled the air. The tavern looked like it came right out of a pirate ship. Outside the window was a view of the river and a power-plant that probably seemed right at the time, but now looking out at it, one would have to wonder what beauty really is. As ugly as it seemed, I thought of it as beautiful. Magazine experts concur.

"Is it always this dead?" Moll asked the barman. There was only one other barfly there and he was doing the classic head-bob with closed eyes. Not that we needed to be around hoards of people, but it was much easier on the psyche to meet strangers than to see old friends, or remember old friends together.

The barman put his hand down as if he was easing down a bowling ball. "In the summer, in this heat, guess so?"

"Where do the locals hang out?"

"Oh there's a couple of places." He wrote down two different places with directions on a bar napkin. Moll put it in her pocket. As we left the tavern, the one other patron woke up and smiled at us. We walked along the river and there was something pressing Moll.

We got to the end of the cobblestone pathway. There was music coming from a closed unmarked door. We entered and looked over a dozen bodies scattered around the long and narrow bar. There was a young man up on a dead-end stage strumming his acoustic guitar. We got some beers and became passive observers. There was a middle-aged couple close to the stage that looked like they just came from the prom. The man was wearing a sky blue blazer, and the woman was in a sequined number. There was a group of hippies rolling joints on a table right in front of us. We were at the end of the bar closer to the stage.

"I'm getting tired of this." Moll started to take a sip of her beer, but put it down.

"He seems pretty good, I mean, I guess he's pretty good."

Blue Blazer yelled requests at the guitar man. "C'mon, pick it up, play something we can dance to." He'd look to his prom queen for support. "Not the folk crap anymore."

Moll exhaled heavily and looked at the floor. The loud mouth kept up his obnoxious routine while the hippie changed a string. He was really getting to me, or maybe it was from the tension Moll was shooting at me. "I should say something to him, or maybe just punch him in the head, or something. You can't talk like that, fucking disgusting humans."

"That's it, that's what I'm talking about! That's what I'm tired of!" Moll yelled at the floor.

"What are you talking about?"

"This, never-ending journey, this," She stumbled with her words. It seemed the road was getting to her. I was getting to her. "Why does everything have to have meaning, have to have you judging, analyzing? Why can't we just be like other people, find a place to live, make friends we can keep, be around our family, do normal shit?"

"Because we don't have a choice! We never had a choice! It's our duty to be different! It's our duty to not give in to the future, to fear of consequence! Who the fuck else is going to do it?" I had much more to say, especially about the part where she mentioned *our family* knowing I didn't have any family.

"Who fucking cares? Can't we just let go of fucking philosophy and just live?" She started up, but was distracted by the Blue Blazer man. "Zeppelin man! Play Zeppelin!" We both looked over at the man.

"What, and be like him, be like that asshole?" I asked and took a slug of my beer.

"Let me ask you something. If I disappeared tonight, how would you react?"

"What kind of question is that? I don't know? I'd be upset."

"That's what I'm saying, you don't even know. The only shit you really care about is chasing some ghost, chasing change, challenging everyone to fuck you over, and if I disappeared you wouldn't really care because that means someone would have beaten you."

It made sense, I'll give her that, but you just can't, "You just can't make up a situation and expect someone to know exactly how they would react, and then accuse them of being a jerk or something." I really did have a problem. The bartender came over and asked, "Ya'll alright?"

Moll looked away.

"Yes, we're just having a political debate." I told him.

"No, I mean do you need another beer?"

"Ah... yes, two, thank you."

"And fucking beer. I'd come in third place if you had to choose between beer, your stupid books, and me."

"Now you love beer just as much as me." It was a bad time for a joke. I wanted to tell her she was going to disappear, that we both were going to disappear soon, and that if I gave into that feeling I wouldn't be able to hold anything in my head. I'd be a complete emotional slob, breaking down every six seconds.

"C'mon, Zeppelin man!"

I jumped off the stool and went to take my frustration out on a stranger. "Hey man, do you mind shutting up and letting him play."

"What?" He was completely oblivious to his own moronic behavior.

"You're being rude. Let the man play his songs."

"Hey, he gets up on stage, then he has to take the good and the bad. He's up there to entertain us." His stupid prom date nodded her head in agreement.

"You don't really believe that do you?" I turned around to check on Moll and saw that she was gone. I walked away from the morons. He said something to me, but I didn't hear him. The barman pointed toward the door and told me, "That way." Moll knew I wouldn't chase her. She knew I would find her, she knew I would sit there stubborn and proud, because chasing Moll would only encourage faster running. I couldn't help but be a jerk sometimes. It was one of my many diseases.

~

I went outside and lit a cigarette, figuring me and Ecc would continue our argument outside. Something had to change and I was ready to face it. After I finished the smoke and he still hadn't come out, I just started walking. There was another bar on that napkin the bartender gave me, so I went that way.

The fucked up thing about this feeling I'd been having, about the argument I was trying to start was... well, it was all my fault.

Last year in San Francisco, Ecc asked me to marry him, and I said no. I wanted to say yes, but... I was already married. It was a stupid fling in France, and I hadn't seen the guy, *my husband* in years. I had no idea how to even find him. I didn't even remember his middle name. So I lied to Ecc. I told him that I didn't want to get married because I thought it to be an antiquated institution for people looking for security in an insecure relationship. He was genuinely shocked and heartbroken. I was so unprepared for the question that I made it a million times worse than it had to be. He walked away without saying anything. Then after a few tequila shots at the bar across from our house, I figured out that the truth would have been the better option. I went home and just blurted out everything, and told him that I did want to marry him, and maybe I could find some legal way to get divorced without my husband involved and if not, then maybe we could just have an independent ceremony. "Fuck the law, we don't ever abide by most laws anyway! In most states it's still illegal to give you a blowjob!"

But it was too late; the moment was shot.

~

After the next song ended I went outside to see if she was sitting close by. There were some shrubs before a small path leading up to the power plant. A tall chain-linked fence eventually blocked the path. It reminded me of fish and how they needed water to live, of how water harmlessly could pass through fences and soil and humans and air. I went back to the bar to drink the two beers. The prom couple passed by me without incident. The acoustic troubadour was now sitting on a stool near me having a can of Natural Light. "Thanks for saying something to that guy." He said looking straight ahead at the warped mirror.

"I probably did it for me than anything else."

"I suppose that's true for just about everything."

That moment almost stood still. I could see his reflection, but couldn't see my own. The mirror faded into a rusty black color in the corners and on the sides. "Do you think that life only exists in the moment?" I asked.

He took a drag of his cigarette. "Well, that with the compilation of the past and the future."

"No, no, those things, I don't think they exist. The future is just the instantaneous present time period. The future is just a concept until it happens, then it's no longer the future. And the past... the past only exists within our possessions."

He didn't know his break from the stage was going to lead him into this absurd conversation, but he seemed halfway up for it. "Well, what about how the past makes us what we are and what about memories? That's our proof that the past exists."

"That's true in a way, but I think memories are also another form of possession. We can either keep them in a closet, keep them on a shelf, keep them around our fingers, keep them anywhere they can be retrieved for use in the present, or they can just be thrown away never to be remembered again. And why I say that the past doesn't exist, is because these possessions, these proofs of the past are always changing with the moment, just so slightly that we could never actually realize it." I stared at his reflection waiting for a response, but he seemed passive. I don't blame him. I was apparently a real asshole in these situations. "Even a rock, to use as an extreme example, is changing every moment. Little by little, oxygen and water and whatever else changes the shape and form of the rock. It may take a million years for the human eye to see the difference, but it is always happening. Every time we recall and use a memory in the present, that exact sensory moment changes the shape and form of that memory."

"That's interesting man, but why are we talking about this?" He pushed out his butt in a red ashtray.

"Oh, unfortunately for others, I'm always talking about this. I'm always trying to capture the ghost. Do you believe in ghosts?"

"Nah, I don't think so, but then again, I live in a place where they have about a hundred different ghost tours for these stupid tourists. No offense." He assumed I wasn't from there.

"Well, I guess I'm not talking about the same kind of ghosts. Same concept though, as in a defiance of space and time. Say for instance, you have a memory of a week in the summer of 1993, and then say your memory of the whole year that just passed. Even though in your mind, you have a concept of blocked time, in this case a week and a year, they are exactly the same because they are gone, and there's no way to grasp it. Ghosts. We can't even grasp the past few seconds. It is just the same as that summer in 1993, gone, without substance and ever changing in the moment. An immortal truth."

He took a sip from his can and then looked down at his hand. "So you're saying the past is like the feces of time."

I laughed, and thought about Moll.

"So if you already have these ideas and opinions about all this, why even contemplate it with a stranger at a bar."

"Oh, probably because I hope that I'm wrong."

"So it goes."

"So the present goes."

We both exhaled deeply thinking about the present too long.

"Are you just visiting?" He changed the conversation to a lighter subject.

"Me and my gal are on a road-trip."

"Cool. Where you headed?"

"Nowhere in particular. Now we're going north. Following a path unformed."

"A path unformed?" He questioned as if he knew.

"Yeah, I mean we don't have any agenda, destination."

"Oh I thought you were talking about *the* path."

"What path?"

"Well, it's more of a trail I suppose." He said comically mysterious.

"What trail?" I bought in.

"There's this mythical trail that starts here in Georgia, it goes north, and it apparently also lacks destination. I thought that's what you were talking about."

"When you say trail, you mean like a walking trail?"

"Yeah, more like hiking, mountains and such. It has all kinds of folk-lore involved with it, healing powers, magic, and such."

"Sounds interesting, cryptic, but interesting."

"Yeah I've heard of stories of people never coming back from it, stories of your ghosts, of spiritual revelations and such."

"Well, we're in a truck for now, so maybe in the next present moment."

The bartender came over to us. "You going play music, or talk about the meaning of life all night." He half-joked.

"Well, I guess I should go play some more shitty folk music." He got off his stool.

"Hey, do you know *Scarlet Begonias*?"

"Yes I do."

"Will you do me a favor, and play it when I come back with my girl?"

He gave me a thumbs-up. I sat there and tried to finish the beers as quickly as possible. There were about a dozen other people sitting around the wooden tavern. They all wore some form of depressed smiles over their dark and oily faces. We were all just ghosts, pieces of dust disintegrating, laughing and crying machines sent here to suffer and hopefully be wrong about everything.

A Soothing Twirl

I crept down River Street in search for Moll. I figured she'd be in one of the handful of pirate bars. There were only a few people out in the creeping evening. Every door or window I stuck my head into held the same scene, a couple old men wilting on the bar-top, ready to pop their heads up in hopes that a beautiful lost gal just walked in. I became manic at this thought that she would be groped and molested with these dirty old men's eyes. She would embrace it on purpose, out of spite, out of need for anyone to make her feel special. My feet moved over the cobblestones at a frantic pace. Each little door of hope was shot down in disappointment.

I circled back to the hotel. I don't know why, but as soon as the key missed the keyhole, I realized that she wouldn't be in the room. There had been other things in the past that let me know she wasn't around. Like once going home, right after a bike ride in Boulder, I couldn't hear one single bird chirping even though it was a brilliant spring morning. Things like that and things like missing keyholes told me she wasn't around.

The sound of a laughing couple came from behind me. My throat clinched up thinking of Moll and another man. I looked down the hall and saw Blue Blazer and his girlfriend. I hated them and everyone else at that time. They fell into their hotel room that was three doors down from ours.

I went inside our room. It smelled like an empty bed. The air condition was on overdrive, dripping excess water into a plastic tray. There were some cups with the plastic wrap around them. I opened a beer, poured tap water into the cup, and sat on the toilet. Sitting on the empty bed would have killed me. Why did we do these things? Just like every other human, I had a nasty habit of screwing up the best things in my life. I shut the bathroom door, hoping that would make the air warmer. That room was so cold. I racked my brain trying to figure out where to find her, but it was all confusion. So I turned to the word of God. I opened up the Bible to my namesake and found: WHAT HAS BEEN WILL BE AGAIN, WHAT HAS BEEN DONE WILL BE DONE AGAIN. My mind backtracked, looking for a clue, and then it hit me. That first barman gave her a napkin with two local hangouts. I remembered the second one was away from River Street, closer to the downtown park. That's where I started.

There were these giant hanging oaks making night shadows. A group of teenagers were hiding in the darkness. I could smell weed and hear whispering. There was one flip-flop lying over the gutter grate across the street. I followed that path. The address numbers started at 18 and then just jumped to 466. I followed that sidewalk. There were noises of humans who didn't know they were being loud. I followed that sound. There was a row of three bars that held some sort of angelic secrecy. Inside the last window of the last bar sat a little brunette. From what I could see, she wasn't doing anything special, but it seemed that every person in the bar was hanging on her every movement, as if she were to fall, the whole structure would come tumbling down with her.

Moll never has had any trouble finding temporary friends. She sat by two guys and a girl. They all laughed at once. Moll threw her head back. One of the guys, the taller one, put his hand on her knee in the moment. I started to react, but then he took it away quickly, as if it was an accident. If I went in, it would have created an uncomfortable situation. So I sat down on a bench across the cobblestone street and took out my notebook. It was enough to be close by her.

~

When I walked into the bar everyone sort of stopped, a stranger, a girl, a strange girl by herself, not a local, possibly a new local, the intrigue of small town life. There was an empty stool right on the corner of the bar where a couple of dudes and a chick were about to throw back shots.

"You mind if I join you?" I asked. It's funny how I had been giving Ecc so much flak about drinking all the time, and as soon as I get away from him I just wanted to get shit-faced.

"Yeah, you want the same?" They were drinking Jagermeister, a shot that reminded me of getting drunk on a mountain while a snowstorm was happening.

"Yeah, fuck it." The bartender, an average boyish looking gal, my type in more difficult days, also did a shot with us. The group obviously wanted to know about me, so I gave them the short version of the journey and the long version of the current night. They of course took my side and became my best friends. It was the power of the one-sided story.

"He didn't even try to come after you? What a jerk."

"Yeah, but I'm married. I'm the jerk."

"Does it even count if an American gets married in France? I mean count in America?"

"That's a good question, I've never really inquired past casual conversation like this."

"Oh, wait!" The bartender said. She went down to the end of the bar and asked a man in a suit about my marriage. "Dan is a lawyer. Lawyer Dan!"

"Unfortunately…" Dan paused, maybe because he wasn't actually sure if it was unfortunate. "If you get married in France, it is recognized by the United States."

My new group of friends all groaned together.

"But!" He made another dramatic pause, so maybe that was his courtroom go-to move. "Odds are that you could marry in this country without any red flags showing your current marriage in France. It's mostly an immigration matter, so if you if were to marry here and your French husband were to try to move to this country, then that's when the shit will hit the fan."

"Yeah, I don't need shit hitting the fan."

I had more drinks with my new southern friends and came to realize that I just needed someone to talk to that was outside of Ecc's circle. Once I made this astute realization, I happened to look out the window and saw him sitting on a park bench and writing away like a madman. I loved watching him write like a madman. Even when he wasn't putting the pen to paper, it might as well have been a torch burning in his hands, and when the notebook caught fire, it very well must have been that.

I figured he'd find me, assuming that he knew I was in the bar. Maybe he didn't? Maybe I found him? These happenings are interchangeable until one of us disappears.

~

The air was so thick, I felt as if I were really a part of everything in the world. I could taste the salt of the Red Sea, hear the fog horn of the tankers coming in the San Francisco Bay, smell the wind coming off the Rocky Mountains, see the old southern porches behind me, and most of all, I could feel Moll's spiteful joy. It's possible that I am delusional nine times out of ten, but who would ever know when that one time would roll around... well, unless they were in touch with everything and nothing at the same time.

I got fed up and started to put my notebook away. When I looked up, Moll was coming out of the bar. She looked over me as if I was a musical note that she had stuck in her head. She took me by the arm and led me back

down the road toward our latest temporary home.
"Where've you been?" Her words were drunk and happy.

"You've been expecting me?"

"Always." She hiccupped.

"Uh oh, someone's a little drunk."

She hit me in the ribs. "You're a jerk!"

"I know, it's all my fault, it's everyone's fault."

"Oh yeah, does everyone feel this?" She stomped on my toes. It didn't hurt that bad, but I pretended otherwise. Then she jumped on my back, and I ran with her until out of breath. I let her go and she went all the way down to the dirty street. A group of sober people walked as far away from us as they could get.

"I have something for you." I said. There was this southern moss powdered over Moll's hands and backside.

"What?"

"It's a surprise."

"C'mon tell me?" She kept repeating over and over until we were back at the unmarked door at the end of River Street. When we walked in, the acoustic troubadour was picking out a bluegrass number to a total of three people. He saw us pull up to the bar and his fingers plucked into *Scarlet Begonias*. I pulled Moll out to an open space near the stage. "What are you doing?" She asked me, knowing the answer. I just shrugged. She tried to fight this slobbery grin as I twirled and slung her around the floor. All I remember of that moment is not being able to see anything but her, no troubadour, no tables, no blue blazers, no stars, no knots, no destination, no past, nothing but my girl, nothing but me inside of Moll.

An Unresolved Dusk

"When was the last time you went home?" Moll liked to ask questions that she knew the answer to.

"You know I don't have a home."

"You know what I mean. Where you lived with your grandmother."

"Since before I met you." I thought about it. "Actually it was just a few months before I met you, but you knew that."

"Maybe. You used to be so secretive that I wasn't sure if you ever snuck back there one of the times that we were separated."

"You can't go home again. You can't go anywhere again."

We were on our way up north, up to Connecticut to visit my grandmother's grave. I was supposed to feel bad about not seeing her for that long, not being there when she died. I was the last person left in the family, just how Sean was the last Hollowbreast; I was Ecclesiastic the last Hetaera. I couldn't feel bad though, because my grandmother was my inspiration for this lifestyle I had been chosen for.

~

Our pace over the land was accelerating. Ecc automatically got into the driver's seat without asking if I wanted to or needed to drive. We were skipping most of the places that we would normally want to stop at. South Carolina, North Carolina, and then we camped in Virginia. It felt as if we were now in a hurry to get to this intangible end. Most of the time we didn't even talk about where we were going even though it was somehow known that we were both going to visit the past, the past before we knew each other. We would listen to a radio station for an hour without changing it, until it went into a choppy static, not even remembering the last song that played.

317

I was smoking less and going to the bathroom more. Going north seemed to change everything. It can be difficult to go to the past, to go look at what you used to be. This one time right before I was leaving for the university in Europe, my parents and I got into a huge fight because I stayed out all night and didn't tell them. I went to stay with my grandmother for the last few weeks before leaving, and barely spoke to them after that. When Ecc told me that his parents were dead it seemed right to say the same. My parents were dead, everything is dead once you leave it, everything is dead once you forget it, everything is dead once it doesn't exist the exact same way it existed the second before.

~

It took us a couple days to get up to Connecticut. We didn't talk much. There sometimes wasn't anything to say. We found the little town of Agartha. We slowly drove down Main Street until getting to a graveyard where most of my relatives that I never knew were buried.

I took Moll's hand and we walked over to my grandmother's grave. These little white rectangular stones separated all of the plots. "A great woman." I read the headstone. It was simple and true, just like her, just like everyone in the yard. They had to survive and procreate. Now, what did we do? We drove cars across the country hoping to find some simple answer to what is already in front of us. Moll placed the palm flower she found in New Orleans on top of the grave. She had to pull me away, because I guess I was lost in a trance. "C'mon, it's almost dark"

"Yeah, it is." I said, but still didn't budge. "She told me when I was leaving, it's what you were born into. Listen to the intense burning in your head, for it is listening to the universe."

Moll tugged at my arm.

"She told me that, and that's what I've been doing. I know that's what she wanted me to do. I hate that I didn't get to see her one last time."

We went back to the Bronco and I could feel the ghosts stay with me. I drove back down Main Street and found the little dirt road once called Avalon Way. It was overgrown, but the Bronco rolled easily over it. The headlights lit up the little cabin in the darkness. I grabbed a lantern and the sleeping bags. Moll was hesitant, but I assured her it was fine. There was a padlock on the front door, so I went to the back and broke the window in the door. This didn't help Moll feel any better. We walked in the cabin and I could still smell all the old books. They were gone of course, along with most everything else, but the smell remained.

There was some graffiti spray painted on the wall and some spider webs in the corners. We found a spot to lay down our sleeping bags. We settled in still not saying much. Then she said, "Why didn't we stay at the house your grandmother lived in?"

"I don't know. Something was telling me to come here instead."

I had told Moll about this cabin since the beginning. This is where I had escaped as a teenager. This is where I had learned about the world. This is where I had learned to be what I was at that moment.

I fell asleep and then half-woke up in a lucid dream state.

I was driving the Bronco in search of Moll. The feeling was desperate. I was out in the country, nothing distinct. The road turned from a smooth pavement to a bumpy and rocky path. It created a vibration throughout the car and my body and mind. That vibration kills words, kills distractions, holds truth and all that amazing stuff that we can feel throughout our bodies.

In the distance Moll appeared as the lone entity in a large field. Moll's head lifted from the ground as she heard the engine shut off. I walked through the grass toward her. She was lying on her stomach and pulling her index finger through the dirt as if she were a child searching for a path. I stood above her waiting for her to look up. When she finally did, we held the same acknowledging expression, smiling sarcastically behind closed lips, wanting to explode, but keeping it as it should be, restrained and paced. I flopped down beside her.

"It took you long enough." She whispered in my ear.

"How long did you wait?"

"Till now." As our lips touched, she caught her breath.

"You know there's no going back now?" I said.

She smiled.

"You know there's no going back now?"

"Take this off." She pulled up my shirt.

"How long have you been here?" I asked again. She unbuttoned my shorts.

"No, there's no going back now." She said and then put me inside her. "Don't ever come out." Moll stayed on top of me, stayed together as if attached. By that time I was awake and looking around the darkness of the cabin. Moll was still on top of me. She may have been dreaming also, but we still found each other as we always did.

"We'll be together again right?" She asked me. I nodded my head. She closed her eyes. I closed my eyes. We saw each other in our dream again. She was on her stomach again, with her finger in the dirt again. I looked over to where she was digging in the ground. It was simply a circle.

A Floor On Fire

The next day I lifted the flower pot on my grandmother's porch and found the spare key. Her neighbor stared over at us. She was obviously trying to assess if we were criminals or if I was the long lost grandson that used to live there. I did not look like I used to look. It was like wearing a disguise. We went inside without explaining. The old familiar smells came rushing back, fresh baked bread, produce, tea, and mint. Moll slowly walked about silently. She picked up all the framed photos of my family and just stared at the faces for minutes at a time. It must have been overwhelming to finally see where someone you've loved for years came from. I also meandered about, looking in rooms and closets. It seemed that no one really had touched anything since her death.

~

I went upstairs and found what obviously used to be Ecc's bedroom. There were small painted canvas' stacked and strategically displayed around the room. Ecc had told me that he painted as a child, but then gave it up when he started writing. Leaning beside a painting of an empty rocking chair was an elaborate looking old book. The cover was made of leather with the words *The Tenth Muse* written around an array of what appeared to be gems. I tried to open the book, but a silver clasp without a lock on it somehow kept the book locked. There were other regular books everywhere, neatly shelved, all seemingly out of order, yet something about the way they were presented had purpose. I asked him about this and he simply replied, "Of course they're in order. Chronological according to the time the story is set in."

I wondered how someone like this man that I loved was going to make it in this world. What kind of human puts his collection of thousands of books in story time chronological order? He would never escape out of the pages. The future and the past were about to collide and it wouldn't be neatly placed on a shelf. I wanted to get a cell phone for the trip, and he couldn't understand what we would do with a cell phone. He really couldn't understand it, just like he couldn't understand insurance, just like he couldn't understand careers, just like he couldn't understand clocks, just like he couldn't understand winning battles. I found a photo of him when he was probably around 12 years old. It was hard to think that the boy in the photo is the person who told me that war was the most essential part of humanity, even more than procreation, or religion, or love, or evolution, or any normal thing you could think of. This 12-year-old boy was dead. His blond hair was gone. His blue eyes have turned dark green. His playful thoughts have turned to philosophical nightmares. He would never make it in this new upcoming world.

~

"Hey Ecc. Are you sure it's alright to be in here?" Moll said from the living room. I walked from the kitchen to see the police car in the driveway.

"We'll see."

I went out to the porch to greet the officer. "Hello."

He had his hand on the butt of his gun. "Keep your hands where I can see them."

"Sure. What's the problem?"

"Got a call that a male and a female were breaking into this residence. What's your business here?"

"This is... was my grandmother's house. She recently died and... I don't know. I came back."

"Okay. Show me some identification. Slowly."

Moll came outside.

"You too. I'll need your identification."

Once we settled who we were and such, he still took us to the police station. Not in handcuffs or anything, just to settle who could legally be on the property. A lawyer eventually showed up. It was my grandmother's oldest friend Ronald. He informed me that they had been trying to track me down from Amsterdam to Paris to New Orleans to Boulder to San Francisco. "You don't stay anywhere too long do you?"

"No sir, my floors are usually on fire."

"Interesting. That's something your grandmother would say."

Then he told me that my grandmother left me everything in her will. It wasn't much more than the house and the stuff inside it, plus enough money to pay the taxes for a good while. "Just sign these papers and you can not only go inside the house legally, you can do anything you want with it."

"Thanks." I told him and I could tell that he was surprised by my lack of enthusiasm.

"You going to stick around awhile?"

"Not sure."

I didn't want to make the situation awkward, but it was all a bit overwhelming and my mind just wasn't reacting to anything said. I was thinking that I should hire Ronald to execute my will. Then as if he read my mind, "I can take care of the house and the legal issues if you'd like. I just need you to be in contact every so often. Do you have a phone number?"

"No, but give me yours and I'll be sure to stay in touch."

He gave me a doubting look.

"I promise! Really. Thanks for everything." I started to walk out after shaking everyone's hand, but it occurred to me that I should probably take care of certain issues also. "Ronald? What's the legality of a will that is handwritten and signed? I mean without going through a lawyer or notary or whatever?"

"It has validity, as long as you don't have someone else fighting for it. Then it could get tricky. Since you're the last living relative in your family, then it doesn't leave anyone to rightly fight for it. Does that make sense?"

"Yes, thank you. And what if there isn't any will at all and I die?"

"The State usually takes the possessions over for auction."

"I see, thank you." Then I pulled out my notebook and wrote down my will. I signed and dated it, and then tore it out to give to Ronald. "Thanks for all your help. I wouldn't want the house to go to the government."

A Big Blue Ox

I stared at a picture of myself when I was four or five. I had straight white-blonde hair, bright blue eyes, and big sad cheeks. I looked at myself in the mirror and saw my dark curly hair, my hazel green eyes, and thin edgy cheeks. How could this have been me? I have been told that this was me, so I have to believe it. A timeless amount of time had passed, I couldn't grasp it, and the only proof is this picture of a boy that doesn't even resemble me.

When I first moved to my grandmother's town, I remember seeing a painting of Mark Twain in the library. I remember how much character his face had, and how much I wanted to look like him. He lived a long life, but for some reason the only photos you see of him is when he was older. I bet you couldn't even recognize him as a child. Anyway, my first test of how this experience gives character would be with Derby the owner of Derby's Garage. It had been almost five years since I told him that I was driving to Amsterdam.

Moll drove the Bronco up to the gas pumps. "So this is your first job?"

"Yeah, a mechanic's apprentice. Wonderful position."

The bell sounded as we crossed over a rubber hose. A kid came strutting out. "What can we get you?" He said politely.

"Fill'er up with regular." Moll said.

"Need your vitals checked." The kid asked.

"No thanks. We are lucky enough to have an on premise automobile mechanic genius right with us." She gestured toward me.

"Oh is that right?" He played along.

"He learned everything right here on this lot, taught by none other than Derby himself."

"Is that right?"

"Yeah." I admitted. "Is Derby around?"

"He's under the lift in there."

I started to go say hi, before the kid stopped me. "Hey? You don't happen to be that guy who dropped out of school right before graduation and then drove to Amsterdam?"

"That's him!" Moll exclaimed proudly.

———

"I didn't know if I really believed if you existed. Derby has made you into a legend."

"Well, that's pretty funny. The legendary high school dropout."

~

I talked with Ecc's replacement while he went to see his old mentor. All this reminiscing was weird, but nice, nice to know he came from somewhere, nice to know he just didn't appear out of a cloud of smoke. A car pulled in to get gas. A pretty girl about my age was driving. She stopped before getting to the pumps, looked at me like she knew me, and then pulled past the pumps and stopped again. She stared into the garage where Ecc and Derby were talking. Then she started to drive away, but stopped one more time before leaving.

"You get that a lot?" I sarcastically asked the kid.

"Nah, they usually stop at the pumps, usually get gas before leaving. Sometimes we get old ladies that just come in to see if the gas prices had changed from the day before, but she didn't seem to care about the prices."

It seemed suspicious to me. It seemed she knew me, or knew Ecc, or knew that I knew Ecc. It would come to light soon.

~

I walked into the garage. Derby was all the way up inside the bottom of a Chevy, so he didn't notice me behind him.

"Looks like the manifold sockets were cracked and drowned."

"What the hell does that mean?" He squatted and pulled his head out ready to argue, but then was stumped by the person in front of him. "Ecc? Is that you?"

"Hey Derby. How are you?"

"Well life is moving right along. And you?"

"I'm doing good. It's nice to be back."

"Good to see you kid." He hugged me. "I thought that I might see you soon enough since the passing of your grandma. She was a good woman, sorry to hear the bad news."

"Yeah..." I never knew what to say to these things.

We walked out to the lot into the sun. "Did you meet your replacement? Or should I say your fourth replacement."

"Yeah he seems nice."

"He is. They're all nice, but after I tell them about you they all work one summer and then they take off on adventures. You're inspiring teenage boys everywhere to get in a truck and see where you can take it."

"Well shit, I don't know what to say."

"Did you do it?"

"Do what?"

"You know kid. Drive to Amsterdam?"

Moll came walking up with the Polaroid camera. "Boy did he. He drove all the way to Amsterdam just to pick me up." She took a photo as Derby posed beside me.

"Moll this is Derby. Derby, Moll. Between the two of you I'm going to be ten feet tall and have a giant blue ox."

"What do you think that is?" Derby pointed to the big blue Bronco. "She's a beauty."

"Yeah, she get's the job done in the most inefficient way."

I told Derby about using the skills he taught me to survive in Europe. He got a big kick out of it. I suppose that was about all to really talk about, cars, girls, and moving on. We needed to have the daily routine of getting our hands dirty together to keep the bond solid. That's just how it goes.

Moll gave him the photo. "It's proof." She said and gave him a hug. We said goodbye once again and probably for the last time. Moll and I went back to my newly willed house.

A False Comfort

Waking up in my old bed with Moll beside me felt good, felt right, felt comfortable. It scared me. I was nearly twenty-four years old and I didn't ever want to be comfortable. I didn't ever want to feel this good about anything, it would ruin every other possibility.

~

Ecc took me to the town diner that held some special place in his past. I'm not sure if he was trying or hoping to run into the girl he chased to Amsterdam, but either way it happened, and no one seemed surprised. Her name was Fran, and apparently he had met her there in that same diner ages ago. Too convenient for my taste, but I try to abide by a strict conviction of never being jealous.

"Ecclesiastes." She called him, showing off her knowledge of his full name. I didn't care. "You're sitting in my seat."

"Hello Fran." He looked up, his eyes on fire, his mouth slightly open. "I think this was technically Janine's seat."

"Oh Janine right. She's got two kids now. Can you believe that?"

"Hey, I'm Moll." I had to introduce myself. She politely shook my hand and told me her name. I imagined her being... I don't know, prettier? Not that she wasn't pretty. She was naturally pretty, not made up in any way.

"No babies for you?"

"God no. There's no one in this town that I'd even consider procreating with. I think I'm going to go back to school. Get out of here again."

"Don't leave on my account." Ecc was flirting right in front of me, but I let him have this moment.

"Don't worry, I'm only leaving for me. How long has it been?"

"Um, like four years."

"Four fucking years. That's nuts. I can't believe I've been back here for four years. I'm hardly ever reminded of my tenure here till someone like you shows up."

"Well, I can't tell you where I'd be right now if you wouldn't have left the first time. I'm helpless when it comes to chasing… ghosts." Ecc said and it seemed that he was going to say something else, but caught himself.

"Wait, you're the girl he was trying to find in Amsterdam?" I finally met the girl, and it also hit me that she was the girl in the car the day before, the one that didn't get gas.

"I suppose so, but I guess you could say that he was really trying to find you. Right? You're the one he found there? You must be, I can see it in your face."

"Yeah, but it's not quite that simple."

"It never is if it means anything."

"We all worked together to get right here, right now." Ecc said uncomfortably, but also oddly confident.

"We should all get a drink later." I said. "This seems too intense for breakfast."

So we planned to meet at the townie bar later on. I suppose we all needed more time to prep for possible loose tongues.

~

I couldn't believe she was still living in that small nowhere town. Fran just seemed too big for it, too big for this world, a force of nature that pushed me to be bigger than this world also.

We went to meet her at the local pub that was called Clemmons after Mark Twain's real name. It was full of townies young and old. I didn't see Fran anywhere, but at the same time I was trying to not seem like I was looking so hard.

"Should we get a drink?" I stupidly asked Moll. She knew this whole interaction threw me off.

"We should get like ten drinks."

We went up to the bar and despite being busy the bartender came to us right away. "Hey, are you that guy that disappeared from here a while back?" I looked over the man and he seemed a little familiar, but I'm sure I didn't know him. I didn't know anyone when I lived there before.

"I wouldn't say I disappeared, but I did leave abruptly."

"No worries. Just checking." Then he got us our beers and shots. When he gave me my change, he told me that Fran had come by earlier to say she wouldn't make it, but she left something. He put a note underneath the stack of dollar bills. I buried it in my pocket. Moll asked what he said.

"He said Fran isn't coming to meet us."

"She's in love with you."

"She doesn't even know me anymore, and I can't imagine her being in love with who I was before."

"That's not how it works *Ecclesiastes*." Moll used Fran's tone in using my whole name.

"Alright, alright, let's just get drunk and then get the hell out of this town."

After a few beers I went to the bathroom and pulled out the note.

THE MUSE ONLY EXISTS WHEN IT'S JUST OUT OF YOUR REACH.

Standing in front the bathroom mirror, holding that piece of paper, I finally knew what this journey was about. No matter how fast I went, I would never catch it, and no matter how still I became, I would never possess it.

A Family

The next exploration was a journey into Moll's past. Finding out where each other came from was never a part of our structure. The past and future ruined frightened people like us, and the beams were readying themselves to crumble.

We drove out to Long Island, New York, where Moll's family lived, where she grew up. I sort of always knew that she was from money, but I guess I never equated it with an actual lifestyle with actual people. It was just a word that she defied and that I never had, so it stayed hanging like a far away planet. That day we went to this planet. It came fully equipped with a mansion and estate. There was even a gate that we had to be buzzed through. A gate? Moll just never seemed like a gate kind of person. I all of a sudden remembered something she told me when we first met that I thought was a joke. She told me that our budding relationship would work out better if I was rich.

Moll could see my immediate discomfort.

"Don't worry, beyond their pretentiousness, they are actually nice people."

"I'm not worried, I was just thinking how happy I am to be put in a strange situation."

"Oh good, then you will be happy this whole time. It will be nothing but strange situations."

We pulled up beside the other cars, the Bronco sticking out amongst the Mercedes, the Range Rover, and the mint condition 1957 Corvette. Even though her parents knew we were coming they made no effort to greet us. I met the butler first. Moll told me they don't call them butlers anymore.

"What do you call him?"

"His name, Pete."

Then we met the house chef. "She actually likes to be called Chef."

"Well now I'm confused."

Then I met her German Shepard, Magnum. He knocked Moll over and licked her all over her face. He sniffed me a little while I scratched his ear, unsure about the stranger in his house.

Then her dad went flying by, half on the phone and half reading the paper. He came back briefly to kiss her on the cheek and give me the once over. He didn't actually say anything as if they saw each other every day. Moll hadn't been back home in a couple of years. Then we went to the kitchen to find her mom. "She always hangs out in the kitchen even though she never cooks."

Sure enough she was sitting at the kitchen island on a stool and staring into a small mobile phone. Everyone around there seemed to be constantly staring at these new pink, orange, green, blue cell phones. When they weren't staring at them they just carried them in their hand like it was some life-assisting accessory.

"Hello mom."

"I can't figure this thing out for the life of me." She said as if we weren't there.

"Hello mom?"

"Molly, we weren't expecting you till dinner." Moll told me she would say something like that. She apparently projected earliness as her biggest crutch. They hugged and then introduced me. Unlike her dad, her mom gave me approving eyes, but it was the kind of approval that seemed like she just didn't care. Moll later told me that she put on an act, but her dad didn't. She said her dad wouldn't talk to her until dinner was served. "He'll build up whatever opinions and advice he has and go on a rant after his second Scotch before dinner."

"Sounds like me, why wonder you love me so much. Daddy issues."

"Funny jerk."

~

"Moll said you were a writer?" My dad asked Ecc.

"Yes sir, and I still am."

"Are you published?"

"No sir, not yet." Ecc used a voice I had never heard before. It was respectful and believable. I'm not sure why he didn't tell my dad that he had been published in several magazines.

"I personally don't think anyone can say they are a writer if they haven't ever published anything."

"Well the great thing about that is that Saint Peter will not be asking me if I had been published or not."

Dad took a long sip of Scotch, a strategic move to figure out what Ecc meant. "That's true, but here in this world Saint Peter doesn't pay our bills."

"If paying bills were a problem, then I'd most likely have several bestsellers by now."

Ecc had an arsenal of witty, yet confusing sayings like this, and Dad would never be able to rattle him. Even though it was uncomfortable, I sort of liked it. Of course mom broke it up by being too drunk. She knocked over her glass of red wine and everyone made a big fuss about it.

Even though the subject was dropped I could tell that my dad was bothered. He wasn't used to anyone challenging him. It was a fault of the system of success. My little brother Joey devoured his plate of food and politely excused himself. I could tell that this is what he did every night at dinner and no one noticed any more. Seems I wasn't missing much, except the irrevocable fact that they were my family, and my family was comforting.

~

Moll's dad did as she said, but it wasn't so bad. He was just concerned like I suppose any other parent, like the dads on television. I just assumed that was normal since I never received that side of life. He wanted to know what she was doing, where she was going, and what she planned on doing in the future.

Moll felt obliged to give them answers that weren't necessarily true, but they were answers to pacify the higher order. No matter how much rebellion she stored up, she still wanted her parents to be proud of her, whether it be putting some ball through a goal, putting some handcuffs on a winning spouse, putting shit here and there, so one day they can buy the womb a comfortable place to die. God, we are absurd. I had it easy though. I had nothing to live up to. I had no one to show how well I can put a ball through a goal, but it was still tough in the presence of those Polaroid clouds in the sky. It was probably the real reason Moll had always been attracted to me, the reason I was so attracted to her. We both wanted to be a little like each other, have a little of what each other possessed.

Later on while we got ready for bed, I told Moll that they weren't nearly as bad as she made them out to be. Moll laughed and told me that her dad made an appointment with her the next day to talk about her life.

"An appointment! What kind of parent makes an appointment to talk to their kid about life?" Moll exclaimed.

"I don't know? It's kind of funny. They're just like everyone else. None of us really know what we're doing, no matter how old we get or how much money we have."

"You know what? That might be the only accurate thing you've said this whole trip." Moll told me, and was unfortunately serious.

A Book

The next day after Moll's appointment with her dad we went to see her grandmother. She lived in a simple three-bedroom house about thirty minutes away from the mansion. Right from the first introduction I could see where Moll came from. It certainly wasn't her parents.

Nana sat on her front porch smoking a cigarette and drinking coffee. She stood up for our arrival, hugged Moll, and then pushed her out of the way to get to me. "Oh my goodness, who is this handsome devil?" She gave me a big hug also, even though she couldn't have been more than ninety pounds. "What is that all over his chin Molly?"

"The beard?"

"Oh good, I thought maybe someone shit on his face." Nana said. "Come on inside, it's hot as Hades out here."

We went inside and it was almost as hot in there. "What you kids having to eat? Tofu? Veggie hotdogs? Broccoli?"

"We're okay Nana. I ate some fruit during my meeting with your son."

"Did your father set an appointment with you?"

"Of course."

"He set an appointment with me last week. He told me that he and your horrible mother wanted me to move into the estate, as if I can't handle myself. Phooey!"

"Funny, he also wanted me to move to the estate. I guess he wants to get us all close, so he can control our every little move."

"He wanted us to move to the estate?" I asked.

"No, he wanted *me* to move to the estate and by his words, 'Get over this silly fling, and find a real man to settle down with.'"

"Ouch. I suppose I should have squeezed his hand a little harder huh?"

"Maybe squeeze his balls a little harder." Nana replied. "I didn't raise him that way, he just found it somewhere after I kicked him out of the house."

"You kicked dad out? How old was he?"

"I kicked him out the day after he graduated high school. Boy you should have seen his face. I just wanted him to survive, I didn't think he was going to turn into such a money whore. Anyway, enough about him. What are you two doing? Racing across the country like a couple of outlaws?"

"Yes! That is what we're doing." Moll said.

"Unfortunately the crimes are few and far between."

"Nana, we're looking for something before it all ends. We don't know what it is, but we're trying to figure it out." Moll sounded like me. I stared at her and thought about how much I loved her, how much I would miss her.

"Dammit girl, you're just like me. You can't sit still for a second, but I tell you, it wears on you, it does honey. My old bones are tired, and I ain't going anywhere anymore."

"But you don't regret it right?" I asked.

"No, of course not. I wish I could keep going."

We looked over family photos. As the pages turned and the pictures of Moll as a child came into sight, I had to hold back my emotions. It seemed so pure, and you know that there was a time when this world hadn't warped our imaginations into analytical thought. Moll's big brown baby eyes stared off into the present.

~

Ecc held my hand while we looked at old photos. It felt as if we were transferring ideas to each other. We had almost become one, after all that effort to stay free and individualistic. That house made me think that there was a point in my life in which I didn't have to fight with time. When I was with my Nana in the kitchen cooking or playing cards or whatever simple activity she would come up with, I didn't know that I was right there in that moment. I suppose thoughts just keep collecting as you get older and twist the moment back and forth until you just stop being in it permanently.

When Ecc went to use the bathroom, Nana gave me a big uncensored hug and looked me in the eyes to tell me she knew something I didn't. It was very typical of her to do this, even though she would claim over and over that she meant nothing by the look.

After we looked through the old photos I showed her all the Polaroid pictures I had taken from the journey. There was one I had completely forgotten about, one that we took a long time ago before the trip. It was an almost transparent image of Ecc and me in the mirror. It was the only one of us together. A stranger wouldn't know it was us in the photo if we were right beside him, but I suppose we knew. On the back of the photo were the words THE REGRET OF KNOWING. It looked like Ecc's handwriting. I wondered what he meant by this.

~

Moll told everyone I was a writer, proud to have an excuse to be bohemian. When she told Nana that I was a writer, her grandma asked me to write her life story, told me that she had seen and been through more shit than anyone could ever make up. She was very sincere and I felt bad that I lied to her and said that I would. I'm sure her story was very interesting, but it wasn't going to happen anytime soon. The immortality of ink on paper is one of the greatest truths.

Later on Moll asked me if I was really going to write her grandmother's story.

"I don't think so, I'd love to, but I have to live and write my own story before I go taking on other people's lives."

"What about me?"

"What about you?"

"Are you writing about me?"

"Of course, I'm always writing about you."

"A book?"

"Yeah, a whole damn book."

"Not like the first one, not the metaphorical novel about me."

I laughed, because I had written a novella about her when I was going through my existentialist phase. That book, *I Don't Belong to Anything*, was now buried somewhere in the floorboard of the Bronco.

"I'm already writing a book about you."

"But not a metaphorical book right?" She laughed.

"No, not a metaphorical book, I wouldn't dare torture you like that again."

"What's it called?"

A Suicide Note

The next morning we woke up to an empty house, made ourselves breakfast, and took a ride to the beach. Moll told me all the moments of her life as we passed them in landmark fashion. Then out of nowhere she asked me about the book again, as if it took courage to inquire about such an easy request.

"Will you let me read it?"

"Sure, if I get a chance to type it up. But first I've got my own suicide notes to finish."

"What the hell is that supposed to mean?" She hated when I talked like that.

"You know, symbolically. But that's all a suicide note is, a document left behind to feel as if you didn't disappear. Maybe an explanation of your plight, your pain, your feelings, I don't know?"

"It's such a selfish act." Moll chugged a bottle of water, spilling some of it down her neck. It made me want to pull over and rip her clothes off, but instead I fought with her.

"That's such a typical reaction. Almost everything we do is selfish and it's the way it should be."

She turned her whole body toward me and then poked me in the side. "You're telling me you wouldn't be angry at me for killing myself? Then you're full of shit. Everything isn't a fight to be different, some things are what they are."

"Oh boy, please don't turn into one of those people who say, *it is what it is*."

"Don't worry, I won't embarrass you with my simpleton thoughts and sayings."

"Thank you."

"But! But sometimes that's the only way to explain things without turning your head inside out. Sometimes people just want to move on in a conversation without spending all day prodding for some immortal truth."

"I love when you say immortal truth. Say it again."

"Shut-up."

"No seriously, say it again."

"Shut-up."

"Can I at least answer your question?"

"No."

"Now?" I asked.

"Okay. What question?"

"I'm not sure? Did you ask a question?"

"Yeah, it was… why are you such a prick about every thing we talk about?"

I hesitated at a stoplight, unsure of which way to go. Moll had zoned out, looking at something off the side of the road.

~

There was a house staring back at me just outside the passenger side of the Bronco. I had practically forgotten about the house. I had never forgotten about what happened in the house six years ago, but the actual structure caught me by surprise. It was yellow, two-stories, a neglected yard, and a front porch where it all seemed fine at the time. The front porch is where I was smoking, where I was drinking, where I met him, where he gave me a pill, where he told me it would be fun and to not worry and to trust him. That yellow house with two stories, with the second floor where he raped me, that second floor where I woke up raped and pregnant. I was in high school and he was much older. He paid for the abortion. He didn't think he raped me, but he paid for the abortion. That yellow house staring back at me, telling me this is where my new life began, this is where everything changed. On that front porch, a handsome older man with drugs. He didn't think he raped me, even after I remembered trying to get him off me, but I was too drugged up and he was too strong. I remember being in the bathroom afterwards, hearing all the voices shouting and laughing. I remember turning on all the faucets to drown out the noise. I never saw him again, after he raped me, after he paid for the abortion, and after the doctor told me I would always have complications with my reproductive parts, after the rape, after the abortion.

I could hear Ecc asking which way to go, but I couldn't answer him. I didn't know which way. After being on that front porch I never knew which way to go. It all seemed an illusion, people, directions, simple answers. Who do you trust after that? After that front porch where everything changed, which direction do you go? I hid away. I hid away playing the cello. I hid away until I had the option to run away. Amsterdam was my first chance to run away.

Ecc was the first and only person I have trusted since then. I told him what happened early on when we were first falling in love. He didn't have much to say about it and he never brought it up after that. I almost think that he repressed what happened as if it happened to him. I don't blame him. LIFE STARTS AT CONCEPTION. Fuck you.

~

I kept asking Moll which way to go, but she couldn't hear me, she wasn't listening to me. The car behind me honked so I just guessed and turned right. "Anyway, I think suicide is to some people a do-over, another try at something they can't comprehend." I said to her despite the fact she had zoned me out.

"No one can comprehend how hard it is to just all of a sudden call a do-over."

"Well, that goes without saying, otherwise everyone would just put a bullet in their head every time they did something wrong. It has more to do with being reborn. We're always being reborn if we're actually living. People who are stagnant in their lives are the ones who are dying. At least people who kill themselves are trying something new for themselves…Can you tell me where to go? I'm lost."

"Go down this little road up here on the left."

"Okay, but what I mean is-"

"I don't think we can always just be reborn after getting through those hard parts."

"Easy to say if you've never been through anything really hard in life." It was a bad poke at her coming from wealth, totally unfair.

She looked at me as if she wanted to kill me, as if I had gotten it all wrong, as if she truly despised me. I didn't say anything else, because I had forgotten something, but I wasn't sure what it was. I just knew it was best to shut my stupid mouth.

"Over there." She pointed to a dead-end road. "Go that way."

A Romantic Afterthought

After that day on the beach I felt strange. Moll had transferred some dark energy to me, and I all of sudden just wanted to hide away. She asked me what was wrong, but I couldn't explain it.

"Let's go get drunk." She had been trying to get me to go out all day, but I didn't feel like being social.

"I don't feel so good, I think I want to just stay in and write."

"C'mon Buster! Don't you want to meet all my awful friends from high school?" She started to walk away. "And my big brother, you still have that one to deal with."

"I don't know?"

"What are you trying to hide?" She surprisingly asked.

"Hide? I just want to be alone for awhile, that's all."
That was the wrong thing to say.

"Fine, be alone then!" She stomped down the hall.

"C'mon Moll, I wasn't talking about you." But as I said that, I realized I *was* talking about her. I wanted her to go see her friends on her own.

"Just tell me what it is!"

"Tell you what?" I really wasn't sure what was going on.

"Tell me what it is! Just tell me!" She began to cry. "Just…" I could tell that she needed to tell me something by the way her mouth kept shivering. She started to come toward me as if to hug me or attack me, but she turned around. "I hate you!"

"Moll, what's wrong?" I followed her and begged for her to tell me, but it was locked away.

~

I went out that night to see my childhood best friend. Carson, like most everyone else from around there, was either home from college summer break or they now worked and lived in the city and spent their summer in the Hamptons. She had already gotten her undergraduate degree at NYU and was waiting for a job to be given to her. We went to some party at a beach house like nothing had changed. I apparently looked exactly the same according to everyone that recognized me. Same question from everyone, "What happened to you? Where did you go?" I guess my story wasn't too different than Ecc's, with the exception of his handful of friends that seemed like real people and all these people from my past all seemed like assholes.

At one point I just had to get away from everyone, so I walked out to the water where it was dark. Carson eventually found me. She sat beside me and put her arm over my shoulder. "Is it hard being back?"

"Yeah, hard in the way that it feels so familiar and comfortable, but like I'm also looking in a bubble that I can't touch."

She paused for a minute before saying, "You know, everyone knows that something happened that last night we all hung out?"

"Yeah, I figured. No one seemed to try to come talk to me though. Not even you."

"I know, and I'm sorry, but you know how it was back then. It was all so wild, and out of control, and when you're a kid it just seems easier to ignore than to confront it."

"It's fine. Some fucked up place in me is now glad it happened. The longer I stayed away from everyone the easier became to never go back, and the easier it was to leave it all behind. I suppose that was the plan, the plan after the other plans were hijacked."

I thought that if I could get through that night, then I could conquer all the bullshit from the past. It seemed to help, but of course everything *besides* being drugged and raped seemed to help.

~

Moll left and I stayed in her bedroom that night. That lump in my forehead felt like a baseball. I wrote all night, not leaving the room. I didn't want to see her parents or the house staff or anyone. Magnum scratched at her door several times. I didn't want to see a dog or any animal. I pissed in an empty water bottle. I wrote until I passed out with the pen in my hand. Moll came in late smelling of whiskey. She curled up beside me and I fell back asleep. There was no way to escape all this sadness.

A Sunny Disposition

After several nights of seclusion, I was forced to go to a wedding. It was actually one of Moll's ex-boyfriends, no one too significant, but still weird enough for me. I stood by the tiki bar on a patio overlooking the moonlit beach, drinking as much as I could while wearing one of Moll's father's suits. We were about the same size except for his gut, but fortunately for me he had his suits tailored to hold the belly in. Most everyone else was under this enormous white tent being served steak and lobster. I had hardly eaten ever since I read that note from Fran. It changed me and I forgot about certain necessities like nourishment.

"Moll says you're a writer." James, Moll's childhood friend asked me. He we go again, I thought. The question was becoming redundant, and I was running out of creative ways to answer it.

"Yeah, most of the time."

"Have I read anything from you?"

"How would I know that?"

"I meant what might I have heard of? I mean that you've written." I could tell James was doing cocaine and it was annoying.

"No, I'm not that kind of writer. I mean successful."

"I have some great ideas for stories, how about this?" He shoved a key into a little bag of white powder and snorted it. "So yeah, this story, about a whore..." He dug back into the bag and offered it to me.

"Oh, no thanks, trying to quit."

"I thought you were a writer?" He asked and contently did the bump himself.

"Right. Sometimes I forget what I'm supposed to do."

"You think Hunter S. Thompson would turn down blow? He would have grabbed the whole bag from me!"

Every dip-shit that considers himself a lover of literature and drugs has to bring up Hunter S. Thompson. He barely wrote anything great his whole life, but he lived the great writer lifestyle that supersedes his actual writing. I was going to ask James what his 3rd favorite Thompson book was just to quickly shut him up. But instead, "Yes, he would have taken the whole bag and wrote his great opus, just like that, magic!"

"Anyway, check this, there's this whore house down the island, open all night, I have my van, we pile in, get some cases of beer, I've got an eight-ball, we'll run down there, dude they're all nude, butt-ass naked, pussy lips and everything, we'll go down there and just get fucked up and tomorrow you and I will write a story about it, yeah."

"Sounds perfect. I'm just going to grab a beer for now though."

He mentioned his whorehouse road trip to everyone else after I dismissed it. I had the feeling that James' whole life was a story of perpetual drug and whore use.

It was an interesting bunch, mostly rich spoiled kids, but not all horrible. I walked up to the second floor deck where Moll was talking to a small group. These were the outsiders of the wedding, the ones who just came to celebrate the party. She introduced me to her friend Raymond.

"Hello Raymond, how are you sir?"

"Things are as well as expected." He said just like James. It was an interesting answer, maybe something from a TV show, or maybe they actually had a chart of expectations. I sort of stood silent while her friends told the funny stories from the years passed, forgetting about the future, maybe grabbing on to something believable.

Raymond and Moll caught up on her travels and his schooling. I was zoning out, but I did hear Moll ask him, "How's your brother, where's he tonight?" But he didn't answer her. He just said excuse me and walked inside the house.

"Dude, what was that about?" Moll asked one of the friends.

"*Dude*, Rick killed himself two years ago…" A guy mimicked Moll.

"Really? Don't fuck around."

Apparently he wasn't fucking around, and apparently Raymond didn't ever talk about it. Moll's first instinct was to try to talk to him about it, so she ran off, leaving me alone again.

"Over here Moll's boy!" One of the old friends called me over to do a shot of Johnny Walker Blue. I went over and ended up doing multiple shots. All of this was happening while down below they were cutting cake, making speeches, and doing all those cheesy dances that seem to happen only at weddings.

At some point after that I jerked out of sleep, passed out in a deck chair. The sky spun so slowly that it seemed that maybe it was just me moving and nothing else. Laughing overdubbed the loud music, a melancholic dust layered over the teeth, and a chatter of the things we already knew filled the space in between drinks. No one asked me about my life beyond the writer question, and when I asked about their lives, it was short and impassionate. Just drink and laugh Ecc, I told myself, just drink and laugh. I needed Moll. I didn't need Moll. The insides of my body itched. I wanted to run out into the ocean, and breathe in those underwater leaves.

Goddamn, where was Moll!

I searched all over the beach, the tent, and then back in the house. All of the strangers just accepted me as another body in the mix. There was a least 300 people there.

Goddamn, where was she?

She was probably comforting Raymond about his brother. She wasn't necessarily good at stuff like that as much as she was persistent in trying it. I tried not to be mad that she left me behind with all these strangers. All of these people of her past, made up her, and she made up me. I didn't want to be them, I wanted to reinvent myself, kill myself, and be reborn into a mind that had no boundaries, no alarm clocks, no agendas, I don't know, it's exhausting… Either way they were me, they were everything that I ate, regurgitated, and swallowed again. Their faces hypnotized me, like sporadic dreams coming to life with daggers and oxygen. I loved them all, loved that they'd one day forget that I was chiseled into this moment with them.

I went back to the beach and passed out in the warm sand.

~

I went running after my friend Raymond. I had just found out that his brother had overdosed and died. They called it suicide. Raymond didn't want to talk about it. Who ever wants to talk about crap like that though? I found him out in the front yard where the valet guys were hanging out and smoking cigarettes. I'm not sure what I planned on saying, so I just said, "Hey, sorry, I didn't know."

"Yeah, it's cool. You've been away." He said like he was disappointed. For some reason I just figured everyone knew what happened, knew why I hid away and then left without saying anything, but maybe no one knew.

"Crazy that Mack is getting married huh?" I said, needing something to change the mood. I told him, "You know I lost my virginity to him?"

"What? To who?"

"To Mack."

"That's right. I forgot that you two were a thing for a second."

"Hey! It was like three months."

"Okay three months. And now he's getting married. The guy you lost your virginity to is getting married." He laughed and we both felt better.

"Jesus that sucks. That makes me feel old."

"I wonder if his wife knows you were the one?"

"Of course not. People don't talk about stuff like that."

"You do."

"That's true."

"So your boyfriend must know that the groom took your virginity?"

"You know, I told him a long time ago about Mack, but I'm sure he doesn't remember. Plus he doesn't like to hear about that stuff, so he kind of blocks out everything that he doesn't want to know."

"Sounds like a lot of blocking." He laughed at my expense.

"It is, but he makes up for it by inventing scenarios that never happened, creating people that conveniently fit into his story."

~

A familiar voice opened up my open eyes. It was James again. "Tell me when you're ready to hit the whore house. Shit is going to get fucking crazy. You know what I mean, Bukowski kind of shit!" At least he mentioned a writer that actually wrote great pieces.

I was laying on the beach in a t-shirt and Moll's dad's pants, no dress shirt, blazer, shoes, or socks. I couldn't recall when I had taken them off or where.

"You have more blow?" I asked him and he laughed while taking out his huge bag of powder. He put two lines down on a cigarette pack and I snorted one in each nostril.

"Can I have a cigarette?"

"All yours. Anything you want."

As I lit up, that statement stuck in my head. Anything you want. Anything you want. I blew out a puff of smoke and thought about how this was something James said without realizing what it meant. The life there was a virtual world of anything you want. I remember nights in

Boulder with Moll. Nights sitting in a big empty room, no furniture but plenty of wine, some weed, and an old boom-box playing one of five cd's we owned, usually Neil Young. I remember we had next to nothing and we would talk about the things that we wanted without really wanting them. Talk of dreams in an empty room felt so good. Then after we got to this odd place where she grew up, it tarnished those moments. At any point she could have made one phone call and had anything she wanted. It shouldn't have mattered, but it did.

"Listen Ecc, let's talk seriously here. What are you and Molly going to do?"

Everyone called her Molly there. I'm glad they did. It separated me from them in the slightest degree. "I'm not sure I understand the question?"

"You guys have been screwing around for a while now right?"

"I wouldn't call it screwing around. We were living, making memories, making stories."

"Christ man, you can't fucking make a fucking living off of fucking stories. It's time to get your shit together, it's time to start thinking about the future." This is the kind of bullshit that only cocaine makes one talk about. This guy didn't give a fuck about my future.

"It's not that simple man."

"Fuck yeah it is, it is that simple! Even right now I could use someone, it's great fucking money, it's work that satisfies you, it's just fuck man!"

I waited for him to finish, but I guess he was. "What kind of work do you do?"

"My family owns a construction company. Building fucking condos all over Long Island. I work for six months, I'm in charge of like fifty Mexicans, they do the work, we make the fucking loot, and I take off for the other fucking six months of the year."

I had no idea what he was talking about. It felt like Moll's father had coerced him to hire me. Maybe he was trying to find ways to keep her around the island? Then I remembered it was just cocaine-talk again. I had never helped build a bird house, much less a goddamn condo or something nocturnal like that.

"I don't know about condos. I'm more into building Cathedrals."

He laughed dismissively as he lit a smoke. "Alright fuck it, you ready to hit this whore house?"

Everything seemed so hazy. I wanted to run away. Maybe we'll all just pass out and I'll sleepwalk home.

Home? Wherever that is? Where the hell was Moll? I was more lost than ever.

I did more blow, smoked more cigarettes, and drank more Blue. James disappeared as if he never even existed. Moll eventually showed back up before I was about to pass out again. What a weird place. She took me to a car waiting to take us back to her house. It was Pete the butler driving. What a weird place.

I stumbled to the bed, dizzy and relieved to be somewhere comfortable.

Magnum came up to me and laid his head over my feet. I fell asleep.

A Very Good Egg

The next night we went to Moll's older brother's house for dinner. It was another giant house close to the water. There were apparently two boys and a wife that also lived there, but you wouldn't have known. Quinn answered the door. He was emotionally reserved. Moll gave him a big hug despite that. I shook his hand. He looked me in the eyes, as a big brother should. He showed us through the miniature mansion. It was the usual set-up, nothing original, the life of people with lots of money, the dream come true, the dead-end of surprises.

We went upstairs. The first bedroom on the right held a little boy that was probably about four. I stared at his focused movements in his room. He didn't look up and Quinn didn't introduce us to him. He just said, "That's Tory." Moll kept up with the tour and I stayed in the doorway.

~

My brother took me around the house. We eventually found his wife, Cara sitting up in bed, reading a novel in a silk robe as if she had no idea we were coming. Maybe she didn't? She got up and gave me a hug. We had known each other forever and had always gotten along really well.

"Sorry, I was just taking a break from the two monsters. It was quiet for five minutes, so I tried to escape in a book."

"Sorry to bother you. We'll catch up later."

"No, it's the story of my life. Interruptions."

Quinn gave me a look behind Cara's back to suggest she was once again exaggerating her difficult life. I all of a sudden got this odd feeling of envy, like I would love to have that house, to have kids, and to have a reason to get away for five minutes to read a book. I couldn't actually believe it myself. There had never been a single moment in which I ever thought about any of this as something I would want.

It was so overwhelming I excused myself to the bathroom after we had seen the whole house. I turned on the water and sat on the edge of the bathtub. Once again out of nowhere I just started to cry. The tears just began streaming down my face. I choked trying to hold them back, trying to hold back the lump in my throat, trying to hold back the hollow feeling in my stomach.

~

Tory had no idea I was there. He reminded me of how I acted when I was a child, off in his own world, imagination running so wild that nothing else existed.

After a minute he asked me a question without looking up. "Are you my dad's friend?" It was strange to hear the word dad in reference to a friend. I had never had a friend who was a dad.

"You know, I've never had a friend that had a son. All my friends are either impotent, sterile, or free."

"Jeez, it was just a simple question." Tory said exaggerating the rolling of his eyes. He had an army man in his hand, playing as if the plastic soldier was flying through the air. I scanned over his room that looked like a tornado of toys had struck down. "Where's your wife?"

"My wife?" I asked.

"Your honey." He snorted a laugh and I laughed along with him. "You have a fake laugh."

"Oh yeah?" I was thrown back. "What's a fake laugh?"

"Like on TV. You didn't really think it was funny, you just acted like this." He did his worst impression of me laughing. It had been so long since I had been around kids that I forgot how honest they could be.

"That may be true. When you grow up you learn to do all kinds of things like the people on TV."

"Like what?" He all of sudden threw the army man across the room. It landed behind his bed.

"Oh, I don't know, dress up, tell jokes, tell stories, and of course, laugh."

"Do you wear that beard because of that one guy on that show?" He asked, confident that I knew exactly which show he was referring to.

"You know, for more than any other reason it is because of that show, but recently I've been thinking about shaving, giving lots of thought to shaving." I rubbed my hairy chin. "It seems that another thing you learn when you get older, is that you have to stop doing what the TV tells you. You learn that the only reality is up here." I tapped my head.

"I have one." He tapped his head just like I did.

"Oh let's see." I put my hands over his head like I was palming a ball. "Yes, yes, this is a good egg."

"A egg?"

"Yes, a very good egg you have here, no dents, no cracks, or anything." I examined closely through his thin blonde hair. It reminded me of my hair when I was his age. "Hey, you want to feel something cool?"

"Yes, of course." He said properly sarcastic, and then exaggerated the rolling of his eyes again. I put his hand over the top of my forehead.

"You feel it?"

"Yes, of course."

"What is it?" I said.

"It's thumping. What is it?"

"It's a caterpillar."

"A caterpillar?"

"Yep."

"How did it get in there?"

"It forms inside brains that become complacent, so what happens is this caterpillar grows inside here and forms a bomb, it forms right there where the mind doesn't know what to do, and it sets itself, and it comes alive."

"Why?"

"It's a secret." I said and he excitedly turned around.

"Oh please tell me, please!" I could tell he was a master at getting information, and decided not to even challenge him.

"Well, alright, but you can't tell anyone except your army man."

He thought about it for three seconds. "Okay."

"It happens to grown-ups that took too many breaths while forgetting it was happening. And the only way to cure it is from the blood of this same caterpillar that lives at the end of the world."

This disease overly intrigued him. "Whoa! Where's the end of the world?"

"Oh, the end of the world is wherever you end up." I said. Quinn came up behind me with a beer. He had been there for at least a few seconds, probably longer. "Thanks." I took the beer and slugged it up.

"No problem. What you guys talking about?"

"Oh I was just explaining to this one here, oh, about life, how immediate and short and dangerously precise every movement must be examined."

"Oh yeah, how'd that go?"

"Ask him." I said, but Tory needed no coaxing.

"He has a caterpillar in his brain that is going to explode."

"He understood more than I thought." I said.

"Ecc." He sounded like he was *my* older brother. "Stop putting weird ideas in my son's head."

"Got it. No problem."

Moll came in the room with her own beer. "What's everybody doing?"

"There's your sweetie." Tory said.

"That's not his sweetie. That's your Aunt Molly."

I could hear Moll breathing heavily. Her face was white. Her eyes were puffy.

4

THE CONFESSIONS

A Faithful Delusion

Moll sat up on a stool in her parent's kitchen. She had such a comfort about her, just like she was still a little girl that came in to eat lunch. It smelled like raisin bread in that part of the house, and the rest smelled sterile. That's probably why Moll, like her mom, hung out exclusively in that area. Pete came in with mail. He sorted through it and handed a letter to Moll.

"Oh wow, look! They responded to our postcard." Moll handed me a letter from Duckwater, Nevada. I ripped open the envelope while Moll told Pete about our two Native American friends. It was written in a barely legible scribble on what appeared to be a torn out blank page that are for some unknown reason, always at the end of novels.

Hi Moll and Ecc. Thank you for the postcard. Lauren and I got into a car accident the night you left Ely. Unfortunately Lauren didn't survive. He really thought you were special people. I hope your lives turn out good. If you are ever near Duckwater please stop by.

Your friend, Sean.

After reading the short paragraph, I handed it to Moll and walked out back to the patio. She came out after reading the letter. "It's not our fault." She said into my constricted face.

"I know, but…it's just weird. I mean we would have never seen him again anyway, but it's just strange that he died right after we said goodbye to him." I slid my hand under her shirt and felt her sweaty back.

"Well, not right after." She said, but I didn't know what she meant.

"Yeah." I felt strange. Moll left me on the deck by myself. The weird part is I couldn't help thinking about how I told him what an Indian Pale Ale was and how he was disappointed that it wasn't his Indians. I kept thinking about how I wished I had lied to him. What if I lied to him and it changed everything? But it was too late, the story had been completed.

~

I left Ecc outside after finding out about Lauren being dead. There was so much death surrounding us. I went to the bathroom with my notebook, and wrote over and over on several pages: YOU HAVE TO TELL HIM. YOU HAVE TO TELL HIM. YOU HAVE TO TELL HIM.

~

Later on that night we sat down in her living room. She was curled up on the couch with her head on my lap. "You know I think I'm done with this?" She told me. "I'm fucking 25 years old with nothing to show that I even exist. I might as well not be here. I'm not getting any revelations, I'm just getting tired and frustrated, and I can't keep going on, changing over our lives again, starting over and over, I need..." Moll opened up as if she had just turned on a faucet full blast. "And when that happens, you won't be able to use me anymore." From the moment we pulled up to her parent's house, I felt the air come out of her as if her destination had been fulfilled. She had made it back home, she had proven she didn't need them, that she didn't need her past, her comfort. Comfort destroys art, but she no longer wished for an artistic life.

We were supposed to go into New York City the next day and as far as I knew keep on moving after that, but...

She went on explaining in the most caring way that she needed stability, needed to know certainties, and needed someone that wanted that. I knew all this before we started the road trip, but, I don't know, I guess I hoped that we would just get into the car and point it at a sunset, point it at a northern breeze, point it at a side of a bridge, and never look back. I was pretty delusional and feverish at the time, and my reality came and went as these sunsets, breezes, and bridges came and went.

I remember back in San Francisco, right after we both quit our jobs, she told me something when we were drunk, "This is it Buster, this it." I pretended that she was referring to leaving California, but I sort of knew that it was more.

Moll fell asleep on my lap like she had done a thousand times before in a thousand different places around the world. I stayed up for hours just staring down on her little freckled cheeks. That night I started to get physically sick, as if my body was breaking down. We didn't go to New York City. For several days I stayed in bed with a chilling fever. My disease seemed to be coming to its destiny. I could hear voices coming from outside the room. One time I heard Moll's mom say, "I took his temperature, and it's normal, but he is cold in some places, and burning up in others, and sweating really abnormally." I put my hand over my head, and opened my eyes. There was no doubt that I was dying.

There was a television and a ceiling fan to keep me occupied. I drifted off while watching the news. I had that nightmare where my reflection was falling endlessly. My body was plummeting toward the ground but the ground kept getting further away as if it was racing me toward its own demise. There were bridges though. I remember bridges. Right before hitting the ground, I woke in a panic. At first I couldn't figure out where I was. All the beds and floors and grounds that I had woken from in my life all of a sudden had all gathered together in order to attack my equilibrium of space. I stood up. I tried to grab the moment, but those goddamn memories, possessions, and false sense of placements all fought each other in my brain. The lump from my forehead grew like a balloon. If only I would have hit the ground. God, why don't you just let me hit the ground! My head started to come together. I heard Moll make a weird noise from the bedroom across the hall, or maybe it was the dog? I went back there and saw her squirming in bed. She was holding her forehead, and twisting back and forth. I wondered if this was our actual destination, would it be like the myth of hitting the ground in a nightmare? I curled up beside her and wrapped my arms around her. She stopped squirming and her mumbling went into a soft snore. As Moll drifted from nightmare to dreamland, I followed the blades of the fan around and around. The moonlight was just strong enough to make it through the blinds. The blades of the fan made these swiping shadows that reminded me of the way Moll danced by herself when she was drunk.

I couldn't go back to sleep, so I got up, blew the blood from my nose, and started writing.

A Broken Set Of Legs

One of my feverish nights in bed I heard Moll and her father arguing. It sounded as if she had done something very wrong and she was being loudly apologetic as apposed to being argumentative. I was so out of it at the time that it was hard to figure out what had happened.

~

I'm not sure what happened. I only had a few beers, but driving back home from a party, I wrecked over a small bridge that I had driven over a thousand times as a teenager. The bridge was low and went over a large creek. The Bronco turned over and landed in the water. I crawled out in a panic, only thinking how Ecc was going to kill me, how my dad was going to judge me. As I ran toward a gas station that wasn't too far away, my mind started to question what had happened and if I had wrecked the Bronco on purpose. It seemed that way, but I couldn't trust my thoughts at the moment.

~

We sat on a humming Long Island railroad train, waiting for it to get moving into Manhattan. Midnight had come and gone. We had been doing nothing but waiting all goddamn day, listening every ten minutes to the announcer tell us something had happened on the tracks ahead of us. Moll was pretending to sleep against the window, but her conscience was way too heavy to do anything but run away. I was conflicted between anger and sympathy.

I sat there on that train with horrible thoughts that Moll may have wrecked the Bronco on purpose. If you take one's vehicle away, whether it be a Bronco, a pen, a book, a set of legs, a bottle, or anything that takes you somewhere else, well, you keep their destiny within your reach. I thought that Moll wanted to control our destiny.

She wanted to stay in the only home she ever knew, but I made her keep going out of guilt. There was a paper-thin tension between us that couldn't be torn by rationalism, so we kept quiet. There had been so many things happen to trap us around her family. The train being held up for hours was the last straw. I was almost ready to jump out and just start running.

I finally asked, "Did you wreck it on purpose?"

It took her a minute to answer, and I wasn't sure if it was out of guilt or out of anger that I would ask such a thing. She had totaled the Bronco a few nights before. She was drunk and no one else was involved. Her family held influence, so nothing happened legally. It was what Moll and her dad were arguing about that night I was drifting in and out of sickness. He had control of her again. He had gotten her out of trouble once again, and she owed him everything.

"I don't think I did it on purpose." She said. "But I couldn't help it. I was driving and my hands froze up and I couldn't stop them from driving off the road. I wasn't that drunk I swear. I knew exactly what I was doing. I didn't want to wreck it, but my hands wouldn't react to my brain."

"Autigo." I said about that disease I had made up. It had come to fruition, invented itself from pure manifest destiny.

"What?"

"Nothing."

"I'm sorry."

"It's okay." I was still pretty mad, but how could I be mad when I had the same disease. I was able to beat it so far. We became silent again.

On cue, right before I was about to ask her the reasoning behind her being unable to control her hands, Moll asked. "Do you think this is a sign?"

"Like as in a sign to stop moving?"

"Yeah, like, I meant what I said before you got sick." She folded a People magazine over her knee. "And this happened, and now we're being held here. All this happened along with me being pretty sure that I want to settle somewhere, and this is as good as anywhere, for both of us if you could ever do it."

"I know you say that now, but you will be here for six months and guess what is going to happen? You're going to be sick of it and you're going to miss the freedom that we had before."

"I don't know? Probably. It's just so frustrating."

"What is?" I thought she was over this part of her mind that fought with her for meaning beyond meaning.

"I don't know? We're going to do this, and then do whatever is next, and then do something else, but never really *anything*. You know?" She knew I knew.

"Salinger said, all we do our whole lives is go from one little piece of holy ground to the next." I hoped someone else's words would be more effective than my own. They usually were. "It's just a better way of thinking about the nothingness of our never-ending flow of actions."

She flipped the pages of her magazine, but wasn't even looking at them. I knew this was an important moment to bandage her worries, before we got to the city. "That's a nice way to look at it, but..." She pushed the hair back off her forehead and kept her hand there. "But, I guess I'm worried about the end. That's normal right?"

"This is the beautiful thing about life... it never ends. Those holy grounds we're skipping to will always be there. Our bodies wither into fearful little bags, but just as the air we breathe becomes a part of us, so does everything that we pass by on our way to the next breath, it is a fluent interconnected line of invisible ropes that connect a human's senses to the world that the senses have created.

So when the reality ending that you are worried about becomes actuality, your spirit will still exist, will still live on in everything, and that is what we can't comprehend until those little moments in life happen in which everything seems to make sense. That's the spirit being infected, that's us living on in the stars, that's us being reborn for the endless time."

"I hate the way you make it sound so easy, like, here it is, this is the way it is, and you should believe this or suffer." Moll didn't like anything that was easy. She was right though, and I was probably wrong.

"I have never said suffer-"

"Quit interrupting me."

"Sorry." I could see it in her eyes, and consequently I could feel the difference in my own eyes. I was beginning to lose my mind, but putting on a good act for her. It was catching up with me. The reality of not having her intertwined in my fingers made me lie.

Then the train jerked forward and began moving normally.

"I swear Buster. One more thing, one more sign, and that's it. I can't just keep ignoring what the universe is telling me, and especially what's in my head." She said while looking out the window.

The tiny Long Island towns passed us by, streetlights and bridges. I looked over and Moll had a flood of tears streaming down her face. I hated myself. We touched fingers. She looked away, and I took the bait. I always took the bait.

"Don't worry, it's not much longer now." I told her. That knot in my head was getting hard, getting solid, maybe it would explode like a star, maybe it would just die out like a star. We always took the bait.

A Jump Into Holiness

By the time we had walked out of Penn Station, it was after 3 AM and the paper tension was torn. We walked down 8th Avenue and before we got to 30th Street, I grabbed Moll and pulled her toward me. She let loose everything she had left in her. I looked back at all of the bright lights of Times Square while she buried her head in my chest. There was this blue haze in between all the buildings that put my mind in a peaceful state. We walked south toward Greenwich Village. I kept looking back toward that blue haze.

"What do you keep looking at?" Moll asked. Her nose was stopped up.

"I don't know, it seems like there's a million souls hovering behind me. Like when you get the feeling that someone is following you, but in this case, like a million someone's are following you."

She turned around with me and stared for a few minutes. Only on my cue did she turn and start walking with me again. There was a feeling inside my head that was progressing by the second. Every person, every skyscraper, every empty bottle of booze, every cab, every rolling street and avenue, every uncompromised voice, and every unmade deal that we passed created this pile of dirt that could fill the Holland Tunnel. I'm not sure what happened, even writing about it now, but as if a stranger had perched itself upon my shoulder and began whispering without pause, about how I should move my legs, about how there's nothing to see on the ground, about how there's only one kind of person to deal with at that moment, the ones that walked on tiptoes loudly, not to say stomping with bricks, ten bricks even, and the ones who you knew, knew that we were all connected, and all they could do is hover over a dirty sidewalk as if they walked on clouds, walked on life, walked on the moment, and all at the same time decided to be deafening about their silence. When Moll looked at me as I looked at the air, she could tell that life was about to get rough, life was about to create those memories that live upon the best years of one's life, yet they were now, they were always there, dancing, levitating above yesterdays antics, passions, and above all, above sore toes. In short, this place was New York, it was like no other place in America, and at the same time it *was* America, fully and majestically how this country was supposed to be, a melting pot, a staggering lampshade of ambition, an oxygen mask that has refused to sleep.

We stopped in a 24-hour diner on Waverly and 6th Avenue. The several older Indian men working there just smiled politely and gestured for us to sit anywhere. We got a booth by the window. "I want French fries!" Moll said, and I made sure she could tell how much I loved her through my eyes. At that moment I was in love with everything, stupid things like the orange cushioned seats, the shiny wooden walls, the tiny static-filled speakers playing a light rock FM station, and even the waiter who came over to take our order. "French fries with cheese." Moll only ate cheese on special occasions. It made me temporarily paranoid what the occasion could be. A gay couple came in and sat behind us. They held the tension that we left behind in Times Square. Moll and I automatically went into eavesdropping on their conversation. "All I'm saying if you're fucking somebody else, then just tell me, but I'm not going to be sitting around home all night waiting for you to come home, you don't answer your phone, you don't tell me where you are…" And so on, until they broke up and left together. We kind of laughed at the situation, but I couldn't help but think about life without Moll. It had nothing to do with her fucking someone else, or her being away, or even companionship and security. It had to do with a muse that was always out there, being without that, not Moll. I couldn't help but think about getting alone with my pen and paper. She sometimes saw that as my own affair, as if I was cheating on her with my hidden thoughts. But… our food came, and we forgot about all that unforgettable stuff. Moll devoured her fries. It made her feel sick as it always did. I had pancakes and bacon, and it also made me feel sick, but just in a tired way. We got some coffee and decided that there was no point in trying to find a room that night.

Out on 6th Avenue the cabs began to come out of the dark. The sky was a light purple. We walked over to Washington Square and sat down underneath the Arch.

The sun was making its way down 5th Avenue. We held hands and refused to say anything. There was a change of the guard between the rats going to their holes and the pigeons coming out of the sparse grass. We were woken up by a cop after a few minutes of sleep. "Sorry, you can't sleep yet." He told us. So we kept moving southward through the Village and on into SoHo. Vendors were setting up on every corner. Dead eyed and lifeless humans took their dogs for walks. By the time we got down to the Financial District the sky was fully lit. There were thousands of suits with hands holding coffee and briefcases. They swarmed in a sleepy panic to their buildings. We looked up toward the fading stars while passing by the World Trade Towers. Everyone else looked down, everyone else had destination, everyone else couldn't have known when to stop and look up. There was so much to take in and I would have to do it a thousand times over to grab it.

By the time we made it down to Battery Park where the Hudson and East River met to show us the Statue of Liberty, we were flat beat. Moll picked out a bench facing Ellis Island, and we went to sleep leaving behind the tragic day that would once again kill who we were, and force us to be reborn under another moment of life.

~

Ecc and I woke up to people shouting. At first I thought I was dreaming when I saw a costumed Statue of Liberty jump off her stand and throw down her American flag. A man was yelling at her in Spanish. Then they began pushing each other. Ecc sat up off of me and I noticed that my legs were asleep and tingly. Then Liberty pulled her rubber mask off and it was a man. They had a brief shoving match while tourists gathered around to take pictures. The man shoving Liberty began walking away, and the unmasked man took off after him. Some people were laughing, some were in shock, and some just walked by without a second glance. Liberty finally gave up on the fight and went back to her stand. He put the mask back on, picked up the flag, and went right back into position as if nothing had happened.

I looked at Ecc and he was wearing this big goofy grin like it was the best thing he'd ever seen. I wish I knew what he was thinking, just a clue to figure out where to go from there. Just when I think I'm done with this lifestyle he brings me back in. I'll never meet someone else that would force me to walk around New York City through the night and then sleep on a park bench while the sun comes up. I'll miss that and will always look upon it as maybe the best days of my life, but all great things must come to an end. His personal motto has always been, 'get uncomfortable.' I think it mostly has to do with some tick in his head that tells him he's going to miss something. Like a child that doesn't want to go to bed, because something exciting might happen while he's sleeping.

I wanted to tell him that I loved him, that I wanted him to join me, that I wanted for him to be with me in this life, but in this new life there wouldn't be moments waking up on a park bench to see a Statue of Liberty fist-fight.

~

"I love this place." I told Moll, and she gave me a strange look of jealousy. I have never said it out loud, but I loved every place that we had been. There was something special about it all, because we did it together, even when we were apart.

"Yeah, but I'm so tired." Moll said with a yawn.

It was still too early to check in a hotel so we kept moving. We walked back up toward Midtown and eventually found an early check-in room in the Hotel Ouse.

A Set-Up Life

We slept half the day. The room seemed filthy in the late day sunlight. It had a window that looked down on the traffic of 5th Avenue. You could hear every nuance of the city even from twenty-two stories up. The ambulances sounded as if they were coming through the door, the smell of honey-roasted nuts was in the sheets, and sweat from the millions of pedestrians lined the walls. I wanted to jump out the window. I wanted to hug the gumdrop sidewalk. While Moll slept, I went out and walked all the way up and around Central Park. I ate a hot dog from a street vendor. I stopped in a tourist-trap Irish pub and had a Guinness. The air possessed an energy that infected me.

There was some sort of conspiracy preacher set up by Columbus Circle. A small crowd gathered around him as if he was a magician act, or a dance troupe. He was telling them that the apocalypse would be happening at the millennium. He said that Y2K was the government warning that the world was ending. His only solution seemed to be to repent which seems silly. How was that going to stop the apocalypse? There were so many ways for the world to end without the world ending.

~

When I woke up, I was relieved to not have Ecc around. There were sharp pains in my stomach, so I went to the bathroom and sat crouched over the toilet. My dad had given me a cell phone in case of any emergency. I looked over it, unsure how to use it even though it seemed just like a smaller version of a regular phone. I pushed 911 and waited, but nothing happened. I held it to my ear, but I heard nothing. Eventually the pain went away and I was relieved I didn't figure the phone out.

I went through Ecc's backpack looking for any sort of pain reliever medicine. I found Ibuprofen and also a small jar filled with what looked like twigs. He had never mentioned the jar, which I assumed had some form of hallucinogenic in it, so he must have been hiding them from me. When he got back I asked him about his secret jar.

"The voodoo lady from New Orleans gave them to me, she said that I would know when to take them, when I needed to know something." Ecc told me. "I figured if I told you about them then it would mess up the powers to send a message."

"Or maybe I was supposed to find them right now? Maybe the message is now."

~

We were walking down Avenue A when Moll pulled out the roots. "It's time." She said. Valier told me to use them whenever I needed to know something, but it wasn't for me. I think she knew the root was for Moll. We both ate the brown twigs and then stopped in the first bar that jumped in front of us. The place was called Doc Holidays. It was an old cowboy dive bar right in the middle of the artsy East Village. There was a Saint Bernard lying on a table, an over-tattooed and aging barmaid that laughed a lot, and several old men that would eventually die at the bar. I got some cans of PBR and Moll loaded the crocked pool table. We played a couple of games and drank a few beers while comfortably telling jokes and chatting like old friends that hadn't seen each other in forever.

I went to the vomit-smelling graffiti-lined bathroom to take a piss. On the wall at my eye-level someone had recently wrote: PAIN CREATES ART. No one does this on purpose as far as I was concerned, but I suppose no one destroys on purpose either. Both ways have a path to follow.

When I came back Moll was talking to a couple that had been making out in the corner for a solid twenty minutes. They wanted to play pool against us. Moll and I loved to play together, but we didn't work that well as a team. Neither one of us took suggestions well. We played a pretty even game all the way up until it was Moll's shot with one ball left for each team. The eight-ball was sitting right by the side pocket, but the space to get to it was impossible to get by without hitting their ball. I didn't say anything. All of a sudden Moll stopped her rhythm and looked back at me. I could feel the power of the root between us. We could hear each other's thoughts, and there was nothing that needed to be said.

After the small victory, we went to the bar to get another beer. As the barmaid popped the cans, the jukebox started to play *Scarlet Begonias* and we became transfixed into each other, not to say that we were each other. Moll started to cry.

"When we started this, I was scared that these moments were over and that I would never find any memories in a smell or a sound or a song, especially a song. I was truly afraid that we were done with those special times that never leave you, and that always haunt you in the best way, but…"

She stopped talking, but I kept hearing her. She said that every time this song came on for the rest of our lives we would think of this moment in the universe. It made the present immortal and it made something valid about this seemingly ridiculous life. As the song played I took her, or she took me, or we took each other and danced as if it would be the last time ever. As I swung us around and looked up into my own eyes, I could feel that pulsating in my brain outside my head and into hers. It was all confusing, comforting, and clairvoyant at the same time. Our spirits had been infected.

A Manifested Destiny

My nightmare was waiting for me to wake, this dream that I never had. At some point I woke very early in the morning, and I opened up the end table drawer. Sunlight crept through the thin curtains and onto the King James Bible inside the drawer. I took it out, found Ecclesiastes, and flipped to a random passage. HE HAS MADE EVERYTHING BEAUTIFUL IN ITS TIME. HE HAS ALSO SET ETERNITY IN THE HUMAN HEART; YET NO ONE CAN FATHOM WHAT GOD HAS DONE FROM BEGINNING TO END. It was a part of this dream that I never had.

~

Ecc was tossing and turning in bed. I could still feel the effects of the root from the night before. My mind was clear and for one of the rare times in my life, I knew exactly what was about to happen. I went to the bathroom and started to turn on the water, but then stopped myself. I didn't want to cover up the shouting and laughing, and I didn't want to be scared of the silence anymore. Whatever happened to me is now done, now a part of me, and I have to accept it as the air I have breathed in. Ecc got me to the top of the mountain without ever knowing it. I waited on the toilet and prepared myself to leave another life behind. Despite all the pain, something about it felt relieving. I wrote my final words in my secret notebook: I KILLED SOMETHING AND THE PAIN WENT AWAY.

~

I woke up later in the morning to the sound of a bag being zipped. Moll was stuffing toiletries into her backpack. She didn't look at me. I got up and stumbled to the bathroom. The reflection in the mirror wasn't a pretty sight, but for the first time in a long while, my nose hadn't bled. Down in the wastebasket there were dozens of blood-soaked tissues.

"Did you cut yourself?" I asked Moll as I came out the bathroom.

"You never could see what was happening, at least clearly see what was happening." She took a notebook I had never seen out of her bag, or maybe I had seen it, but not clearly. "I wasn't sure what to do with this, but now I know." She threw it on the bed. I wondered if it was one of my old notebooks that I had forgotten about and she had found something horrible written in it.

"What's that?"

"It's finished. It might be the sign, but I think that it's in my head, in your head. We don't have to look for it. The sign is in our head."

"I don't understand?"

"Me neither. Read it and you'll know what to do with it."

Then I remembered the notebook that I found when we started out this journey. It was the same one.

"Maybe you'll understand for both of us."

I understood. Just like at the pool table the night before, there was nothing else to say. There were only motions pulling actions from thoughts.

She walked to the door with her bag, and then turned around to look at me. I sat down on the bed and stared up at her. She seemed to be in an immense amount of pain. I couldn't figure out for the life of me how all this got started, and where it was going from there. We had been in this position before, many times over, but we usually just disappeared without explanations. Moll came back toward me without her bag. She was just out of my reach. I put out my hand for her to take it, but she couldn't do it. And at that moment it made sense, that she was right at the tips of my fingers, that she wasn't gone, and that I wasn't done searching, so we found the space in between our holy grounds, that train in the mind, that same moment that we kept trying to catch was turning into a new world.

Before leaving the room, Moll took off her necklace. She cut a small piece off of the black cord with her nail clippers, and put the raindrop shaped stone in her pocket. Then she tied the cord around my left wrist while holding her crooked lips tightly together. I could hardly tell what was going on. My body went into a convulsion of crying. The blood that once decorated my beard changed to clear drops of rain. She sunk into my chest feeling each thump from my heart against her forehead. With all senses gone we felt the pains of not existing together any longer, of what we built crumbling to the earth, a million buildings burning, oceans drying up while the land drowned, every soul silently saying goodbye, the sun turning into a the head of a pin, and everyone that I had ever passed by just turned into words. It was all so fast, this journey, our lives together, her putting that cord around my wrist, and even the time afterward when I kept thinking she was across 2nd Avenue in the East Village or under the Arch at Washington Square or hanging from a cloud in Central Park. And the thing is, she *was* there, always dreaming in those slips of moments, always waiting somewhere under the sun, always rubbing the glass rain drop around her neck, she was there, she was always right in front of me just out of reach, she was always there.

THE END